The Chocolate Korndog:

A Gustometric Adventure

A Balona Book by
Jonathan Pearce
http://www.balona.com

Cover Art by Allyn Holt

Copyright © 2002 by Jonathan Pearce

ISBN 0-7414-1127-X

Published by:

PUBLISHING.COM

519 West Lancaster Avenue
Haverford, PA 19041-1413
Info@buybooksontheweb.com
www.buybooksontheweb.com
Toll-free (877) BUY BOOK
Local Phone (610) 520-2500
Fax (610) 519-0261

Printed in the United States of America

Printed on Recycled Paper

Published May, 2002

To Derith C. P. Foreman,
having often borne heavy burdens
but also having always maintained the
cheerful optimism of the True Balonan

One

I, Joseph Oliver Kuhl, a tall blond community college sophomore, "handsome in his way" (as described by a bunch of women in my history) am puzzled. I am ashamed about how come the discovery of the chocolate korndog by my dad, Kenworth O. Kuhl, created a state of mind in my little brother Richie that caused such miserable outcomes in our hometown of Balona, CA 95232. And I'm worried about what my little brother is going to do that will maybe put me in jail.

But for the parts that turned out good, I have to give credit where credit is due, so I would say that the arguments and the uproar—if not the invention itself—all started when my schoolmate over at Chaud County Community College, Patella Sackworth, wrote up a column that finally got printed in the *Courier*. Although she has been known around Balona for her diligence in pursuing me as a romantic prize, her column now shows that she no long appreciates me as an object of romance. The column also points out that she has taken up with a younger man, who happens to be my Cousin Zack. This unromantic development is not exactly a disappointment.

> Patella's Patter
> by Patella Euphella Sackworth
>
> Who could imagine not having snack time? This columnist becomes faint just thinking about the possibility. So when I ran out of maplenut ice cream the other morning, and couldn't make my usual morning snack-time milkshake to have with my usual morning snack-time korndog, I took my korndogs along and drove Barney over to my new boyfriend's house and did something unusual.
>
> Since he objected to getting his blender all messy, like he said, and since he didn't have any maplenut ice cream anyway, I went and made myself a pot of

cocoa, him watching. And so then I had cocoa with my morning korndog snack. He also joined me in this pleasure.

What I am writing about in this column here is that the scales fell from my eyes when I did that. What I mean is, cocoa and korndog beats maplenut milkshake and korndog, hands down! So that's what I am recommending all you snackers do, instead of drinking milkshakes. Drink cocoa. Or you could drink chocolate drink, too. Either the kind in the box that you stir up with milk. Or the kind that you buy in a carton or bottle already liquid, sometimes called chocolate milk.

I have tried all those kinds, and I recommend the cocoa made with real cow's milk and a little sugar to taste. If you use too much sugar, I found, you probably will drink too much cocoa since it tastes better that way. And you might finish it up before you got through with your korndog. The ideal way of a morning snack is to have your korndog and your cocoa finishing up at the same time.

Anyway, this is my discovery which I shared with my new boyfriend, Mr. Zachary Taylor Burnross, a handsome red-haired young fellow, almost graduated from Balona High School in another few months. Mr. Burnross was impressed with my discovery and said my taste was pretty good and he was changing his snacking habits, too. So maybe I have started a revolution!

You will notice that Patella is not talking about a chocolate korndog. What she is talking about is having a regular korndog with cocoa. That's a different thing entirely. But it is what started it all. Probably.

Saturday, I was doing my part-time job as Assistant Chief Boxperson at Mr. D. H. Carp's Groceries & Sundries where both Patella and Zack were looking at the magazines. Actually, Zack was examining the condom display, but I happen to know that Zack doesn't believe in sex, since it leads to reproduction, and he has expressed his opposition to reproduction on general principles.

So his interest was just a matter of curiosity with him, as he explained later. Zack pointed out that it was unreasonable that there should be so many "extra-large size" condoms for sale, since any modestly observant guy in the locker room will note that the manufacturers have overestimated the market and will probably go broke.

Anyway, then Mrs. Bellona Shaw came in and started looking at the magazines. She may also have glanced at the condoms, too, because they are propinquitous, but she didn't remark on the fact. (You will soon discover that I am practicing using Doctor Fardel's favorite vocabulary list, and will probably make an A soon if I continue to strive on thus and maybe show her the product, including my original and creative variations on her words.)

"What'd you think about my snack-time idear in my column, Bellona?" went Patella, fishing for compliments, since Mrs. Shaw is a regular columnist for the *Courier* where Patella is only the publisher's granddaughter.

"Well, dear, I thought the column was fun. I cannot imagine having cocoa with a korndog, since they have completely different tones, but it was interesting." Mrs. Shaw started examining the magazines and humming, like she was too busy or disgusted with the combination to think about Patella's snack idea.

Patella's lower lip immediately shot out and hung there like Binky Swainhammer's belly. She obviously felt dissed by Mrs. Shaw. If you thought about it, you could predict that here was a real feud in the making. If I was a betting person, I would bet that Patella would find some way to diss Mrs. Shaw back. As it turned out, I was right.

Since it was sort of related to Patella's snack idea, I guess I started the part that became a big problem by mentioning my dad's discovery of the chocolate korndog to Patella and pointing out how she was responsible for stimulating the creative thought.

"Eeeeew!" she went when I described the delicacy. "Even the thought of it makes me sort of sick." I forgave Patella for her remark, since she was probably still affected by Mrs. Shaw's dissing. But then she went on to say, "Ugh. Like your famous tunafish milkshake."

Patella was being downright insulting, disrespecting the creative discovery which I happened to invent in my head at Frank's Soupe de Jour one day when I was showing off for Claire Preene, a local heiress that my ma believes I am pre-destined to marry someday. Claire was there, and Patella, and probably Sal Shaw and somebody else, maybe Jack Ordway.

Everybody in the crowded booth ordered korndogs and ordinary maplenut or chocolate or strawberry milkshakes, except me. "I'll just have a tunafish milkshake with my korndog, Frank." This happened one day when we were all still in high school, me and Sal and Patella being two years more mature than Claire and Jack.

Old Frank didn't raise a sweat about my jokish order. He just went over to his soda fountain, got out a milkshake can, filled it with ice cream and milk, then added a couple scoops of tuna salad, and whirred it on his machine. This type of a salad is supposed to go on bread to make a sandwich. When you put it in a milkshake, all the lettuce and fish oil floats on top. Very pretty sight as Frank plonked the finished product down in front of me.

"Eeeeeew!" went all the guys at the table. So to show how suave I was, I had to drink it down, smacking my lips and going "Ahhhh!" after each slurp. Actually, it wasn't possible to slurp through the straw, since the lettuce and pieces of fish sort of clogged up the instrument. But I got it all down without throwing up, thus creating a legend in my own time. Even today, Balona guys who are especially suave will once in a while order a tunafish milkshake at Frank's, just to keep up the famous tradition.

Anyway, back to the present, Patella claimed that the scales fell from her tongue as she tasted the combination of cocoa and korndog. She said she had started a new breakfast fashion with that column, since guys called the *Courier* and either bragged that they had been having cocoa with their korndogs all their lives. Or else called to complain that the combination made them sick, even to think about it, and that they had hired Uncle Kenworth Burnross to work up a lawsuit. Or to suggest that if you dumped the Balona Special Secret Korndog Sauce into the cocoa and stirred it around good, it made the breakfast experience that much more interesting. Maybe those guys were joshing, since the Balona Special Secret Korndog Sauce is made of ketchup, mustard, and peanut butter.

But when my dad heard about the cocoa and korndog breakfast idea, he started thinking about something even more chocolaty. It was him who finally came up with the chocolate korndog idea that has led to him getting chickled and disposed.

It was natural that poor Dad would get chickled out of getting credit for his discovery. Anyway, he is out of the picture now, only temporarily I hope, since Ma committed him first to the funny farm over at Delta City and then, more recently, to the Jolly Times Rest Home down on First Avenue near King Way.

The funny farm experience was because of his noisy dreams and fantasies about his discovery and his constant drooling. The drooling was the feature that got sort of unpleasant around the house whenever he forgot his towel. Dad's still enthusiastic about his creation, but he's not so unhappy now. Even though the County billed us for his stay over there, old Grandpa Daddy Kon Chaud will eventually pay the bill. And Dad is finally getting a good rest where Ma doesn't get to natter at him all the time.

I guess Dad getting screwed out of his discoveries all started years ago when he invented his earpick. This was actually only a paper clip which you bent so you could stick it into your ear to get satisfaction. Uncle Kenworth Burnross was our family lawyer, and he said he would "research" the idea, but he never got back to Dad. And then Uncle Kenworth Burnross started losing his memory. The rest is history.

The other discovery Dad got chickled out of wasn't really a discovery. More of an advertising promotion. Which was to advertise our address in the papers and advise guys to "send in your dollar before it's too late." Then, Dad said, everybody would send in their dollar, and Dad and us would be rich, since guys who sent in their dollar would be giving us a gift and so would not really expect to get anything in return.

It was a true Balona idea. However, my Cousin Nim who is also Pastor Nim of Balona's BoMFoG Tabernacle said he thought the idea was unethical and illegal and went *tsk* and wagged his head. So Dad set the idea aside, but felt screwed then anyway.

I'm told that the idea of a chocolate korndog does capture the imagination. Ordinary corndogs produced in other places have a stick stuck up their long end so you can sort of gnaw on them like a popsicle, mustard leaking off and crumbs falling around you, and a stick to dispose of when you finish.

But true Balona King Korndogs don't have a stick. They just sort of lie on your plate where you can smother them with the Special Balona Secret Korndog Sauce. Then you either pick them up and eat by hand, or you cut them up with a knife and fork.

As I have already disclosed, but it bears repeating, the basic secret sauce is made out of ketchup, peanut butter, and mustard. It's the variations of the amounts of each ingredient that everybody around here varies that makes the sauce "secret." Also, some guys add weird stuff into their sauce, like honey or soy sauce or chopped-up mint or parsley or even the leaves off of a bush I won't mention here in a story meant for families to read.

I suppose it was Claire Preene and her painting who really made the chocolate korndog something everybody got to talking about. And the painting and the talking and my Cousin Zack Burnross was what finally got a famous San Francisco chef involved. And the chef was the one who finally made my dad's discovery world famous. Almost. But that comes later.

In between came Richelieu Oliver Kuhl, a kid who should remain in infamy forever, him and his punky friend Ricky. They thought up ideas that have made a blotch on the good name of Balona, not to speak of the good name of Kuhl.

But the first thing was the involvement of Zack, and then the intrusion of Mr. Sam Joe Sly, a guy who has a natural interest in the chocolate korndog since he produces the regular korndog over at the King Korndog Korporation Kastle Keep on King Way just off Eighth Avenue. And then came the part where famous radio talk show host Buddy Swainhammer horned in, or at first failing to horn in. And of course my ma, the well-known Bapsie Kuhl, had to make an unusual deal out of it all, because of her fabulous flatulence problem.

The thing about my brother Richie is what is worrying me most. I was passing by Richie's bedroom and I overheard him and his buddy Ricky talking. They didn't know I was listening since I sort of used some tradecraft which I practice from time to time, just to stay in shape for my eventual career as a secret agent.

It was Ricky who started it by saying, "Hey, let's get your brother in on it. Let's fix it so Joe takes the rap."

And my dear little brother Richie went, "Hey, yeh. That's a good idear. Let's work on that!"

I'm going to have to keep my eyes and ears open, that's for sure.

Two

Claire Preene plays the flute. In fact she is going to be a pro flauterist some day, she says, and is studying the flute big time even while she is a senior in high school. Claire is pretty tall and has long blonde hair, which every normal flute player has to have. She has very blue eyes and pink spots on her cheeks. When she plays the flute she sort of tosses her head and her hair flies around. That is when you can see that her ears are both pink and pointed.

My ears are sort of pointed, too. That makes sense, since me and Claire are related. We are not related so much that we couldn't get married some day. That's what my ma hopes and is always striving for, since when me and Claire get married, that will bring the huge Kuhl fortune back from the Preenes and into the broke Kuhl family, instead of in Claire's bank accounts where she inherited it from my dead Great-uncle Oliver.

But this part is not about Claire's flute or her money. She has got another talent. It's her painting. In an interview in the *Courier* about good students, Mr. Rimshot over at Big Baloney said that he thought if Claire ever got tired of the flute, she could "make it big" as an artist. Mr. Rimshot teaches art over there, but his main claim to fame is his portraits of sugarbeets which he tries to sell at our annual Sugarbeet Festival. Since sugarbeets don't typically look like movie stars, Mr. Rimshot's own fame is probably going to stay pretty local. We Kuhls do have a sugarbeet portrait hanging on our living room wall, but I think Dad won it in a raffle.

So when I happened to mention to Claire about my dad's discovery, and sort of described it to her, she laughed up a storm and went home and right away painted a chocolate korndog as part of her sense of humor. Of course, it wasn't an actual chocolate korndog, since there wasn't such a thing. It was just Claire's version of it.

Which was pretty juicy looking, on a white plate, with lots of shiny frosting running down the sides, and the dog part peeking out of one end. She even put a little pile of Balona Secret Korndog Sauce on one side of the plate. People who don't live in Balona wouldn't know what that was, since it actually looks sort of repulsive looking. Also, why would a guy want to spread that Secret Sauce on a chocolate korndog? I couldn't imagine.

But the painting was pretty good size, and Mark Ordway, the guy who finally got married to Claire's ma, said she ought to take it over to Mr. D. H. Carp's Groceries & Sundries and have Mr. Carp display it in his window. Mr. Carp displays all kinds of stuff in his window. He even displayed my ma's posters when she lost the mayor election a while back. So a painting of a chocolate korndog wouldn't look out of place. Besides, Claire owns Mr. Carp's building, so the poor old guy didn't have any choice.

"What *is* that!" everybody said who went by or who came into the store. "That isn't a maple bar, is it?"

In my capacity as Assistant Chief Boxperson every Saturday, I usually answered the customer, "Well, that's chocolate on it there, and you can see it's got the dog there sticking out from inside, so it's a chocolate korndog, a discovery of Kenworth Oliver Kuhl, painted up by Claire Preene."

Everybody knows my dad, so they would say something like, "Well, Kenworth Kuhl. That figures." But then they would look at the painting again and go, "Hmmm." And then they would say, "Looks good enough to eat." Which of course was the idea in the first place, even though Claire probably wasn't considering that.

Mr. Carp said over and over, "It's a joke. It's a joke. There's no such thing. Yeccch! Who would eat such a thing!"

But guys would just look at the painting and go, "Hmmmm," like they were considering the possibility. And the women viewers would also go, "Hmmmm!" like they were looking mostly at the chocolate part and not thinking about the weenie inside.

After the portrait in the window, Mrs. Shaw got into the act again.

Bellona's Balona
by Bellona Shaw

The painters busy on the flat roof of Hannibal Chaud's Funerals are painting a giant target bullseye up there. Why? Mr. Chaud tells us that from now on, every aircraft pilot who flies over Balona at whatever altitude will ask that same question, and the answer is, "That's Balona!" What a productive idea.

Yet another painting, the new one in the window of Mr. D. H. Carp's Groceries & Sundries is an original by young artist Claire Preene. Claire is a senior at Balona High School and an art student of Mr. Rufus Rimshot, who calls Claire "one of my best students of all time."

The painting is of an imaginary confection said to have been invented in the imagination of Kenworth Kuhl, local real estate agent.

When one sets aside the disparities of taste, texture, and appearance between the imaginary confection and the real King Korndog, one realizes that Mr. Kuhl must absolutely be joking. Perhaps it is better to remain with Ms Patella Sackworth's version of a good snack, cocoa with your korndog, although in this columnist's opinion, that combination does little for either the cocoa or the korndog.

One may hope that the chocolate korndog will soon find its way into legend and its conclusion there.

You could hear Mrs. Shaw smacking her lips after finishing that column. *That should end all argument and also shut Patella up*, she seems to be saying. She also disses my dad. But that's not unusual. Everybody disses Dad.

But Mrs. Shaw was wrong about ending argument. One of the guys who stood in front of Mr. D. H. Carp's window hunched over and scratching in a bunch of places was Mr. Sam Joe Sly, owner and operator of King Korndog. Also dad of Sammy Jack Sly, a rich kid who is sort of a student over at Chaud County Community College, a place we usually call C4, where I study Criminal Justice.

Mr. Sam Joe Sly finally came inside, since it was pretty foggy outside. He stood with his head crooked to the side so he could see the picture better, since it was pointed mostly towards Front Street.

"That's a pretty good looking thing," he went, nodding his head like it was on a flexible wand. "Yep. Pretty good looking thing." He looked around to where Mr. D. H. Carp was sleeping back in his office and Mr. Sackworth was just coming out of the toilet and nobody else but me was in the store. "You think it might taste pretty good, kid?"

"Huh?" I went, since I am not used to having rich guys ask me my opinion of stuff. "Well, I guess so, if it had a lot of chocolate slathered on top."

Mr. Sly mumbled, "Have to change the dog, though. Maybe inject it with some chocolate? Whaddya think? Stick a chocolate weenie in there, too?" I guess I must have made a face. "I mean, not a chocolate weenie, but a chocolate-flavored regular weenie. Something like that? I could do that, no problem now that Simon's out of the country. He's so conservative."

Simon, stylish Mr. Simon Burberry, is Mr. Sly's partner and also Mayor of Balona, but he's back in England now, negotiating to make King Korndog the national dish of England. Mr. Burberry's not expected back in town until he clears up his inheritance back there and returns to Balona a billionaire.

Mr. Sly took off mumbling to himself and nodding his head like he was agreeing with what he was saying.

I mentioned all this to Zack when he came by the store to get dogfood and snacks for Harley. Mr. D. H. Carp doesn't want dogs in the store. He's always giving Mr. Keyshot's dog Lamont hard looks, but he lets Harley come in because when he talks to Harley, Harley gets a thoughtful expression on his face and nods his head and looks like he's taking your comment under his advisement. So Harley now enjoys a carpet scrap that Mr. D. H. Carp laid down near the door especially for him, so Harley doesn't have to rest his little butt on the cold floor.

I get surprised every once in a while by people doing stuff that you don't expect them to do. Mr. D. H. Carp, for example, is a mean old cuss usually. He doesn't give to charity. He's a true tightwad to his employees. He's insulting to his fat old wife. He puts his thumb on the scale when he's weighing meat. But he goes and puts that carpet scrap down on the cold vinyl tile for a little black dog with blond eyebrows. Go figure.

Anyway, about Zack. When I mentioned that Mr. Sam Joe Sly seemed really interested in the idea of a chocolate korndog, Zack looked interested, too. Zack is sort of a gourmet cook, inventing weird dishes that taste pretty good, especially if you don't ask him what's in them. If you ask, he'll tell you stuff weird enough you might throw up.

"He was really interested?"

"He kept mumbling to himself and nodding his head and talking about injecting the weenie."

"Aha. Injecting the weenie. He's serious. I think I'll go home and do some experimenting." And off he went to his house, where he's got not only all kinds of computer equipment and a private phone and a copy machine and his own microwave and blender, but also he's got a whole new Binky Swainhammer-remodeled kitchen his ma lets him work in. Copper pots and cooking tools hang from racks over the chopping island where there's another small sink for washing your hands. The sort of thing you see in *Sunset* magazine. Before he left, he went, "C'mon over to my place after work and I'll let you taste some of my experiments."

So after work, that's what I did, instead of going straight home where my ma, the worst cook in Chaud County, would probably be finding something old to throw into the microwave for our dinner.

At Zack's, which is only across the street and down a ways from my house, his ma was still at her garden club meeting and his dad was napping, which is what his ma and dad mostly do. Zack was in the kitchen, and the place smelled pretty good when I let myself in the back door. Smelled like something in the oven.

Harley was sitting on a chair at the kitchen table, watching Zack mix something in a bowl. "How's things?" I went, the usual Balona greeting.

"Yeh, how's things?" went Zack, the usual Balona response. In Balona that's all there is to it. You don't really want to know details about the other guy's warts and athlete's foot, so the tradition is you stop right there. "I'm mixing up a *ganache* here."

"I hope I don't catch it," I joked, not knowing a *ganache* from my uncle, but not wanting to admit it to this young high school kid.

He explained and spelled out the word, which is what he usually does, whether you're interested or not. "It's what Davy Narsood taught me how to do. It's a real high-class frosting, see?" He pointed the bowl at me so I could see the chocolate he was mixing up. Davy Narsood is the famous San Francisco chef that Zack is always watching on TV and learning how to boil snails and hummingbirds and earthworms.

"Looks good enough. What smells so good in the oven there?"

"Just in time." Zack put down his bowl and turned to the oven. He opened it slowly so all the good smells would come out and capture your nose sneakily. "See what I got here! My chocolate korndogs. One for you and one for me. Also one for Harley." Harley closed his eyes and smiled.

They didn't look like any korndogs I'd ever seen. They looked like maybe jelly donuts, round like that. "That's a korndog? They don't look like a korndog."

"Well, honk! As you may well know, it's an experiment, so it's not exactly a finished product since I mixed it up out of regular pie dough. That's why they're sort of pale looking and sagged down."

"So it's not really a korndog. And where's the weenie sticking out, like my dad imagined it? It dut'n look like Claire's painting at all."

"The weenie's curled up in a circle inside each one there. I tied it together with some string."

Zack was sounding a little peeved, like he had made a great invention that was not appreciated, and his ego was damaged. I hastened to calm my young cousin. "Well, maybe it's not a true korndog, but it sure smells good!"

"Well, honk! Of course it smells good. All quality materials. I even scraped the dogs out of regular korndogs and used them for the weenies. Just wait till you taste it. I bet it'll knock off your socks."

Zack slid the baked things—I wouldn't call them actual korndogs—on a plate. He grabbed a spatula and started spatulating the things with the goo in the bowl.

They did look sort of tasty. A lot like sagged-down chocolate-covered jelly donuts.

"As you may well know, we now got to wait a little for the *ganache* to set up. It gets firm and crisp and it has a nice sparkle to it. You'll see." Zack shoveled more *ganache* on the tops and some ran down the sides. They looked very tasty. My mouth watered. I heard a sudden loud *slurp* and looked over at Harley. He had both paws on the table and was looking at the things with a very beady eye. Harley's mouth was watering.

"Yeh," went Zack, "there's one for you and one for me, but Harley can't have any since, as you may well know, chocolate is very bad for dogs."

Harley frowned, a disappointed dog for sure.

"Hold on there, Harley. Soon as it cools off, you can have the un-frosted korndog here. I'll cut it up for you in a minute. In the meantime, here, you can have a nice carrot." Zack peeled him a raw carrot which Harley started munching on "Harley likes carrots. They keep his breath sweet and his teeth sparkly." Harley is a clean dog, all right. I wish I had a dog.

Three

❈

About Zack's version of the chocolate korndog, I went, "Well, it does have a certain *jinny say kwa*." I was using the sophisticated Chinese saying we guys use over at C4. It means, *I don't know what*, but I figured Zack would be impressed.

"How's about the chocolate?"

He wasn't impressed with my sophisticated saying. Probably concealing his true impression. "The chocolate is great. I must say that for it. Yeh."

Actually, though, the whole thing was kind of gummy, especially where the pie dough didn't get all baked up on the inside. The weenie was sort of shrunk and dried-out tasting. Just as well, since the weenie taste didn't fit with the chocolate at all.

But I have learned that it's better not to say anything if you can't say something nice. I learned that from my ma. Actually, I didn't learn it *from* my ma. I learned it *about* my ma, since if you criticize anything she does, she might grab you by the hair and throw you down the front steps.

"I got to do something about the weenie, though."

"Yeh. The weenie could use something, all right."

Zack frowned. "But you liked the *ganache* okay, right?"

I kissed my fingers, the way Davy Narsood does on TV after he's just invented something especially tasty. "The *ganache* was superb." I burped a little to show my sincere appreciation.

"I'm gonna try to make up some korndog-type dough. Like stiff waffle batter with a little cornmeal mixed in. And then I'll work on the weenie part. Maybe I should put it in some kind of a mold or a little pan so it doesn't sag down so much around the edges. I could make a mold out of aluminum foil."

"Yeh. Also, you might try to make it look like Claire's painting, since her version looks more like what a chocolate korndog is supposed to look like."

Zack frowned again. "There's no such thing as a chocolate korndog, so the first guy that makes one gets to make it look any way he wants it to look. That's a matter of logic." Zack smacked his lips again, exactly the way his dad, Uncle Kenworth Burnross, does after he makes a big important saying.

"You smack your lips the way your dad does," I pointed out, trying to be an honest cousin.

"No, I don't."

"Yes, you do. Ast your ma, if you don't believe me."

"Mummy dut'n pay attention to stuff, so she wut'n know." Zack always denies any relationship to his dad, who he calls "Da," like a little kid. He also calls his ma "Mummy." Zack believes he's really a prince of a foreign country, child of his true parents of royal blood who got lost in Balona and left Zack behind by mistake on a stormy night.

Zack will be a new high school grad in a few months and acts like he knows everything there is to know about everything, so there's no use arguing with him. He also has a habit of sort of thinking faster than me. But since he is only a half-cousin, once-removed (according to my genealogical Cousin Nim) and once in a while sasses me, I am searching for a way to take him down a peg or two. Of course he is also my James Bond-type Q, and makes up secret inventions for me, so I take that into consideration.

"When you get your actual chocolate korndog baked up and *ganached*, you ought to bring it around so my dad can taste it. He's the one responsible for the whole idear in the first place."

"The first guy I'm gonna take it to is Da, so he can patent it for me. And then I'll take it over to Mr. Sam Joe Sly and let him taste it. I'll sell it to him for a million bucks." Zack rubbed his hands, gnawed at his donut-looking chocolate weenie thing. He went "Mmmmmm," like it tasted like a world champion confection. "Needs a cup of cocoa to go with it." He got out a pot and made us cocoa which we sat around and drank.

"If you get rich from the korndog idear, you won't have to go on to more school. You can just lay around and spend your money."

"Oh, no. The idear always behind getting rich is getting richer. And anyways, I *like* school. I am debating myself whether I should go to Harvard or Oxford. Oxford has got more class. If I went over there to Oxford I would probably get all kinds of great weird idears for inventions and foods and stuff. I would come back with a great accent and suave clothes, eksedra."

"You could get idears like that here, too, just laying around spending your money. You could have your own tailor and speech therapist."

"I am determined to become Chief Justice of the Supreme Court, and you can't do that by laying around spending money. And by the way, you're supposed to say *lie* around, not *lay* around."

This argument was going nowhere, and I was getting depressed with Zack's remarks forcing me to think about school.

Being as how I sort of flunked a few classes last semester, I am having some make-up work to do this semester. It is especially disappointing that I flunked English 1B, since it was my favorite class and had my favorite teacher, Doctor Fardel.

Doctor Fardel said, "It pains me to register this failing grade, Joseph, but I don't know what else to do, given the considerable number of your absences from class. And also the missing assignments." She then flashed her gradebook at me, where she had a paper covering some of the other student names and grades. After my name there were a few blank squares. I gave her a bunch of alternative grades she could apply, but she just made a small smile with her lips closed and wagged her head. "See you next semester?" she went. "Yeh, I guess so," I went. So there you are.

I got by Mr. Dainty, my Criminal Justice teacher, by getting notes from my Uncle Anson and my (distant) cousin Cod, both lawmen who mentioned that I was working day and night to fight local crime, so was necessarily detained from class(es). My Uncle Anson is Sheriff of Chaud County and Cod is Balona Constable, and they are both very flexible guys, so their comments carried enough weight with Mr. Dainty to get me a passing grade.

Zack made a big *slurp* and an *aaaaah*, very much the way guys at Ned's Sportsbar do after chugging a Valley Brew. He put his cup down firmly on the table and looked me in the eye. Zack's eyes are so brown they are almost black, which is always a surprise, since both his ma and his dad are blue-eyed. He also has bright red hair, which is also a surprise, since both his ma and his dad don't. "I am considering getting me a tattoo," he announced.

This was also a surprise, since it wasn't connected to anything we had been talking about. "What brings that on?"

"Well, honk, Joe. It is the suave thing to do, anybody will tell you. All the big sports stars have tattoos on their shoulder. And movie stars, too, have them—often in other places, as you may well know. Next, you will see members of the Supreme Court flashing their tattoos. I intend to be on the ground floor. My tattoo will be distinguished. I shall welcome any reasonable suggestions."

"How's about a chocolate korndog?"

Zack looked at me with his eyes squinted. "I am serious about this. This is a big deal decision for me. You shut'n poke fun at a guy's serious decisions."

"Who's poking fun? If you have to have a tattoo, why not have a unique one? What I mean to say is, everybody's got a heart or a dragon or Mother or a Born Loser tattoo. Who do you know who has a chocolate korndog? See what I mean?"

Actually, I think tattoos are sort of dumb to get, since they are permanent. They are also fashionable, which is a reason a lot of guys have them. Only problem is, fashions change, where your tattoos can't. All you can do is wear a long-sleeve shirt to cover up *Hilary* when *Jasmine* is now your girl friend. I mentioned these truths to Zack.

"I know all about that stuff. I am not going to do it to be fashionable. I am going to do it to get even with Da who keeps telling me it's a stupid idear and forbids me. It's *my* idear. I am not stupid. Ergo, my idear is not stupid. Da's stupid."

"Anyways, you'll have to wait."

"How come?"

"You got to wait till Halloween anyways."

"Oh, it's got something to do with my birthday. You're gonna make me a birthday present of a tattoo."

"No, I wut'n, since it'll give you a disease where your shoulder'll rot and fall off. The point is, you got to be 18 or it's a crime."

"How come you know so much about tattoos?"

"I'm a student of Criminal Justice, Young Zack. It's my duty to know such things." I didn't mention that at one time I, too, was considering getting me a tattoo, but that Millie Wong snorted in her nose when I said how I was considering it. And how she went on to say that in her opinion, and the opinion of her psych teacher, only idiots and convicts and dopers and dumb athletes do it, on account of the health and esthetics hazards, not to mention the fashion risks.

I inquired about the movie and sports stars, and she classified the sports stars as among the health hazard idiots, and the movie stars among the esthetics hazards doper idiots. Besides, she went, it shows a general weakness of character and a childish need for the attention of the crowd. "A tattoo seems to give their lives meaning, gives them something that makes them feel distinctive for a miserable little while. Yecchh!" Millie sounded disgusted with tattoos and people who had them, or wanted them, or were just *thinking* about getting one.

So I sort of changed my mind. Also, it was expensive and I didn't have any cash.

Zack was at his kitchen sink washing out the cocoa pot when we heard snarfing and shuffling from the porch. Harley only raised his eyebrows. He knew from the sound that it was Uncle Kenworth Burnross, Zack's ancient dad. "Hey, boys! How's things!" went Uncle Kenworth, not sounding mentally impaired at all, the way his own son and my ma always describe him.

"Hey, Uncle Kenworth. How's things!"

Zack didn't bother to look up from his household chores. Zack is a guy that got his driver's license right away, gets a regular allowance, can keep his dog in the house, and is generally spoiled. If I treated my ma the way Zack treats his ma and dad, my ma would grab me by the hair and, well, you know the rest. One thing, though: Zack is neat. He washed not only his baking stuff and the cocoa pot, but he also washed our cups and put the makings back in the cupboard and the fridge.

"What're those things?" Uncle Kenworth leaned over Zack's creations—now mostly crumbs and pieces of weenie, except for Harley's portion—but still recognizable as a creation.

Zack finally recognized his dad. "Those are crumbs from my latest culinary invention, a chocolate korndog." Zack smacked his lips, exactly the way his dad does.

"I have just seen a chocolate korndog," Uncle Kenworth said, as he sat himself at the kitchen table, his Humphrey Bogart hat still on his head. He wagged his head. "I cut'n believe my eyes, either."

"Oh, well. You saw Claire Preene's painting of a chocolate korndog in Mr. D. H. Carp's window. That's not the same thing as seeing a real artistic product fresh from the oven like I just made."

"No, I just saw a real chocolate korndog, son. Sam Joe Sly brought it over to my office in an iron box with a lock on it. Opened it up with a key, took it out and cut a piece off for me, and stood there and watched me eat at it." Uncle Kenworth Burnross belched a good loud burp. A distinct smell of korndog then perused the air around us. "And it wat'n all that bad. Not good. But not all that bad, either. Had a tang to it, y'know. He wanted me to start procedures to patent it, y'know."

"Oh, honk! No!" Zack was right away upset. You could tell from how he hollered. "You're not gonna patent it for that guy, are you?"

"No, son, I am not. But only because it's probably not patentable. It *might* be, maybe, but in my legal opinion it's not a *useful* thing. Maybe edible, but not useful. I wut'n patent it if I was the patent mogul. But then, I'm not the patent mogul. On the other hand...." Uncle Kenworth Burnross mumbled for a while, looking at the ceiling and sort of arguing with himself. "I dit'n tell him that right away, of course. You got to let clients know you're thinking about their best interests, researching the law, eksedra, y'know. I'll get back to him with the bad news later, after I apply for the patent and collect my fee." Uncle Kenworth looked at Harley's korndog sitting on the baking sheet. "That's your version of a chocolate korndog, Zachary?"

"No, no. Harley can't eat chocolate, and that's Harley's." Harley nodded his head in agreement, then looked at Zack as if to say, "Well, is it cool enough?" So Zack put Harley's korndog on a saucer, cut it up nice so you could see the weenie inside, and put it on the table in front of Harley. Harley dug right in, holding the saucer down with one paw, occasionally wiping his lips with the other paw, and making little appreciation noises as he ate.

"Sam Joe Sly's chocolate korndog looks sort of like a maple bar, a nice golden brown, with the weenie sticking a little ways out of it at the end, and chocolate frosting all over the top of it. Tasted sort of like, uh, chocolate and something strange. The something strange was from the weenie, I guess. Sam Joe said something about 'injecting the dog'." Harley stopped eating, looked alarmed.

"Sure," went Zack. "He meant making the weenie have some weird flavor so it wut'n taste so much like weenie. Chocolate and weenie don't match." Zack frowned his whole face and wagged his head. "I've got to do the same. If I'm going to win this battle, I've got to be more creative!"

Zack is now determined to come up with a better chocolate korndog. I bet he is secretly dreaming of such a creation as his motor vehicle to fame and fortune.

Four

It was sort of a shock to see how quick everybody is reacting to Claire's painting. Well, not everybody. But the guys who are the movers and shakers of Balona. I have to include Zack in this category, since he went and moved and shook. He now says he is going to try to inject different stuff in korndog weenies to see if he can't get a taste into it that won't cause the eater to gag and throw up.

He has also made up a bunch of different styles of what he calls "molds." Molds are things like you pour Jell-O into so it comes out when it's all set up looking like Santa Claus or a Valentine or Uncle Sam or whatever. Zack's molds maybe will let the chocolate korndog look like Claire's painting. Which is like what my dad's dream originated in the first place.

Dad is doing better, not drooling so much, sleeping most of the time. "How's things, Dad?" I went when I was over there to see him at the Jolly Times where Ma has stashed him, which is also where she stashed her dad, old Grandpa Daddy Kon.

"How's things, Joey, uh, Joe. It's just that all the guys over here are so old. Makes me feel like I'm gonna die any day now." He pulled the sheet up to his chin which had gray stubble on it. His face was paler than usual, his thin tan mustache needed a trim, his hairpiece was on crooked, as usual.

"Well, it's a rest home. You're supposed to rest here. You getting any actual rest?"

"Well, I can't keep Killer here, and I'm used to feeling his warm body up against my feet, y'know. It's a cold feeling not having your dog up against your feet. Also smells different. Sort of an old-person smell around here. Know what I mean?"

I sniffed a whiff and figured out what he was talking about. "Well, at least the fleas aren't as bad."

"Oh, no, Joey, uh, Joe. The old guys and old ladies here got as many fleas as Killer has. Maybe more." Dad looked sad again. "Maybe you can bring me a fleabomb?" We both laughed at that,

since the last time we used a fleabomb at home, it made Ma calm and decent for a change. Except it probably would have melted her bones if we'd kept it up.

"I guess you're playing pinochle with Grandpa Daddy Kon."

"He dut'n even know who I am. He lays there in his bed and looks at the wall all day. Dut'n even look out the window. Once in a while he will pinch one of the attendants on the butt and laugh like crazy. He will pinch even a guy attendant, he's that far off. You know."

"Oh, well," I went, not wanting to talk about Grandpa Daddy Kon any more.

I had brought Dad some copies of the *Courier* and a few magazines, since he's my favorite dad. He perked right up and we began a decent conversation, more or less.

"So, Joey, uh, Joe. How's things at home?"

"Well, Richie's home again."

"Oh. Yeh. Well, that's nice, I guess." Richie is my little brother. He should be a high school senior, except for all the classes he's flunked, so he's probably actually a sophomore. And he's spent a lot of time at Runcible Hall, which is the place kids get sent for crimes and misdemeanors not quite bad enough to get you sent to the Chaud County Jail or San Quentin. Richie is not my dad's favorite kid.

Richie is my ma's favorite kid. I am my dad's favorite kid. It is a good feeling being somebody's favorite, especially when they act like you are and actually, once in a while, tell you so.

Richie most often wears his tan pants from Runcible Hall, along with a sweatshirt and, if I haven't hid them or don't have them on at the time, my Air Jordans which are too big for him. But lately he's got himself a white police-type motorcycle helmet and black pants and a black shirt, so from a distance, he looks like a motorcycle cop. Richie's buddy Ricky has got the same outfit, plus Ricky has got a red spotlight they flash at night to stop motorists and scare the spit out of them. Especially if the motorist is a teenage girl or an old lady. Since both those guys pull down their helmet faceplates, you can't actually tell who it is behind the helmet.

"Somebody's gonna run you off of the road one of these days," I mentioned. "And then you'll be sorry."

"Nah. They're always too scared. We're gonna start collecting fines next." Meaning the scaring part isn't enough fun for those guys.

The worst part is, he says that when him and Ricky drive away from their victims, he hollers back, "Joseph Kuhl rides again!" Which is going to put me in jail one of these days. So far, even though they've been doing this trope for a long time, no lawman has interrogated me about those crimes, so maybe Richie is joking me about these crimes. But any way you cut it, Richie is a liability.

"Yeh, Richie's home again. He's mostly out with Ricky, as usual, riding around on Ricky's motorcycle." Ricky's full name is Ricky Placock. He is Mr. Placock's kid, who is a teacher at Balona High School and is probably embarrassed to have a kid like Ricky. Except that Richie is the one always caught doing the crimes, and Ricky never gets caught. Ricky has never been in Runcible Hall, a fact that Richie jokes he is working on to change.

"Well, some day Richie'll grow up, and maybe then we'll be proud of him. Who knows. He might grow up to be Mayor of Balona."

"Yeh, well, speaking of which, since Richie got home, Mayor Burberry's box is missing off of my bureau where I put my hair stuff and pimple cream on it. I woke up the other day and it was gone. Richie said it wasn't him, but who else would steal a nice box like that right off of a guy's bureau?"

Mayor Burberry is Simon Burberry. He is an Englishman who builds really neat Burberry Boxes that look like art. What you do with them is put them on your mantel or on your bureau and put stuff on top of them, since you can't open them up or you will die from the fumes inside. At least that's what Mr. Burberry said before he left for England. He went back there to claim his inheritance.

"I hope Mr. Burberry comes back soon," went my dad. "He's got a lot of style."

"Yeh," I went. Which is true. Richie probably did steal my Burberry Box, which I got fair and square in the raffle at the Sugarbeet Festival, and which I swore to Mr. Burberry I wouldn't try to open it up. These boxes are maybe a foot or so square each way, and heavy and shiny, like furniture. If you got one of those boxes you had to *swear* that you wouldn't open it up, and you had to sign a paper to that effect, or Mr. Burberry wouldn't let you have it. Even if you won it in the raffle, fair and square, which I did, more or less.

The problem now is, I can't prove Richie stole my Burberry Box, and my ma won't believe me. She believes either I misplaced it during a nightmare or else an art-loving burglar slipped upstairs one night and spirited it away. "Richie's a good boy," she is always saying. "Not like some around here I could name." She is referring to me, even though I never got shipped off to Runcible Hall for my minor youthful indiscretions, just put on probation a couple times.

"So, how's Chaud County Community College, Joey, uh, Joe?"

"It's fine, Dad." I can't let on to Dad that I flunked a few classes, since he is proud of me going to C4 and working to get my Criminal Justice certificate.

"Uh-huh. You doing any sex?"

"What?" Dad sometimes changes the subject on you. We don't talk about sex much, so this was a surprise.

"Well, I mean, that little fat girl always follows you around and I thought, well, you know."

"You mean *Patella?* Dad! I'm shocked! *Shocked!*" I was not really shocked, since I'm a sophisticated guy and talk about sex always interests me. But *acting* shocked at their questions is always a good way to get your parents off of your back and feeling guilty for asking. Dad right away turned bright red and seemed to be thinking about changing the subject again.

I have to admit that the idea of actually going out and *doing* sex sort of scares me. Even though on the tube, kids a lot younger than me are constantly swapping spit and climbing in and out of each other's beds a mile a minute. But a regular Balona guy has got to swagger about and brag he has done stuff he has not done, simply in order to maintain his manhood status.

So finally I went, "Well, Dad, I'll just say—I get by! Ha ha ha." Dad looked satisfied with my suave response to his sex question, and that was all that was necessary.

But to get back to techniques I learned from Richie. Actually, the Acting-Shocked Technique is one of those few useful things. Richie uses the technique whenever any adult asks him about his doping habits. He puts on a good act, and the adults always look ashamed of themselves for doubting that good boy. Then Richie goes off to do crimes with Ricky Placock, both of them snickering and snorting about how dumb parents are.

The other useful technique I learned off of Richie is the Holy Look. This is where you make your eyes as big as possible and cast them toward Heaven—or directly into the eyes of whoever you are trying to impress. It makes you look innocent, if sort of stupid.

Another technique I have *not* learned from Richie is his way of getting around my ma, since it doesn't work when I do it. For example, he will bring her gifts. I will bring her a gift, but she will be suspicious right away. Richie will bring her a gift, and she will tell everybody about how nice and good Richie is. Hah!

For example, the plastic head of Shakespeare. Richie got this plastic head at the Delta City Fleamarket recently, he said. Probably he stole it. It is about the size of a regular human head with part of the neck, only it's made out of plastic. I think it's pretty repulsive looking, pale and fat and gray and with its eyes closed, not like it was made of stone and gazing at you like a regular statue of a head.

It looks sort of like Grandpa Daddy Kon, except that Daddy Kon is skinny and still breathing. But when Richie brought this head to my ma, he had it sitting up on one of our good dinner plates. Ma was lounging with a toddy at the kitchen table, and he set the head on the plate down in front of her.

"See what I brought you, Ma. Just for you."

"Hey," she went, "it's just like a Shakespeare head. We can put it up over the fireplace in the living room, and everybody will see we got some class after all." She practically cracked her face with a big smile. "See, Kenzy, see what little Richie brought me!" She was hollering at Dad in the living room, but she had forgot that she had packed Dad off to the Jolly Times Rest Home, "for his own good," she said.

So, up there on the mantel it sits, sort of shiny. A fat bald head with the eyes closed. Doesn't look like Shakespeare at all, since I think Shakespeare always wore something friggly around his neck, which was longer than this plastic head's neck, which is pretty short.

After I left Dad, I went back on up to Mr. D. H. Carp's Groceries & Sundries to see what was up. Carp's is one of the places where you go to find out stuff in Balona, since everybody passes by there sooner or later. The other places are Ned's

Sportsbar, Peeking Peek-Inn, and the *Courier*. There's another place called Veterans Hall, but mostly veterans go there, and also Uncle Kenworth Burnross who considers himself a veteran, since he was on the draft board a long time ago, an army thing.

I found Zack at the magazine counter and Mr. Carp himself hollering at Zack not to get fingerprints on the magazines. "If you want to look, you got to buy," Mr. Carp always says. Only nobody pays attention to him ordering you around.

Kind of like the way a parent will say to their kid, "Don't do that, Junior. Quit doing that." And Junior goes right on doing it. His folks don't pay any more attention, since they are happy that they did their duty and *said something*, the way the parenting books tell you to do. That makes them feel better. Junior is also happy since he gets to go ahead doing what he was doing, knowing that his ma and dad are happy and off of his back.

It's great that kids now have this way of ignoring what their parents tell them. If they work it right, the kids can use the same technique at school, since teachers know they can always get sued and lose their shirts if they insist on having it their way.

"So, Zack. *Tell Gort, Klaatu barada nikto!*" This is a sort of code me and Zack have. We first heard it on an old space movie. Nobody knows what it means, but it sounds suave and people passing by think we're big scholars talking a foreign language. I say it first, and then Zack repeats it in hushed tones.

"Yeh," went Zack, looking into his magazine. "You ought to quit using that dumb saying. It's childish." Zack was not using hushed tones. Zack was sounding depressed.

"How come you're sounding so depressed?"

"I tried three different formulas and all it did was made the weenies taste weird."

"Like what kind of formulas?"

"I just made 'em taste like onion and garlic, but the taste dit'n go with the chocolate. Also, I feel sort of bloated."

Zack also *looked* bloated, but I didn't want to mention that and increase his depression.

Just then, Mr. Sam Joe Sly came in with a big box and a loud voice. "Hey, Mr. Carp, I got a bunch of chocolate korndogs here for your customers to try out for me."

Mr. Carp came out of his office rubbing his hands, and the two of them started putting Mr. Sam Joe Sly's creations into trays in the bakery cabinet.

"You wanna be one of my guinea pigs, kid?" Mr. Sam Joe Sly handed me a chocolate korndog and I found myself biting into it even without looking at Zack. Zack was standing there with his mouth open.

I chewed and chewed. "Hey," I went. "I tastes pretty good!"

Five

"I got my people working on this day and night, and Mr. Kenworth Burnross is going to patent it. You say it tastes good? Say, ain't this red-headed kid Mr. Kenworth Burnross's kid?" Mr. Sam Joe Sly was looking at Zack as if he might be a foreign spy or have some kind of a disease.

"Yeh, he is. Name's Zachary. Yeh, this here's not bad. Maybe needs some sugar."

"I need to try it, too," went Zack, his hand out.

"What's this taste you got in the dog part?" I asked.

"It's a bunch of secret ingredelents. This is just for trial and error, y'know. We're gonna mess around with it until we get it right. Then we're gonna go public in a big way."

Mr. Carp was peering at Mr. Sly's korndogs like they might get up and march away if he didn't tie them down. "Those things look a lot like the painting the young Preene girl did that's over there in my window." Mr. Carp waved his hand toward the painting in the window.

"Well, they ought to, since that's the model I used. Cut'n bake 'em in the regular King Korndog pans, so I had my staff make up some special molds. But I frosted 'em myself in the lab we got over at the Kastle Keep. Pretty tasty looking, huh!"

"Well, since I'm hosting the inspiration in my cabinet there, that ought to be worth a cut of the profits."

Mr. Sam Joe Sly snorted in his nose and laughed a huge, "Ha ha ha! You got a rich sense of humor, Mr. Carp. But I will give you exclusive rights to give away the trial balloons here."

"Give away? You can't give away stuff and expect people to pay for it later. I say charge *more* for it at the beginning and then slowly lower the price, the way they do with cars."

"Or the way they do with computers," went Zack. "The day after I bought mine, the price went down $200."

I thought of a creative idea: "Or you could give *cash back* to everybody who tried one, like you get when Mr. Pezmyer sells you one of his Buicks."

"Hey, you're getting your own money back when he does that. Dit'n you know that?" Zack is always showing off how much he knows about the way business works.

Mr. Sam Joe Sly wagged his head and gave me a hard look about my *cash back* idea. "Nah. This stuff is too experimental. Who knows, maybe it'll make somebody gag, and they'll sue."

Mr. Carp turned pale. "I better make 'em sign a waiver, you think?" Mr. Carp is mean, but he's also pretty crafty.

"Yeh, go ahead. Whatever. Only I want 'em to write up a comment if they take one."

We didn't notice Mrs. Bellona Shaw standing right there until she chimed in. "I bet you could make a pile of money if you called them the *Burberry* Korndog, since Mayor Burberry is so sweet and stylish and attractive." She tittered and lashed her eyes at Mr. Sam Joe Sly.

"Hey, if we call 'em anything other than King Chocolate Korndogs, it'll be King Slydogs. Don't that ring a bell with you guys, huh? *Slydogs?*"

Actually the Slydog tasted pretty good—sort of weird and chocolaty both, if you overlooked the sort of heavy meat taste hanging onto your tongue, a feature which did tend to gag you. I suggested an experiment. "Hey, Mr. Sly, me and Zack here really need to see if your quality control is working. So how's about another Slydog?" I winked my eye at him, which is what he does to everybody he talks to.

He didn't wink back. "I'm gonna reserve these dogs for Mr. Carp's actual paying customers. But maybe Mrs. Shaw would like to try one?" He showed his crooked yellow teeth at Mrs. Shaw who was using her comb to touch up her practically white new blonde hair-do with the black eyebrows.

"My!" went Mrs. Shaw, "It looks sort of, uh, masculine." Her face blushed bright cherry red all the way from her neck to her hairline. She began to sweat. "Tee hee," she went and grabbed up a chocolate korndog, giving it a good bite and talking with her mouth full right away. "Hm. I wonder if it would be better warm."

"I tried it hot from the microwave, but the chocolate frosting got all runny and stuck to my fingers, eksedra, see?" He turned and showed everybody where the chocolate dripped onto his shirt and wrist. He also had some on the corner of his lip, but nobody wanted to say anything about that since Mr. Sly is so rich.

Everybody was watching Mrs. Shaw masticate her korndog. I noticed that she chews only on the left side. I notice stuff like that because of my training in tradecraft and Criminal Justice in general. Mrs. Shaw looked at the ceiling as she chewed. She looked at the floor. She looked at her watch. I made a few notes in my notebook. "Well?" went Mr. Sly.

"Oh, it's interesting. Yas. Interesting. The taste is sort of like..." She giggled, "parsley, sage, rosemary, and..."

"Parsley! That's what the weird taste is." Zack hollered so loud that Mr. Sackworth jerked on his stool and started chewing on his jerky again.

Mrs. Shaw looked disappointed, gave Zack a hard look. "Well," she went, "I have to toddle off now."

"Oh, first you got to put your observation in writing. That's in sort of payment for trying it out and, like, voting."

"Oh. Oh, well." Mrs. Shaw got out her fountain pen, held it up to the light, maybe to show off the fact that she uses a fountain pen when everybody else in Balona uses a ballpoint or a pencil. She looked at the ceiling. She looked at the floor. She looked at her watch. She wrote a few words on the slip of paper Mr. Carp had handed her, waved it in the air to dry off the ink, made a big deal out of putting her pen away, and trounced off through the front door.

"What'd she write there?" Mr. Sam Joe Sly looked interested.

"I don't know that I should show you."

"Hell, I'm the owner. I'm supposed to know."

"I thought maybe it was supposed to be anonymous, like an election."

"I seen her writing it. I seen she used a fountain pen. How many people in Balona who will taste my Slydogs there use a fountain pen. C'mon, Mr. Carp, don't be a old fart."

Mr. D. H. Carp turned pink as a monkey's butt and handed over the slip of paper.

"*Tastes okay* is what she wrote. Now what kind of criticism is that! That's not a criticism." He turned to me and Zack. "Hey, you guys write out your criticism, too."

So each of us did. I was feeling sort of jokish by that time, after watching Mr. Sly twitch about Mrs. Shaw's criticism.

"Lemme see what you wrote, kid." I handed him my slip of paper where I had wrote, *Tastes okay.* Mr. Sly said a rude word and grabbed Zack's slip. He said another rude word and stormed out, not saying another verb.

"What did you write, Zack?"

"I said it *tastes okay*, of course." We high-fived and laughed a lot. Even Mr. D. H. Carp who never laughs except at accidents and funerals smirked through his nose.

"Hey, Zack. Mr. Sly said your dad was going to patent the Slydog."

"Ahhh. My dad will tell a client anything. Mr. Sly doesn't have a lock on this thing, so I'm going home and perfect mine. Maybe I'll use parsley, too. Maybe I'll get some weed from Aunty Pring Chaud's greenhouse. That'll make people sit up and take notice."

"That'll put people to sleep and you in the pokey."

"Oh, well." Zack picked his nose, a sure sign of keen thought. Then he snapped his fingers. "I got it. I know exactly how I can get the upper hand in this struggle." Zack's eyes got beady and he had a cruel smile on his lips, like Kiefer Sutherland. You could hardly see the bead in his eye because of the smudges on his glasses, but the cruel smile was easily visible.

"Well, how?"

"I don't know if I should tell you, since you will right away blab to the whole neighborhood."

"You should talk. You, the boyfriend of the biggest blabber in Balona."

"You mean Patella? That boyfriend business she wrote up in the *Courier* was her idear, not mine. I deny it categorically. Alls I do is have milkshakes and korndogs with her. Or nowdays, cocoa and korndogs. She dut'n even know this latest idear."

Mr. Sackworth, Patella's dad, was crouched on his stool right there at the cash register, overhearing all this gossip about his daughter. You hardly realized he was there, since he is very fat and sits statue still, hardly breathing and with his little fat eyes closed, chewing on a cud of jerky. He does this all day long, and comes to only when his sensors detect a customer approaching the register. He wheezed and swallowed. "Patella's a good girl, boys. You shut'n talk bad about her."

Me and Zack both got red in the face. Since Mr. Sackworth is sort of my Saturday superior, him being Mr. Carp's Chief

Boxperson and me being only Assistant Chief Boxperson, I apologized right away. "It was Zack here said the bad stuff, Mr. Sackworth, not me."

"You're the one called her a blabber. Alls I said was it was her idear to have me known as her boyfriend. If you want to know, she said her idear was to make you jealous."

My personal UITS Manual (Universal Intelligence Training School—Pronounce it *WITS*) tells me it's wise to change the subject when you get the feeling you're losing the argument. "Well, I am trained to keep secrets, Young Zack, so you can tell me in confidence about your winning idear."

Zack's beady-eyed expression returned and he sort of relaxed. I have learned that when you are in a tight spot, all you have to do is give a guy a compliment. It can be an indirect compliment, like my *winning idear* remark. It doesn't have to be about how sweet his breath is. "I'm gonna notify somebody that I got a winning invention over here. Somebody influential. Somebody...." Zack looked out of the corner of his eye at Mr. Sackworth. "I'll tell you later, when we're alone."

All the way back to Zack's house I kept after him to reveal me his secret, but all he did was keep on whistling Mr. Burberry's favorite tune, "Going Home." We were climbing Zack's front steps when I finally realized that Harley was not with us.

"Where's Harley?"

"Harley is already up in our room studying for his test."

"What test is that?"

"Harley is going to be a lost and found dog for Mr. Preene over at the *Courier*. He's going to find lost dogs."

"Whose idear was that?"

"It was Harley's own idear. He's full of idears, but this one is a winner all right."

"How do you mean he's studying? Dogs don't study."

"Well, honk, Joe. Harley studies a lot like you do."

"I actually don't study much, relying mostly on my powers of retention."

"That's what I meant. But Harley also *thinks* about stuff. Then, after he's thought a while, he's ready to take his test. He's been sitting in his window seat this morning, looking out the window, thinking about stuff."

"Well, that's the way I do it, too. Only I don't always pass."

"Well, there's bound to be differences of intelligence there."

THE CHOCOLATE KORNDOG

I didn't say anything for a while, thinking about that, and about what Zack might have meant when he said it. Finally, I stopped thinking about it, since I couldn't find anything positive in it and didn't want to start a big argument with Zack when he was about to reveal his secret.

Up in Zack's bedroom, there was Harley, sitting in his window seat, looking out the window. He turned his head, looked at us over his shoulder, frowned a little, then moved himself right back to looking out the window. A thinking dog.

"So, what's your big secret?"

"What secret is that?"

"The secret you dit'n want to talk about in front of Mr. Sackworth."

"Oh, that secret. It's nothing. I'm just going to become rich and famous is all."

"C'mon, Zack, you said you would tell me when we were alone."

"Well, we're not alone. There's Harley there." Zack and Harley both snickered.

"Well, I guess I'll just go on home."

"Okay, okay. I'm gonna call up Buddy Swainhammer and get interviewed on the Buddy Swainhammer Show, live. I'll reveal that I am the inventor of the Chocolate Korndog and that a corporate conspiracy is trying to rob me out of fame and fortune."

"Wow. But probably Mr. Sam Joe Sly will sue you."

"So? I got my own in-house defense lawyer, such as he is. Nothing to worry about. Besides, a minor's got immunity."

"You don't have a factory to produce chocolate korndogs."

"I don't need to produce chocolate korndogs. Alls I need to do is tell everybody I got screwed out of my invention. Then the thief will have to pay me a settlement."

Zack is planning to get Mr. Buddy Swainhammer and his Talk Show to set up Mr. Sam Joe Sly for a settlement about who invented the chocolate korndog. I am beginning to think that maybe Zack has criminal tendencies.

"Hey, Zack. You got to mention my dad on the talk show. How he was the one had the vision and the dream."

"Yeh, I might." He picked up his phone and called the Buddy Swainhammer show. Since he knows a lot of telephone numbers from memory, he didn't have to look it up. It took him maybe two minutes to convince Buddy Swainhammer's program director that

Zack had something unusual to say. "Buddy will be ready for me when I call him up live day after tomorrow night." Zack smacked his lips. "Joe, I need to be alone so me and Harley can work up my script for then."

Zack, my young cousin, a high school kid, my Q, dismissed me. What a downer. I dragged myself home and sat in the basement for a while, thinking sad thoughts. I was hardly able to wait till when I will hear what Zack has to reveal to the public.

Six

When Zack finally got on the air with Buddy Swainhammer over KDC-FM, I was so tired I could hardly keep my eyes open. Buddy had spent almost the whole late-night talk show bragging about Mr. D. H. Carp, and how Mr. Carp was going to be a great Member of Congress. And how Buddy was going to Washington, D.C., with him to be one of his advisers. Only problem with that is, Mr. Carp will never get elected because he has a reputation for telling lies. He will look you right in the eye and tell you a fantastic lie. Everybody knows that, so nobody will vote for him.

Lots of Balona guys tell lies, but they never look you in the eye when they're doing it. You'd think Mr. D. H. Carp would have learned after all these years.

Anyway, when Zack got on the air he was nailed right away by Buddy Swainhammer who likes to nail all his callers. "I understand somebody over there in Balona is trying to steal an idear from Mr. Sam Joe Sly, the fine owner of King Korndog. Is that the fact, caller?"

"No!" Zack practically squealed his answer, since Buddy Swainhammer had twisted Zack's idea backwards and was now putting Zack on the anvil to get hammered. "No, that's not the fact at all. The fact is that Mr. Sam Joe Sly has stolen the idear from me!" Zack really sounded convincing, so Buddy led him on a dialog about the "Balona Secret Invention." Zack wouldn't describe the chocolate korndog, except that it was something secret.

"Well, what is it you're talking about exactly? We got to know what it is, if we're gonna take sides in this argument."

"If I reveal the invention, other guys might steal it, too, besides Mr. Sam Joe Sly."

"So, you think so little of our fine audience that you'd call them thiefs in advance? That's a fine thing!" Buddy always does this to his callers. Makes them squirm.

"If they knew what this was, it is so neat they would all be tempted, yes. So that's why I'm saying only that Mr. Sam Joe Sly is trying to steal this great invention away from me so he can stuff his pockets with even more gold, which he's already got a lot of."

"Well, we'll just have to get Mr. Sam Joe Sly on the horn here, and see what he has to say." And then followed a few minutes of Buddy Swainhammer trying to raise Mr. Sam Joe Sly on the phone. You could hear the phone ringing, but nobody answered it. "We'll just have to continue this exciting discussion when we can get Mr. Sly to respond in person. In the meantime, you better tell us your name, ma'am."

Buddy always does this, too. He accuses guys with sort of high voices, like Zack, of being a female. He does this to make them mad, so they will squeal.

Zack squealed. "I'm a guy, but I won't reveal my identification until I'm talking ear to ear with Mr. Sam Joe Sly."

Well, that ended it. We have to listen on the next broadcast, which happens to be tomorrow night. Everybody will be listening then, which is probably Zack's intention.

But right away Zack called me up. "You got to try my latest, Joe. It'll knock off your socks."

"You're referring to your latest in the secret-invention line, I trust."

"Exactly. I baked it up tonight while I was waiting for Buddy to get on with it. C'mon over and try it."

"Zack, it's 11:20PM. I got to get my beauty sleep."

"Then make it tomorrow soon as you can. You just got to try this."

"Will do." I was pleased that Zack thought so much of me that I would be the first to try his new achievement. I went to bed feeling that I had something fine to look forward to. I even stopped feeling miserable over possible different fates of my Burberry Box. I was grateful that tomorrow would be Saturday, and that the only thing I had to worry about was my job at Mr. D. H. Carp's. I decided I could be slightly late for that, in the name of science.

In spite of wondering what new flavor Zack had dreamed up for the chocolate korndog, I went right off to sleep and woke up feeling refreshed and ready to *carpe diem*, like Doctor Fardel says.

First thing Zack said was, "You better sit down when you eat this." He was looking at me as if I was going to fall down on him.

I chuckled. "There, there, Young Zack, never fear. After eating my ma's food for a lifetime, I have the digestion of a dog." I crinkled my eyes at him, but he frowned and made a secret gesture with his hand, meaning I should not talk that way in front of Harley. "For petesakes," I went, but sat down at his kitchen table. I took one of the paper napkins Aunt Pippa's got stuffed into a container on the table there, tucked it in under my collar, ready to do my duty.

"I'll zap it in the microwave for a few seconds to give it a little twitch. Not too much, so it won't run all over your fingers, though." We waited for the microwave to bong, and Zack presented it before me like it was his new treasure. He handed me a fork. "You shut'n eat this with your fingers. This is too high class."

This new product finally looked like Claire's painting. It was sort of golden brown all around, except on top where it had nice gooey chocolate frosting. The dog stuck out a little on each end, like a pair of brown noses.

"That's a two-dog chocolate korndog," Zack joked.

I was tempted to make a clever remark about brownnoses, but Zack stood there looking serious again, so I looked serious, too, figuring out where to start in with my fork. Harley sat on his chair at the other end of the table, his front paws up on the table, him leaning forward, like he expected something to happen.

I felt I had to do some sort of criticism so I wouldn't look like an experimental dummy. "Chocolate frosting is sort of gooey. Is that what you want, instead of *ganache*?"

"That is *gananche*. It's just warm *ganache* is all. Cold *ganache* would crackle when you bite on it. You'll like it!" Zack was now leaning forward, like Harley. He pointed with his finger. "Eat that end first." They were both expecting my criticism, like I was a professional taster, sort of.

I felt very pro, cut off a piece with my fork where Zack indicated, took a bite, chewed it up, tasted it. "Hey, it's chocolaty and, uh, uh, minty! It's *minty* tasting. Hey, it's pretty good, Zack. You got something here, all right." It tasted a whole lot better than Mr. Sam Joe Sly's parsley-tasting korndog "It's got a corn texture, too, sort of like a real korndog. And the weenie doesn't have a heavy meat taste. Just sort of, uh, minty and meaty." I ate up some more. "Yeh, minty and chocolaty and meaty. Yeh."

"Is that all you taste, Joe? Just chocolate and mint and meat? You sure that's all?"

"Yeh, well...." My tongue was sort of thick all of a sudden. And the light over the kitchen sink was blinking, sort of red, then pink, then yellow. And I was feeling woozy. Comfortable, but woozy. And Harley and Zack were both laughing. I felt like laughing, too, but felt more like taking a nap. "You got something to drink with this?" I went, hoping for some hot cocoa, maybe.

"Did you say something, Joe?"

"I said, I said. Did I say something?" I couldn't remember saying anything, but the whole situation seemed funny and I laughed and laughed.

Harley spoke right up. "Say, Joe," Harley went, sort of surprising me at first. Then I realized that Harley is a pretty smart dog and probably has been staying quiet so as not to astonish humans who wouldn't understand. "How come you don't have a dog, Joe? Everybody should have a dog."

"I know, Harley, but my ma is just getting so she can stand Killer, what with his ripe smell and his fleas and all. She wut'n let me have a dog of my own. She'd probably shoot it."

Harley frowned. "Well, that wut'n do at all." He wagged his head. "I understand, Joe. You got it rough at home. Maybe some day your ma will kick off. Then you could have your own faithful friend, like Zack here has got me." Harley squinched his eyes. "And I got Zack."

"Yeh, that would be nice, Harley. And maybe then you could recommend a particular dog." I thought for a minute. "Mr. Keyshot's dog is a nice clean dog. Maybe I could find a dog like that out at the shelter."

"I would be happy to recommend a dog for you, Joe. Of course, Mr. Keyshot's dog does have some psychological problems, y'know. You have to watch out for that when you get dogs from the shelter. Yes, I would be happy to advise you."

"Well, I appreciate that, Harley."

Harley smacked his lips and closed his eyes, exactly the way Zack and his dad both do. Then I fell out of my chair and ended up on the floor, where it felt pretty comfortable, so I went to sleep right there.

I woke up alone and with a headache. Somebody, probably Zack, had dragged me into the living room and had thrown one of Harley's blankets over me. Nobody ever goes into Zack's living room any more, so nobody saw me laying there, out of it. I staggered upstairs to Zack's room, still floating some.

"What's the idear!" I went, feeling like I should maybe bust my little cousin one, since it was obvious he had doped up his chocolate korndog and had used me as his guinea pig.

"Well, it was tasty, wat'n it?"

"What was that stuff?"

"Richie gave it to me before he, uh, went away the last time." Zack was being delicate, unusual for Zack. "Some pills he lifted from the working counter in Mr. Vibrissa's drugstore. He said if I wanted some fun I should grind one up and put it in Harley's water dish or my backyard birdbath. But I figured I'd better try it on a human being first, y'know, since Harley's pretty sensitive. Get the right dosage. Richie said it wut'n hurt."

"Richie's an idiot. He'll tell you anything for fun. You cut've killed me or fried my brain."

"Well, honk, Joe. You're still alive and I don't smell fried brain. And you had a nice conversation with Harley until you zonked out." Zack looked at me with his beady-eye look. "So, how was it?" I guessed he meant the korndog, not the conversation.

"The korndog was fine, if I remember correctly. It tasted like chocolate and mint, with meat in the background. Sort of like one of those candies that make you sick when you eat too many, the way kids do. And, what, sort of chewy. And tasty. Yeh, tasty. And with the added attraction, you got a hit, all right."

"You mean by added attraction, the ground-up pill."

"Yeh, of course. Oh." I realized what I was saying: The ground-up pill sort of made the chocolate korndog a tastier experience. "Well, you could maybe market it as a sleeping aid. Or a conversation aid for shy guys." I looked at Harley out of the corner of my eye, but he was sleeping in his window seat, not in a conversational mood, I guessed. "On the other hand, maybe you could end up in the pokey."

"I wut'n do it, except as a joke. I put it in there as a joke, Joe." Zack actually looked sort of worried.

"Yeh, dumb kids will do that once and a while, don't they."

"It's no big deal."

"It happened not to be a big deal, except for my headache and the fact that I didn't get to my job. But you dit'n know what that pill was. It cut've been a poison. Maybe it was a poison and it just dit'n affect me." I breathed a sigh of relief. "I think I just missed dying maybe. Or maybe it will happen this afternoon."

"Well, that's sort of dramatic. I was gonna try it out on myself first, but then I decided maybe there better be somebody to watch the experiment in case Richie was in a bad mood when he gave it to me."

"Yeh. Richie dut'n usually give away *anything* for free. I think you did a dumb thing, Young Zack. And I think I'm just a lucky guy I dit'n die or turn blue or start drooling. Yeh, that was a dumb thing."

"Well, you said it tastes good."

"That's about the chocolate korndog, not about the pill!"

"Oh. Yeh. Well. Sorry."

At least I got an apology out of Zack. Pretty rare for him. Usually he won't ever admit he's wrong. This time maybe he saw the error of his way. He started looking sad. I decided to let him sweat a little. "I won't mention this experience to Cousin Nim," I went.

"What? You wut'n of mentioned this to him in the first place, would you?" Zack respects Cousin Nim a lot, especially since Cousin Nim is Pastor Nim, and it was just a flash of my genius to mention his name. I bet Zack started thinking in the back of his head how he would explain to Pastor Nim what he just did. At least Zack will now feel a little guilty about feeding pills to unsuspecting guys.

It's something a stupid high school kid will do for fun, but it's a really dumb thing to do, since strange pills are liable to do strange things to guys. Maybe even kill them or cause glands and organs to swell up and burst or fall off.

First it was tattoos. Now it is pills. Maybe I should figure out how to do some advising to my young cousin.

Seven

It turns out that Buddy Swainhammer never even bothered to call Zack back. He never got Mr. Sam Joe Sly on the line, either, which is probably why he never called Zack. Mr. Sam Joe Sly refused to talk about "his" invention, is what they told Zack when he called the station. Buddy Swainhammer dropped Zack's whole sensational story. Zack has to think of a whole new strategy to bring Mr. Sam Joe Sly to his legal knees. So now Zack is pouting and eating pizzas with Patella, which is what they always do when they are depressed. Actually, they go in Patella's purple Ford coupe "Barney" to Mello Fello and eat pizza whether they're depressed or not.

But the thing that is more interesting is about the turkeys.

When I got to work, finally, nobody paid any attention to the fact that I was sort of late. Actually it was after lunch when I finally got there, and Mr. Sackworth was already asleep at the cash register, Mr. Carp was asleep with his feet up on his desk, and the regular customers were all shopping at the Mall in Delta City. What you do when there is nothing to do is stand at the door and look at the sights.

Uncle Hannibal's painting crew of Junior Trilbend and Bobby R. Langsam was still slopping paint on the giant bullseye up on his roof. I went out in back and climbed the outside ladder up to Mr. Carp's (and Mr. Keyshot's) roof, got a better look at their progress. Not bad. Colorful. Of course, I remained covert while up there.

Zack mentioned that when you're in an airplane, and you see that bullseye down there, what you will think is, *that's Hannibal Chaud's Funerals.* Smart advertising. Junior and Bobby R. look like they're having extra fun, since every once in a while they frisbee hunks of tar paper at each other, or sail big hunks across the parking lot.

I climbed back down, went into the store, put on my green apron, and took up my station where I could reach the jerky jar

41

occasionally.   What you do when there isn't much going on is think erotic thoughts.   So I chewed on jerky and thought some erotic thoughts about Willow Runcible, a cute long-legged girl from Delta City who is on the newspaper staff at C4.   Willow is tall and blonde, wears short skirts and has nice thighs.   But like all newshounds, Willow is more interested in getting famous as a reporter than having a meaningful relationship with a guy from Balona.

Then I thought erotic thoughts about Millie Wong.   Millie's real name is Amelia Earhart Wong.   She is Mr. Wong's kid who lives in their place over Peking Peek-Inn down the street here. She is also my Criminal Justice classmate at C4, plays the piano, and is almost as tall as Willow.   She has creamy skin and sweet-looking pink lips and long brown hair.   Only she likes Sal Shaw who is six-four and smart and has abs all over and a Plymouth.   Of course, I have a car, too, but I can't drive it without gas, and gas is too expensive to let you drive around with no place you really want to get to.

Those guys are not the turkeys I referred to earlier.   There is Richie, a guy who is a different kind turkey all right, but more about him later.

Then there is Claire.   I have mentioned before that I am supposed to marry Claire, according to my ma.   But Claire is not only tall and blonde, sort of like the way Willow looks, but she is also smart and is sort of cool to me.   So it is not a sure thing that Claire would ever want to marry me.   Besides, she likes Jack Ordway and hangs out with him.   Besides, she is my cousin.

There is always Patella hanging around, hinting about being your girlfriend.   But who would want to consider Patella his girlfriend?   Patella is too bossy to be a guy's girlfriend.   She always has got something to say that makes a tall guy feel short. If you don't do right away what she says, she'll make you pay. Zack once said something about Patella that I keep remembering.

"When Patella grows up," went Zack, "she'll be just like A'nt Bapsie." Meaning Patella will be just like my ma.   My ma has already got my dad walking on his knees.   Forget that.

Clare and Patella and even Richie are not the turkeys which I was referring to earlier.   The turkeys I am talking about came running down the middle of Front Street in a huge cloud, from the south, barreling towards Airport Way.   I had wandered from my post over to the window to observe Balona life on Front Street. Once in a while you can see something interesting.

But on Saturday afternoon, when all the kids have gone into the New Oliver and are busy in there flicking Milk Duds at the screen (no matter what picture is showing), and there's no funeral going on at my Uncle Hannibal's, and Cod is slumbering away on his bench outside his office, and there's no traffic at all, then is when you don't usually see anything interesting. What you do is stand there at the door chewing on jerky and nodding off.

But about the turkeys. I'll regale about the Mysterious Balona Turkey Run.

First, I need to mention that, although the korndog is the national dish of Balona, our town has got another big industry. We do have a sewer plant and a dump, which are also enterprises of note, but the other big one, besides King Korndog, is King Turkey. No relation to King Korndog, but everybody suspects the turkey factory just wants to trade on the famous King name, which Mayor Burberry and the Sly family are busy doing right now.

King Turkey feeds and slaughters and cuts up and freezes thousands of turkeys a day all year long, not just at Thanksgiving. My dad once worked at King Turkey where he rose to the rank of Assistant Featherman's Helper. That was before he went in the Army over to Vietnam where he rose to the rank of REMF (a secret job I cannot disclose since Dad said he might be executed if I ever did).

Anyway, King Turkey has a huge plant up off the West Levee Road that uses water out of the Yulumne River. After they wash off their turkeys with it, they dump the water back into the Yulumne. Then the town of Fruitstand which is downriver never fails to complain about the turkey taste of their drinking water, since they get it out of the Yulumne.

Fortunately, our water company sucks most of our water out of the Yulumne *upriver* from King Turkey, so us Balonans don't get to enjoy turkey-flavored water. When the river is low we also get some of our water from wells in the ground, one of which is next to the dump and the other of which is next to the sewer plant.

The sewer plant also discharges their end product ("Our End Product is Sweet and Clean") into the Yulumne just upriver from where King Turkey sucks their water supply out, and just *downriver* from where our town water supply is sucked out of. You can tell this is a profitable enterprise for all concerned. You could also get an idea that if the Yulumne ever goes really dry, a lot of people will be in trouble.

Anyway, there came the turkeys making a huge gobbling noise. You'd think they'd lay off the gobbling while they run, but no, they gobble even louder while running. They gobbled loud enough to wake up Constable Cod, since it took them a full minute, running at top speed, to pass by Cod's bench. When they were gone, it was like a tree had fallen down in the forest and there was nobody there to hear it, it was so quiet.

Guys came out of the bowling alley, looking both ways, wondering what that noise was. Mrs. Bellona Shaw came all the way out of the *Courier* office, waving her fountain pen. Frank Backhouse came out of Frank's Soupe de Jour, his Franksburger spatula clutched in his hand. Even I made my way out of the door and peered after the turkeys now passing Pezmyer's Buick and the first of them turning east onto Airport Way.

"It was the turkey run again!" I hollered.

"Oh, that." everybody went, and returned to their labors.

How come is that? you will ask. And I will answer: It happens about every three or four weeks, or sometimes more often. Somebody over there at King Turkey leaves a door open, and all the turkeys in the feedlot take off in a group. Some guys say that turkeys are stupid, but I believe they get a feeling about what's on the other side of that Green Door, the famous factory door that leads to them becoming frozen turkey parts. They decide they don't want the honor. And then something strange happens.

Curious thing about The Mysterious Balona Turkey Run is that the birds—a different group each time—always follow the same route: They start at the factory up there on the West Levee Road, run down into town, turn north on Front Street (instead of going straight down Fourth Avenue), turn east on Airport Way, then south on King Way where they dash by the King Korndog Kastle Keep to Eighth Avenue, then back up Eighth Avenue to Front Street again where they slow down quite a bit, and then they make an *S* and return to the lot at the Turkey Factory.

Nobody you can see is leading, chasing, or directing them.

Of course when they return from their 2-K run, those guys are all breathless and worn out, and probably they have lost body fluids and a couple of pounds, the way runners do when they run. They have also lost their gobble, so they are quiet. And, as my dad himself has witnessed, when the Green Door slides open, the athletic turkeys then march quietly through to their doom.

Right after the turkeys disappeared, Zack showed up. He was driven to Mr. D. H. Carp's Groceries & Sundries by Patella Sackworth.

Zack looked serious, pushing the door open for himself where he was walking in front of Patella and not holding the door open for her, something his ma is always after him about. I always hold the door open for women and pull out their chair, the way James Bond does. Zack came right to the point.

"Patella says I shut'n do it, but I think I'm about ready to bring in the big guns." Zack took off his glasses and wiped the glass on his shirt tail, a sign he was truly serious since he usually doesn't care if his glasses are smeared-up or not.

"Alls I said was you should think it through first, before you call him, since maybe the same thing will happen with him as happened with Buddy Swainhammer

"You said I shut'n do it, is what I remember you saying." Zack was arguing. It is not wise to argue with Patella, as Zack will some day find out. She will always get even. "Anyways," he went on, "I thought I would get your opinion, since I got Harley's and now Patella's. Harley thought my idear was brilliant."

Patella wasn't finished. "I just thought I would write up a nice column first, and prepare everybody for the event."

"You could still write your column and prepare everybody for the event. It's just that the event will happen sooner my way."

"If it happens at all." Patella always has to have the last word.

"So," I went, "what's this big event you're talking about?"

"It will be bigger than Sugarbeet Festival, bigger than Fourth of July, bigger than Halloween."

Since Halloween is Zack's birthday, I guessed he was being really enthusiastic. "So? What is it?"

"It's a great idear I had."

"Yeh, so?"

"It's going to establish a tradition. And it will also establish my fame as its inventor."

"Yeh, so?"

"I am speaking of the Great Balona Chocolate Korndog Bakeoff." Zack closed his eyes and smacked his lips as he finished his sentence. "I'm gonna have people out-do Mr. Sam Joe Sly. We'll give prizes so everybody will know Mr. Sam Joe Sly's product it'n the best." Zack closed his eyes and smacked his lips. "Probably my own product will win the big prize."

"It dut'n sound fair to win the prize if you're the one running the contest." Patella is always finding fault with a guy's ideas. "So, who'd you get that cut'n be bribed by Mr. Sam Joe Sly, who everybody knows, would bribe his mother to win any prize."

"I plan to solve that problem this afternoon, after I get home and relax a little, loosen up my lip for the important phone call."

Zack was sounding more and more confident. I had to take him down a peg or two. "Just remember how confident you felt when you went to get Buddy Swainhammer to sandbag Mr. Sam Joe Sly."

"That's all in the past, Joe. This is bound to be a winner. I am sure to get the best judge in the world, so now I have to go prepare myself." Zack sounded like Jack Ordway preparing himself for a piano concert where Jack goes into zenitation and won't talk to you.

"Okay, so you got somebody in mind. I guess it it'n my dad, even though Dad being the inventor of the chocolate korndog in the first place would be the logical choice, except he's got to get his rest."

"No, it it'n Uncle Kenworth. It's. . . can you guess, Patella? Even Patella dut'n have a clue."

"Who cares? I think I'll go over to the office and write up a column about Mr. Keyshot's dog Lamont, a smart dog who dut'n look at you like you've just done a social error." Patella now is criticizing Harley, a trope that won't endear her further to Zack.

"You better move Barney then, Patella, since you're partways into Mr. Carp's handicapped zone."

"That's where I always park. It's just that Barney's a little wide."

I resisted making a smart-mouth remark.

"Well, I'll tell you who the expert guy is, so you don't die of anticipation. It's Davy Narsood, of TV fame."

Davy Narsood is just the most famous TV chef of all time, him being famous not only in San Francisco where he hangs out, but all over television-land. They say so at the beginning of every broadcast. I know so, even though I'm not a Davy Narsood fan.

Me and Patella both gasped with appreciation. I went, "If you can get Davy Narsood to come to Balona and judge your contest, you'll make the chocolate korndog world famous."

"Well, honk, Joe. Of course," went Zack. "That's exactly what I intend to do."

Eight

"So, is Davy Narsood coming to Balona?" Me and Zack were having a rare lunch on Zack at Peking Peek-Inn, where Zack has a whole hour off for lunch, and I have only a couple of classes on Tuesday, neither of which is all that important to a guy with heavy stuff on his mind.

Lunch on Zack is "rare" since it is Zack paying for it. Zack usually pays for stuff with coupons, if he can, or gives IOU's written in his own invented ink which looks fine at first, but naturally disappears in about a week. Zack is a champion grinch.

Today was especially rare since Zack had some genuine greenbacks out and already on the table, evidence that he intended to actually pay. Harley sat on the floor since Mr. Wong says that a dog seated at one of his tables, wearing a napkin around his neck, and eating neatly from a plate might have a delusional effect on the other customers.

"Is Davy coming? Who knows? I haven't heard all week, so who knows?" Zack looked disgusted over his chow mein, picked out a piece of something with his fingers, and slipped it to Harley. "I phoned him up, but he wasn't there. 'He's taping right now,' a lady said, 'and then he'll be taping some more, so write him a nice fan letter,' she went."

Mr. Wong brought me my *saimin*. "How's Millie, Mr. Wong?" I went.

"Amelia's over at Chaud County Community College attending classes, as this is a school day." Mr. Wong was hinting that probably I should be over there at C4, too. I suavely addressed my meal.

"So, Zack," I went, "you wrote Davy a nice fan letter."

"I did not. I sent him an e-mail, a long e-mail that detailed the situation over here, more or less. I told him it was practically a national defense thing it was so secret. I told him it was a subject that practically would guarantee him an Academy Award. But I dit'n get an answer. Yet." Zack slurped at his food, looked a little

47

worried. "Of course, I signed Mr. Burberry's name to the e-mail. Maybe I shut'n of done that."

Mr. Burberry is not only the builder of those famous Burberry Boxes and possibly a retired secret agent from England, and a very suave guy, he's also the new Mayor of Balona. But Mr. Burberry is not only out of town, he's out of the country, and who knows when he'll be back? "Well, how come you signed Mr. Burberry's name?"

"It seemed like the right thing to do at the time—to finally get some attention. I mean, who'll listen to a high school kid when they've got a mayor handy? Who'll listen to a high school kid when there's *any* adult around?" Zack was sounding like Richie now.

"So, what's gonna happen to the Great Balona Chocolate Korndog Bakeoff?"

"Gimme a while. I'll think of something. Right now I've got to finish my chow mein or I'll have hunger cramps all afternoon."

Mr. Wong always has somebody eating something at his place. Sometimes at lunch time Peking Peek-Inn is really crowded. Not today. Only a couple guys from the *Courier* and Rose from Roseway, eating by herself and reading a magazine, four mousy-looking high school girls who gave me the eye, and Carl from Carl's Shoe Repair getting so close to his soup you'd think he'd drown in it. My dad says that Carl has retired on the job, since when you give Carl a pair of shoes to fix, and then go back to collect them after a while, he'll look for the shoes and finally find them and go, "Oh, *these* shoes. Yeh. When you want 'em?"

So when a customer comes in to Peking Peek-Inn, everybody sort of looks up to see who it is. So the door opened and me and Zack and Harley, all three of us, looked up from our lunch. There in the doorway was a big guy wearing a raincoat and a hat with a brim, like Sam Spade in *The Maltese Falcon*, a favorite old black and white flick that Claire includes once every so often at the New Oliver Double Feature that always sucks in at least a dozen customers. Usually senior citizens, she says. Even with the light from outside behind him, the guy looked vaguely familiar. Could it be Mayor Burberry was back?

No, it wasn't Mayor Burberry. Mayor Burberry is skinny. This guy was fat.

Zack hissed a whisper at me. "Joe, it's him!"

"Who?"

"It's him, himself."

"Who? *Who?*"

"It's Davy Narsood!" Zack almost strangled.

And it was Davy Narsood. He came right in like a regular human being and sat down at the counter, not six feet away from us so we could hear everything he would say to Mr. Wong.

"What's good?"

"Everything's good. Clean, too. Fresh today. What do you like?"

"Ah, stir-fried fresh crab with some salted egg-yolk sauce?"

"Hm." Mr. Wong frowned.

"Deep-fried fish with pine nuts in sweet and sour sauce?"

"Uh, you're talking Shanghai-type food, sir. I run sort of a Peking-style place here, y'see."

"I see. Sure. How about, uh, spinach-filled won tons and some sliced lamb and cucumber?"

"Well, I can give you some won tons and some sliced pork and some saimin…. You seem to know your Chinese food."

"Yes, well. Is your saimin Vietnam type or Hawaiian saimin?"

"Actually, it's neither. It's Wong-type." Mr. Wong showed his white teeth. He is a huge tall guy with muscles you can see through his T-shirt and was in the U. S. Navy.

"Well, I'll have a bowl of the Wong-type, then!" Mr. Davy Narsood showed his teeth, too, and took off his hat, put it on the stool next to him. Mr. Wong moved off to the cash register and then to the kitchen, and Davy Narsood swiveled around on his stool and looked right at Zack. Zack just about fainted.

"Hello," Zack croaked.

"Hi. Maybe you can tell me where I can find Mayor Burberry's office."

I piped right up since Zack was in no condition to respond, him having a huge frog in his throat from the surprise of seeing his hero in the flesh, et cetera. "Mayor Burberry's back in England. Been there for a few weeks where he's claiming his fortune." I thought it was necessary to give Davy some background there so he'd know the story.

"Oh?" Davy frowned his entire face. "Mayor Burberry just a week ago e-mailed me from Balona. This is Balona, isn't it, home of the Sugarbeet Festival?" Davy showed his teeth again, probably out of respect for one of Balona's chief products, the sugarbeet. Then he frowned. "Maybe somebody's playing tricks again. That happens, and when it does it upsets me so that I can hardly cook." Davy looked like he had an upset stomach.

"Here's your Wong-type *saimin*," went Mr. Wong, sliding the bowl in front of Mr. Davy Narsood. "You look familiar. You got relatives in Balona?"

"No, this is my first visit. I had intended each year to come over to cover the Sugarbeet Festival. But today's visit is probably my last. Someone's been playing tricks, and I don't have time for that."

Mr. Wong kept looking at Mr. Davy Narsood while wiping the counter and wagging his head.

I mentioned to Zack, "You better tell him right now, while you got him trapped behind his saimin." I guess my whisper was sort of loud because Zack hushed me.

"Hush," he went. "I can't, since I got to go back to school right now. If I tell him, I'll miss Mrs. Carp's senior English, and she'll give me a flunk for the day. She hates me. If I get even one flunk, I won't get my A. If I don't get my A, I won't get into Harvard or Oxford." Mrs. Carp is the wife of Mr. D. H. Carp, my part-time employer. She is known to hate lots of kids, Zack in particular, since Zack is widely known as a smart-mouth, always correcting the teacher, a feature that teachers are known to hold in despite.

I decided to do the only heroic thing possible. "I'll tell him for you. You just go ahead and pay for our lunch, like you said, and then you can take off, and I'll tell Mr. Davy Narsood all about your baking triumph, eksedra."

Zack looked at me with a real beady eye. "I have to trust you, I guess."

"I am trustworthy as the day is long."

Mr. Davy Narsood is an expert with the chopsticks. You could tell from the way he eschewed the spoon and slurped up the *saimin* with his chopsticks and the bowl held up to his chin. A true pro. Mr. Wong stood back and admired the exhibition.

Zack started to get up, then sat down again and leaned into me. "You can take him over to my house, since Mummy is playing bridge with A'nt Bapsie. There's a couple of fresh new ones in the fridge. Alls you have to do is put 'em in the microwave for 30 seconds, just long enough to get 'em warm."

He gave me another serious look. "But you got to give me credit, understand?"

"Of course, Young Zack, of course." I smirked reassuringly at my young high school cousin who was not able to establish his priorities so as to give himself some credit.

"Let's go, Harley!" And Zack left, leaving just enough money to pay for the both of us, a fact I appreciated, since I had only a quarter in my Levi's.

"Is it always so foggy over here?" Davy was starting a conversation with Mr. Wong, something a polite person learns how to do, maybe at home, but which I never learned since my dad always waits to be spoken to, and my ma always insults people first thing.

"Only in the fall, winter, and spring. In the summer it's hot and dusty." Mr. Wong laughed a hearty *ha ha ha* at his own humor, which is more accurate than humorous.

"It took me two hours to drive over here from the City. I asked at the studio, and they said it shouldn't take more than an hour and ten minutes or so."

"Oh, the traffic. Yeh."

"The traffic and the fog and the roadsigns. Somebody has reversed the road signs just out of town. If I hadn't followed my instincts, I would have ended up in Manteca or Modesto."

"Teen pranks."

"They should take teens out on the desert and leave them, is my opinion about teens." Mr. Davy Narsood was maybe unaware that the handsome manly blond blue-eyed fellow sitting at the nearby table was still enjoying his teen years. Maybe I don't look like a teen, but I am still one.

I cleared my throat, and Davy Narsood turned and looked at me. "You're Mr. Davy Narsood of TV fame," I went, giving him a Holy Look.

"I have that distinction, yes."

Mr. Wong horned in, "Aha! I knew you looked familiar. The saimin's on the house!" Mr. Wong looked happy he had served the famous chef. "What do you think of my saimin?"

"Pretty good. Could use maybe some *ngoc mam*?"

"Oh, no, sir. That would take it too far into Southeast Asia. This one is Hawaiian. I was stationed over there. That's where I picked up the recipe. My saimin is authentic."

"Well, okay. I'll take authentic over experimental any day." Mr. Davy Narsood was hinting that he is a conservative. Maybe he was not the guy Zack intended to break the story to, after all. "On the other hand," he went on, "after the authentic is said and done, I do like to experiment." Ah. Zack's plan was okay after all.

"Well, what brings you to Balona, Mr. Narsood?"

"Call me Davy for David, Mr. Wong."

"Call me Ben for Benjamin Franklin, Davy."

"Call me Joe, Davy."

Davy turned around so he could talk to both of us. "I got this e-mail from your mayor, saying he had a great surprise for me and my program, and that I wouldn't regret making the trip. And now I understand it was a fake e-mail, so my trip was for nothing. Except for the fine saimin, I very much regret making the trip."

"Well, Davy, maybe you dit'n make that trip for nothing after all, since I am an operative of Mayor Burberry, and I know exactly why you're over here." Both Mr. Wong and Davy looked at me like I was maybe exaggerating, which I have been known by Mr. Wong to do occasionally.

"Are you exaggerating again, Joseph?"

"No, sir. Well, not much. It was Zack e-mailed Mr. Davy Narsood here, in the name of Mayor Burberry, so Mr. Davy Narsood wut'n throw away the e-mail if he knew it had came from a teenager."

"So it was a fake after all."

"No, sir. The e-mail was real, all right."

"I know the e-mail was real. I mean the deal is a fake. The secret is no secret at all."

"The secret is still secret, and it is my job to tell you about it, if you will listen."

Mr. Davy Narsood turned all the way around on his stool. He leaned forward. "I'm listening." He looked at his watch. "I won't listen for long. I've got to get back to The City."

By *The City*, Mr. Davy Narsood means San Francisco, which guys who live over there always pronounce like it was a holy word.

I decided to be suave. "Well, c'mon over here and sit at my table, and perhaps Mr. Wong will do us the honor of serving us a cup of tea."

THE CHOCOLATE KORNDOG

"I'll serve Mr. Davy Narsood a cup of tea." Mr. Wong was sort of pouting since I was taking over the guest of honor.

Mr. Narsood slipped from his stool to Zack's chair at the table. He is not a real tall guy, but he has a big chest and a bigger belly to go with his curly hair and beard. I got right to the point. "I am Joseph Oliver Kuhl, and I am Mayor Burberry's representative in this matter." I presented my business card to Davy. "I shall now tell you, in confidence, all you need to know."

Nine

❈

Mr. Davy Narsood was soon convinced of my genuinity, since I walked him the three short blocks to Zack's house. I was planning to tell Davy all about my private eye career intentions, but he spent the whole trip gabbing and complaining and otherwise giving orders to somebody named Francine on his cellphone.

Harley did not give Davy a bite or a sniff or even a hard look when we made our way through the back door of Zack's house, since the great chef was with me. Harley knows I am an honest person, and most guys don't lock their doors in Balona.

We went right into the kitchen and I sat Davy at the table, first taking his coat and hat and hanging them on the backporch where you hang your stuff at Zack's. At our house, you would just throw your coat over a chair. Davy was interested in all the cooking stuff hanging over Zack's kitchen.

"These folks seem to like to cook."

"Zack is a champion chef, even though he is only a high school kid who's got a lot to learn. He is also my Q, which is what any self-respecting private eye has got to have, as you may well know." One of my problems is I tend to talk too much. I could tell since Mr. Davy Narsood kept looking at his watch.

"So, why are we here, Joseph? What's so damn special about this particular kitchen?" I had never heard Davy curse on the TV.

I then explained how my dad had thought hard about a curious invention. About how he thought so hard that he had a breakdown and was now resting. I then explained how a young woman artist took my dad's imagination in hand and created a painting. I said I would show Mr. Davy Narsood that very painting later, after we had experienced what he was about to experience.

"Okay," he went. "Maybe I could start experiencing it pretty soon?" Mr. Davy Narsood was being polite, but obviously he was in a hurry.

"You may have heard of the famous King Korndog?" I mentioned.

"I know about it. It's a variety made here in your town, I understand. Has a reputation of making people sick every once in a while, but nobody's been able to pin any specific impurities on it yet."

This was news to me, but I strived on.

"Well, my dad's creative visions have inspired Zack to create another variety yet, one that will knock off your socks." I nodded my head vigorously. Harley was also sitting up now, his paws crossed on the table, giving Mr. Davy Narsood his most intelligent expression.

"For petesake, Joseph. Let's have it. I'm ready to leave right now."

I paused at the door of the fridge. "What you are about to see will take away your breath." I felt that was the right thing to say, but later I wondered if it maybe hinted that Davy had bad breath. He didn't wince or twitch, just looked at his watch again.

I flung open the fridge door. Milk carton, pickles, orange juice, bottles and jars. Probably mostly stuff for Zack's ma and dad, since Zack has his own little fridge up in his bedroom. Where was my objective? There is was under plastic. I fetched the tray out and set it on the table in front of Davy. I drew away the plastic that covered the chocolate korndogs, three of them. The chocolate gleamed.

"A maple bar? A chocolate maple bar? That's what you're showing me?"

"Ah! A moment!" I slid the korndogs onto a plate and put them in the microwave. We both watched as the machine sizzled the dogs for 30 seconds. I removed them and set them before Davy with a flourish. "Vwa-la!" I went, using sophisticated language.

"Well, it smells good, anyway. What are the, uh, the little brownnoses there?"

"Aha! Those are a key to the confection. This, Mr. Davy, is a chocolate korndog, and the chocolate korndog is why you are here!" I slid one onto a saucer and set it before him. I gave him a fork. "Try it."

I held my breath, since I wasn't sure if Zack had perfected his injection, and if he had restrained his urge to use the rest of Richie's pills. Harley was watching carefully.

"Hm."

"Good?"

"Hm. This is certainly the strangest thing I've tasted all week." This was really saying something, since Mr. Davy Narsood is famous for tasting weird stuff.

"Strange. Well, okay. But how's it taste?"

"Not bad. Interesting. Sort of minty. Orangey. Chocolaty. Yes, quite interesting. Some cornmeal texture. Not too sweet. Strange backtaste. A very nice *ganache*."

"Zack says he learned about his *ganache* from you."

"Undoubtedly why it's so tasty. Best thing about this confection is the *ganache*."

"How's about the korndog part?"

"Well, it's strange, that's for sure." Davy took another couple bites. "Probably I ought to try another one, don't you think?"

Which he did.

Then I told him about Zack's plans to have a huge Chocolate Korndog Bakeoff, where guys from all over would come to try their best to beat Zack's product. I asked Davy if he would consider being the famous host of the Bakeoff.

"I'll have to think about that."

"You'd become famous overnight."

"I'm already famous."

I'd said the wrong thing. "I mean, of *course* you're famous. What I meant was, you'd become even *more* famous. *World* famous."

"I'm already world famous."

Davy Narsood has no ego problems. "Oh. Well, sure. But you'd be recognized as a sort of a sponsor of the chocolate korndog, a guy who made it all possible."

"That's what I'm afraid of. Well, I have to be off...."

Suddenly, the door from the porch crashed open and Constable Cod bashed his way into the kitchen, his huge shiny black Beretta 9mm automatic in his hand, hollering: "Keep yer sands in hight! Don't move a muscle!"

We hadn't heard Cod creep up, really something considering he weighs about 400 pounds. Even Harley hadn't heard him, but now Harley was still sitting in his chair, wagging his tail. Harley probably felt Cod was no threat.

That wasn't how Mr. Davy Narsood felt, obviously. His face was white as a ghost. He wasn't moving a muscle.

"Yer expanding yer criminal tendencies, are you, Joey?"

Cod obviously misunderstood.

"Mr. Davy Narsood here is a guest which I brought over here to see Zack's invention."

"Pippa Burnross called me on her cellphone. Told me she had kobbers in her ritchen, heard 'em talking and carrying on, called me up and told me to come over and nail 'em." Cod was busy tying up Mr. Davy Narsood's wrists with his special plastic handcuffs. It has been my experience that those cuffs will actually cut you up if you try to squirm out of them, as Davy was sort of trying to do.

"Zack told me to bring Mr. Davy Narsood over here, Cod. It's no crime."

"I'm doing my duty, and you're lucky I don't hustle you off, too. When this criminal here has paid off his fine, then I'll listen to the arguments." This is Cod's usual trope. You are guilty until he figures out that maybe you're not. Since Mr. Davy Narsood was in a strange kitchen with me, he was probably guilty, according to Cod's reasoning. I hoped Mr. Davy Narsood had a pocketful of cash.

On the way out of the house, Cod shoving Mr. Davy Narsood ahead of him, Harley skipping along side, and me trying to argue Cod out of his stubborn way, we saw Aunt Pippa standing across the street on Judge Ordway's sidewalk, wringing her hands and weeping up a storm. "You got them, you got them, the criminals. Oh. Who is that criminal? That dut'n look like a criminal. That looks like Mr. Davy Narsood, the world famous chef!"

Even though he was being hustled along, Mr. Davy Narsood managed to get into a pose where he was able to be admired. Mrs. Pezmyer from down the street, a person who is always interested in knowing what is going on, was standing there with Aunt Pippa. "It is him, Pippa. It's Mr. Davy Narsood himself, coming out of your house in handcuffs. Who wut've thought Mr. Davy Narsood would become a Balona criminal!"

"Serves him right," went Aunt Forey, who lives next door to Aunt Pippa and whose husband is my Uncle Anson Chaud, who is Sheriff of Chaud County. "We should be glad we got good law enforcement in Balona. Good work, Cod!"

Then my ma actually came out of Kuhl Mansion, clambered down our front steps, barefoot naturally, and joined the group witnessing the crime. She squinted across at Davy since she's real nearsighted, and she leaned into Aunt Pippa. "Want I should go over there and bust him one?" My ma is always ready to come to the aid of anybody not personally willing to use force and violence.

"That is actually Mr. Davy Narsood, the world famous chef?" Aunt Pippa is a fan of Mr. Davy Narsood, watches him every day on his TV show.

"Tell Cod this is a big mistake, A'nt Pippa," I hollered. "Zack told me to bring Mr. Davy Narsood over to your house to sample the chocolate korndog."

"Chocolate korndog. What chocolate korndog? Joey joking? Somebody said chocolate korndog?" This from Aunt Forey, who I guess hadn't been over to Mr. D. H. Carp's Groceries & Sundries to see Claire's portrait.

Patella's purple Ford coupe screeched to a halt nearby, Patella emerging with her camera in hand. "Wait! Don't move. Lem'me take a nice photo for the *Courier* here." And she snapped a bunch of flashes, Mr. Davy Narsood showing his teeth and turning this way and that for each shot. "Hey," Patella went, "this is actually Mr. Davy Narsood of TV fame. I bet I win a prize!"

"This is absurd! I have to get back to The City." Davy tried to get a peek at his wristwatch, tough to do when your wrist is locked behind you. "Young man! Joseph Kuhl! Tell the officer here that this is a terrible mistake."

"This is a terrible mistake, Cod." Cod didn't mind getting his picture taken, but it didn't seem that he was interested in letting Mr. Davy Narsood go.

"I think maybe I made a mistake in calling you, Cod." Aunt Pippa was whining now, in her very high mosquito voice so everybody in the community could hear. "I bet Mr. Davy Narsood came here to help my Zacky with his little baking project."

Mr. Davy Narsood pulled himself up to his full height. "I have been called here, Madam, on false pretenses, I believe. I received an e-mail from your Mayor Burberry, and now I discover that Mayor Burberry could not have sent that message."

"Hey, Davy, uh, Mr. Narsood! I already explained that. Zack dit'n mean to convince you. He was just trying to make sure you got over here since you are so famous and important and necessary to the success of the Chocolate Korndog Bakeoff!" I was laying it on pretty thick, since I have learned that guys with huge egos do respond nicely when you slather on the compliments.

"Well, perhaps the young man's intentions were good."

"Cod!" went Aunt Pippa, "this is Mr. Davy Narsood, a famous TV chef who is famous for cooking stuff. He wut'n be interested in burgularing my house. I made a mistake. I shut'n of called you. You need to let him go."

"He created a scene where I had to get up and respond. So he's got to pay."

"How much? I can't get to my wallet with my hands tied like this."

"Oh, that's simple." Cod untied Mr. Davy Narsood's handcuffs, and the famous chef felt around in his coat for his wallet. "Uh, a hundred bucks."

"What? What!" These exclamations from everybody. "Too much, too much!"

"Uh, okay. Twenty."

"Twenty it is." Davy fished a twenty out of his wallet and handed it toward Cod who reached out for it. But Davy was too quick for the lawman and snatched the bill back. "Or do you want I should cook up something for you? Something sweet and tasty. Something chocolaty and yummy?"

Davy had got old Cod's number. Cod was drooling.

"Yeh, okay. What you got?"

"It's still back in the kitchen there. You let me go and I'll bring it out for you."

And that's what happened. Everybody took off in different directions. Patella buzzed off with her camera for the *Courier*. Aunt Pippa and Ma went back to Ma's bridge game, Aunt Forey went back to her house, Mrs. Pezmyer went down the street and back into her living room where she can use her field glasses to spy through her window on Ma's bridge game across the street. And Cod sat there in his squad car munching on Zack's chocolate korndog while I accompanied Mr. Davy Narsood back to Front Street where he had parked his car.

The car had one of Cod's pink parking tickets tucked under the windshield wiper.

Mr. Davy Narsood said some rude words about Balona. But he also said something weird. "Who was that gorgeous big woman with the bare feet?" I was too surprised to answer him.

I couldn't tell you right now if we're going to get Mr. Davy Narsood to be host for the Big Chocolate Korndog Bakeoff.

Ten

⧉

Brrrraaaaap!

My ma's flatulence took its toll on her bridge companions, who expressed their dismay by pushing themselves back from the tables. All moved to another part of the room, except for Aunty Pring Chaud who stayed dozing in her chair. Aunt Sarah rose up and cranked the window open. This group experience was nothing unique for the Kuhl living room since, once after Taco-Time takeout, Ma regaled the whole family a brief variation of "My Country 'tis of Thee" on her unusual instrument.

"Good heavens, Bapsie!" went Nancy Sporlodden fanning herself. Nancy is Coach Kork's wife who is always lashing her eyes at me. She is super skinny, has a big mouth, and talks in a loud voice, like her husband on the football field.

"What? Helping of what?" Mrs. Crinkle is about a hundred years old and doesn't hear so good. but she, too, got up and retreated. "My god, Bapsie, was that you again?"

"So?" went Ma. "It's a purely natural thing, farting is. Everybody does it." She looked at Mrs. Trilbend. "You ever have a little gas, Anna?" Mrs. Trilbend looks like she's a lot younger than the other women here, turned bright red, played with her hanky, didn't answer back. "Maybe Bellona don't, since she's so pure. How's about it Bellona. You never fart?"

Mrs. Shaw talks through her nose. "I never heard of such a topic. Not at a refined place, anyway."

"She won't answer the question, girls. Now that's a dead giveaway!"

"Perhaps I should find a way to report on this in my column."

That was a threat if anybody ever heard one, so everybody went back to their table, looking at their cards or reaching for a horse-derve or a hanky or messing with their purse.

"Yeh! Why don't we change the subject and get back to our game?" Nancy has got allergies and was blowing her nose pretty vigorously.

Ma pursued her point with alacrity and verve. "It's that chocolate korndog Joey brought over from Pippa's house where that dumb Zack's been making 'em. Chocolate does it every time. Better than beans." Ma demonstrated with another blast, this one sort of restrained as compared to the first one.

"Mercy, Bapsie. Let's leave this, shall we? This is hardly a topic for a group of ladies." Aunt Pippa is always mentioning how ladylike she is. She speaks high up in her head and looks past you when she talks. You'd think she never passed a gas in her life.

"I was just mentioning that it's also that *dum-shik* Joey's fault." My ma was having a good time with this, and using her homemade swearwords which she believes are a lot more refined than the cusswords generally found around Balona. She hollered into the kitchen where I was enjoying not only the subject, but also a can of Hires. "Joey, go get some wood from our new garage and stoke the fireplace. It's getting cold in here what with Sarah needing all that fresh air for her pure lungs. You can close the *futzin* window, Sarah."

"Well, I don't know...." Aunt Sarah rumbled her answer down in her chest, like the base-baritone she is, looked worried, as if Ma might be ready to strive on again with her organic concert.

"I got the furnace turned down so we can enjoy the fire, so close the window." Ma barked her order like a drill sergeant in the movies, so Aunt Sarah did like she was told, and I set down my Hires and went out and did like I was told.

Our big new two-car garage is a gift of Uncle Oak Runcible who tried to chickle us out of our phantom fortune a month or so ago. He thought he was buying off the Kuhls with a new garage. It turned out that Uncle Oak chickled himself, and we kept the free garage. The garage has a nice hole up on the front for Dad's magpie to get in. Nobody but Dad has ever seen his magpie, but if it should ever show up, it's got a little house up in our garage with a little door to get into it.

The regular front garage door you open with a zapper. You just point the zapper at the door, press a button, and the door clanks up or down. Dad spent a lot of time, when it was first installed, mostly after dinner, zapping the door up and down, until ma took the zapper away from him and hid it.

I went in the garage through the door to the house. The garage also has attic storage we haven't filled up with junk yet, and another door that goes into the back yard.

We had the carpenters build us the woodbox on the side when they made the garage. In the woodbox we keep logs and trashwood to burn in the fireplace. It's got a neat door that opens up in front, so you don't have to lean down into the box to lift out the logs. I opened the door and grabbed a log, and then another one, since I didn't want to have to come back. I saw something there under the fireplace logs.

Moving some logs aside for a better view, I saw what looked like pieces of my Burberry Box. That's what they were. Pieces. Somebody had broke my Burberry Box and thrown the pieces into the woodbox. Who could have done such a crime? Could it have been the famous burglar of my ma's fantasies. A guy who crept into our house and up the stairs into my bedroom, and moved my pimple cream and Aqua Velva and hared off with my Burberry Box? I do not think so.

I think it was Richie did it. There in the woodbox was all the evidence. Probably had Richie's fingerprints all over the pieces. But Mr. Burberry said the box shouldn't be opened because of the lethal fumes inside. Richie was lucky. Somehow he missed the lethal fumes. Right at that moment, I thought to myself, *too bad*.

In a low mood I carried the logs into the living room and stoked the fire. Sparks went up the chimney and I squatted there for a while, enjoying my gloom.

"Joey's making us a nice fire, but he looks like he just lost his best friend," went Nancy Sporlodden, who always pays attention to my face expressions and my moods in general.

"He always looks like that when he's got to do some work. It's just his *dum-shik* nature."

"Joey's not a *dum-shik*, are you Joey!"

"Somebody stole my Burberry Box."

"My word!" Exclamations of concern. "Who would do such a thing!" All except Ma and Mrs. Bellona Shaw exclaimed an exclamation of concern at my loss.

"Naaaah, we had a local burgular crept up to Joey's room and took it, is all. No big deal." My ma never considers my losses or Dad's losses as a big deal. She only considers her losses or Richie's losses as a big deal.

Mrs. Bellona Shaw changed the subject away from my welfare to a subject interesting to her. "Well, Bapsie, I see you have installed a bust of someone famous up on your mantel. Is that a bust of Handel perhaps?"

"It dut'n show the bust, you *butt-head*. It only goes down to the neck, and the neck's sort of short."

Mrs. Shaw didn't drop a stitch at the *butt-head* remark, sort of ignoring it, only raised up one black eyebrow. "Well, I dit'n know you folks were interested in classical musicians. How charming." Mrs. Shaw got out her notebook and fountain pen and started making some notes.

"That's a gift from my little Richie, that good boy."

"Ah, and where is little Richie?" Mrs. Shaw mumbled while she was writing in her notebook. Mrs. Shaw reads all the crime reports at Cod's and over at Uncle Anson's sheriff office. She knows exactly where Richie is and probably why he's there at Runcible Hall. She is asking so my ma gets embarrassed.

Nobody embarrasses my ma. "Little Richie is doing some community service like all teens should, once and a while." My ma actually doesn't believe in community service, except for guys on welfare and jailbirds, but this sounded like a good excuse for Richie.

"What're you all looking at?" Mrs. Crinkle not only doesn't hear anything unless you holler, she doesn't see much, either. She turned around and looked at Richie's statue on the mantel, now sitting right down on the wood instead of on the dinner plate. She frowned, took off her glasses, polished them up on a paper napkin, peered back up at the plastic head.

"It'n that classy!" went Nancy, sucking up to Ma, as usual. Ma's face expression glowed like a cat. Ma likes compliments. I need to compliment Ma more, only I usually can't think of anything to compliment her about.

"Actually, it ought to have a base of some kind, instead of just sitting there on its neck." Mrs. Shaw is not only a columnist for the *Courier*, she is also the critic of art and music, as well as writing about travel and pets and guys who are sick and die. Obviously, she was wearing her art critic hat today. "Must be pretty heavy, that neck, to keep the head balanced like that," Mrs. Shaw added finally.

"Well," went Nancy, "I wut'n look a gift horse in the mouth, huh, Baps! I think it's nice, even with a heavy neck."

Mrs. Crinkle had been looking at the statue for a long time, squinting and frowning and wagging her head. "It sure reminds me of somebody, but I can't remember who."

"It's probably supposed to be the composer Handel, a German musician of the Seventeenth Century who wrote Baroque music." Mrs. Shaw likes to show off her knowledge. She leered to herself and waggled her head. "He wrote the *Messiah*, y'know."

"Except it's bald, it looks to me more like Davy Narsood than Handel. No, more like Marlon Brando. Marlon in his late period, of course." This from Aunt Pippa, a movie fan. "Davy Narsood was so handsome and so gracious. Who wut've thought we'd have Mr. Davy Narsood at our house. In our kitchen."

"I'll need to interview you about that, Pippa," went Mrs. Shaw.

"Who cares!" went Ma. "He'll never come back. Let's play cards."

Mrs. Crinkle was still turned around, looking at the statue. "It looks like Bena." She said it in a small voice. Then louder, "It looks a whole lot like Bena. I wonder who cut've made it."

"Bena Splinters has long curly red hair. Probably touches it up some, but lots of it." This from Aunt Pippa.

"Bena's red hair? Lost all her hair when her first husband divorced her. Thirty years ago. Got herself a wig. Bena's bald as an egg. Just like that statue up there. Looks just like her, except the neck is too short for Bena. Fat like Bena's, but too short. Wisht I had that statue for my mantel. Reminds me of Bena a whole lot. Made by an expert, all right." Mrs. Crinkle sniffed, blew into her paper napkin. A sentimental person. "I hope she likes it up there in Montana. I hear it's cold as sin up there. I hope she's got a nice fireplace to keep her warm."

The statue does have a passing resemblance to old Mrs. Splinters, but it actually doesn't look like her since, as Aunt Pippa reminded us, Mrs. Splinters is red-headed and besides has moved to Montana to be with her son Cardamon Splinters. Besides, old Mrs. Splinters never had a smile for anybody, and this statue of Handel has got a nice pleasant smile on his lips, eyes closed like he's got a secret. Looks like he's thinking pleasant thoughts, which is more than you could ever say for Mrs. Splinters.

"My Kenworth got another postcard from her not long ago. She's doing just fine, she says." Aunt Pippa relays a lot of information about her husband's correspondence. If I had a wife, I would tell her to keep her lip zipped about my business.

"She never writes me, and I'm her best friend." Mrs. Billa Crinkle is still sniffing.

"Well, the postcard is actually addressed to you, Billa, only my Kenworth has probably left it in his overcoat pocket, forgotten for the moment. Things slip his mind lately, y'know. He forgot Zack's birthday. He forgot my birthday. He's forgot our anniversary." Now Aunt Pippa is sniffing into her napkin, since Uncle Kenworth Burnross is about a hundred years older than her and is lately forgetting to put his pants on when he goes to work. Everybody clucks in sympathy. Except Ma, of course.

"I wonder if your mystery statue cut've been made by Mark Ordway. He's always making statues." Mrs. Trilbend finally said something. "He's so handsome."

"He makes huge statues out of stone that get showed off in banks and museums. He dut'n do—what is that up there, plastic?" Aunt Pippa frowns at our statue of Handel. "Looks sort of wet."

"Whoever made Bapsie's statue might be persuaded to make a nice chocolate korndog statue, if we could find out who he is." Nancy again.

"That makes me hungry," went Ma. She hollered for Mrs. Earwick, her part-time housekeeper. "Bring us some more horse-derves!"

I hollered back from the kitchen. "You sent Mrs. Earwick home on account of she had a hangover." I had forgot that Mrs. Trilbend is Mrs. Earwick's granddaughter. "Sorry," I went.

"Hell, let's play cards," goes Ma. "Wake up Pring there, Anna."

Aunty Pring Chaud tends to go to sleep at the drop of a hat, and, by agreement of the players awake, was dummy at every game at her table today. Mrs. Anna Trilbend who hadn't said much, sort of shook at Aunty Pring's shoulder. "She's out like a light," went Mrs. Trilbend.

"Okay, my deal again," went Ma, rubbing her hands.

Eleven

Patella's Patter
by Patella Euphella Sackworth

Was it really him? Was it the famous chef of TV fame tied up there by Constable Lafcadio H. Gosling in front of Zachary T. Burnross's house and complaining of hurt wrists from the plastic cuffs put on him to keep him from running off to San Francisco where he is World Famous?

Yes. But even though he looked criminal, Mr. Davy Narsood of TV fame was not held by our Constable for long, since he paid his fine like a good citizen should and left Balona right away. Mr. Davy Narsood is a famous TV chef who is on TV practically every day where you can see him cook up stuff that most people cannot make in their own homes but feel better when they see Mr. Narsood make it so easily, since it looks so tasty.

Mr. Davy Narsood was in Balona for the day at the invitation of Mr. Zachary T. Burnross who has a secret project going on that this columnist has promised not to divulge, except to say that Mr. Davy Narsood has something to do with it, if he doesn't end up in jail somewhere.

This columnist must confess that she is a real fan of Mr. Davy Narsood, now especially since she has seen him in all his flesh.

"We need to say 'flavor enhanced,' not just, like, 'whisky-flavored.' Instead, we'll say *flavor enhanced with fine bourbon,* like that." Zack was expatiating his version of how chocolate korndogs ought to be described.

THE CHOCOLATE KORNDOG

I went, "Why describe it at all. Why not just let guys discover for themselves? What I mean to say, everybody's going on about choice, how you got to have a choice in everything. So, go ahead and let guys have a choice about the flavor of their korndog."

"Their *chocolate* korndog."

"Yeh, that's what I mean now when I say korndog."

"You got to be more specific or you'll never get rich. Rich guys are always specific about their riches. If you just say korndog, guys will not know you're talking about the chocolate version."

"Okay, okay. Then we should say, *your flavored chocolate korndog*, right?"

Zack picked at his nose. Harley *hmmmmd*. They were thinking about my suggestion. "I do believe you're right, Joe."

This was just about the first time Zack actually came right out and told me he thought one of my ideas was okay. Usually he demoans my ideas.

"So, what flavors you come up with so far?"

"In my kitchen I have tried whiskey, of course, using dregs from Da's *Early Times*. And beer. What you do with the beer, instead of injecting it into the dog, you stab the dog with a fork a few times and lay it in Valley Brew overnight. That sort of soaks up the beer taste. Dut'n do much for the chocolate part, but beer drinkers will groove on it right away, I bet."

"That's two flavors. Is that all?"

"Oh, no. You got your fruit flavors: orange, bubblegum, and guava. All taste good with chocolate, I think."

"You classifying bubblegum as fruit?"

"How would you classify it? Fuel? Fabric?"

"Oh. Well. Okay, if you can get your hands on some bubblegum flavoring."

"If they can get it into toothpaste and bubblegum, I ought to be able to get it stuck into a korndog. It'll become a great hit."

"Say, how do you get the stuff into the korndog?"

"Well, I use a hypodermic syringe, of course." He lifted up the lid off of a little black box, and there was the instrument under discussion.

"Where'd you get something like that? It'n it illegal for a kid to have something like that?"

"Ast Richie. Ast your little brother. He's the one I got it from. He's got a whole boxfull. Needles, too. I don't think he's gonna use 'em to inject korndogs though. Anyways, it works best, and I'm not about to try something else when I've got this."

There's no arguing with Zack when he says he's right. He must have picked up that trope from Patella. He strived on with his explanation.

"Then I went and thought up some weird flavors, too, but I don't know that they'd go over so good, except as novelties, y'know. Vomit-flavored, for example."

"Eeeeeew!"

"Well, I figured if Harry can do it, so could I. Guys would order it to joke their friends."

"Dirty Harry makes up vomit-flavored chocolate korndogs?"

"No, not our Dirty Harry. The book Harry—Harry Potter—where that Harry sells vomit-flavored beans. I was just using an example, not a real thing."

I don't know about the book Harry, since I am too busy with academic things and so don't have time to read books. *Our* Harry is Dirty Harry Runcible. He is one of our old-time Balona characters. He is always referred to around here simply as Our Dirty Harry to distinguish him from the old-time movie star.

When the first famous old-time Dirty Harry movie came out, our Dirty Harry made a fortune from his stool at Frank's Soupe de Jour, autographing baseballs, books, napkins, and anything you can think of, while charging a quarter for each autograph. Nobody every complained, since it was a genuine Dirty Harry autograph.

My dad right away talked about changing his own name to Ronald Reagan, Jimmy Carter, or George Bush in order to make a bundle autographing stuff. My ma said she preferred the name Chaud, and if he was going to change it to anything, he should change it to Chaud, my ma's maiden name. That ended that.

Our Dirty Harry is 70 years old, has one good eye, walks with a limp, and was retired from the Turkey Factory as Chief Featherman. Spends part of his days at Frank's Soupe de Jour and his nights at Ned's Sportsbar, promoting turkey over korndog as the key ingredient of a healthy diet. He wears turkey-skin cowboy boots, claims to sleep on turkey feather pillows, and says *make my day* maybe twice a week. Frank Backhouse, owner of Frank's, said he thought Dirty Harry had a private detective's license, but if he has, he doesn't flash it around like I will when I get mine.

"If we could convince Dirty Harry to endorse my chocolate-flavored, I mean, flavored chocolate korndogs, I bet I could convert the population. Think about it: a big sign on the wrapper, 'eaten daily by Dirty Harry himself'. Something like that."

I suddenly realized that Zack was using "I" a lot, instead of "we," when talking about the project. He had also just said "*my* chocolate-flavored korndogs." I pointed that out to him.

"So? It's my invention."

"It was my dad's creation, in his imagination. And then it was Claire's imagination made the painting that has inspired all the attention. And I been helping think up plans and stuff. And it was me met with Mr. Davy Narsood, since you had to sag off to class. So, how do you get off claiming the whole thing is yours?"

"Well, was it *you* who baked up a chocolate-flavored korndog? Possession is nine-tenths of the law." Zack smacked his lips again. His lip-smacking habit is as bad as Mrs. Billa Crinkle's sniffing habit.

"Well, then, Mr. Sam Joe Sly has got you beat hands down, since he possesses a whole factory that could be full of 'em."

"If it had been me who hosted Mr. Davy Narsood in my own kitchen, things wut've turned out different. Probably you dit'n say something right."

"I did so. I said everything right. It wat'n me called Cod on her cellphone, remember." I then recreated for Zack my entire conversation with Mr. Davy Narsood. Actually, I couldn't remember a word of what I said to Mr. Davy Narsood, since a week had already gone by. So I had to be real creative in my memory as I strived on. "Anyways, I also wrote your cellphone number on the back of my business card, and gave it to him before Cod hustled him off."

Zack was impressed with my thoroughty and showed his approval by nodding his head several times. "Well, we got to think of another strategy now, since Patella's column was probably the last straw in Mr. Davy Narsood being a master of ceremony at my Big Balona Flavored Chocolate Korndog Bakeoff and Carnival."

"What's with the carnival part? Is that something new?"

"A guy might as well make a little extra money out of the Bakeoff besides the entry fee."

"What entry fee?"

"Well, you just can't bake an entry and enter it. There's expenses involved. Like, I got to record stuff and take my valuable time to judge it, eksedra. Stuff like that. Expenses. All contests got expenses. Honk sakes, Joe."

"Okay, okay. So what's with the extra money besides the entry fee?"

"Well, I figured some games—a skateboard race for the kids and bingo for the old folks, and ring tosses, stuff like that, a quarter a throw. Just so's guys would have something to do while the judging was going on." Zack is always thinking. Of course, that's why I selected him to be my Q.

"What are you doing there with those little houses?" Zack had a big board on his bed with model houses and stuff from his dad's backyard model railroad.

"This is a model of the Bakeoff and Carnival. See, here's Mr. D. H. Carp's Groceries & Sundries. Here is Uncle Hannibal Chaud's Funerals and his parking lot. The parking lot is where most of the Carnival will be, I figure."

"Where are people going to do their baking?"

"Well, at home, of course. I'll have to figure out some rules so everybody brings their korndogs in the same kind of container."

It suddenly occurred that something was missing in Zack's bedroom, which is a whole lot bigger than my bedroom and has a king-size bed and its own bathroom, where I have to go down to the end of the hall in my house to get to the john.

"Something is missing here." I had on my puzzled face expression.

"What's that?"

"Something you had in this room a few days ago when I was here is missing now."

Zack looked around. "Oh, yeh. My Burberry Box."

"Aha! Somebody burguled it?" Maybe the Burberry Boxwood in my woodbox was Zack's and not mine. Maybe mine wound up at the Delta City Fleamarket after all.

"No, I stuck it up on the closet shelf. Still there. Take a look, if you don't believe me."

"You did? That beautiful artistic thing? You stuck it in the closet? Why would you do that?"

"It stunk."

"Huh?"

"Well, honk. It was giving off a bad smell. Leaking out of it. So I thought it might be lethal and maybe strangle me and Harley in our sleep, so I stuck it up on the shelf in there." Zack was rearranging cars and people on his model. He didn't seem to be bothered that he had disgraced a fine piece of art. "It was Harley actually discovered the smell."

"You mean it was dripping something?"

"No, just smelled bad. I dit'n want to take a chance with Harley's lungs and stuff."

"Mr. Burberry used some strange chemicals in his glue."

"I guess. I'm glad he was a waiter and not a chef. I wut'n want to eat anything he made if he was a chef and his boxes smelt so bad."

We argued for a while about whether the suave Mayor Burberry was a waiter or a writer or a secret agent, since he always kept his coat on and stood up straight like a waiter, and had a great vocabulary, and one time mentioned that he worked for MI-6, and was in Balona because he was escaping assassins.

Zack's cellphone made a peebling noise. Zack ignored it. The phone peebled again. "You got a call on your cell phone," I pointed out.

I have my own cellphone clipped to my belt on the side, so it shows that I've got a cellphone. Everybody in Balona has got a cellphone. Only I don't turn mine on, so I never get any calls. If I did turn it on, it wouldn't work, since the battery is dead and I haven't recharged it for a while. Even if I re-charged it, the thing wouldn't work since I haven't paid the bill for a while and the company sends me rude letters about that. But wearing a cellphone on your belt makes you look suave, and that is important in Balona.

"You never want to answer your cell phone right away, Joe. You always got to show you're suave about getting calls." He picked up his phone and poked it once. "Yes?" he went in a deeper-than-usual voice. "Who? *Who* is it?" He looked up at me. "Wow!"

"What! What?"

"He's actually calling."

"Who's calling?"

"It's Davy Narsood on the phone."

Twelve

So, if I overheard the cellphone conversation aright, Mr. Davy Narsood is actually going to come over here to Balona to host our big Chocolate Korndog Bakeoff. Of course, hearing one side of a conversation isn't always fluorescent. Also, since Zack kept turning away and sort of whispered into the phone, almost as if he didn't want me to hear.

The first thing Zack said after he got off his phone call shocked me. "He dut'n want Joseph Kuhl involved in any way, he mentioned, Davy did."

"What? I was the one introduced him to the whole idear in the first place. How come?" I felt wounded, especially since this news was on top of the *D* that Doctor Fardel just awarded my best poem ever submitted to an English teacher. ("Spelling errors" she wrote in the margin, as if spelling would make a poem better or worst.) I would include the poem here except it's sort of romantic and doesn't really belong in a chocolate korndog book. Maybe I will include it later, if I can figure out how to regale the romance.

"Why Mr. Davy Narsood dut'n want you involved is since you were the one introduced the whole idear in the first place. He's afraid he'll get arrested and fined again."

"I'll call him up and give him my personal guarantee."

"No, no, you don't want to do that. There's a better way. I can keep you sort of involved, providing you stay in the background and don't try to hog the spotlight, the way you usually do."

"Oh, yeh?"

"Yeh. You can be my assistant. My gofer."

Now this was insulting. It is Zack, this young high school kid, who is supposed to be *my* gofer. He was turning the tables on me again, just when I was trying to think of a way to take him down a peg or two. But, since I couldn't think of a quick response, I decided to play along with him, see what he was up to. I could insert myself later. "Well, Young Zack, I'll just take that under advisement. In the meantime, I'll play along with your plan and use tradecraft to disguise myself as your assistant. On this operation only, of course. After this, we go back to where you are my Q and assistant."

I looked to me like Zack was smirking to himself. "You got to always agree with me, show guys that I'm in charge, okay?"

That burned. "Well, okay. That'll be part of my tradecraft disguise. Except everybody will know it's not a very good assistant who'll agree with everything you say, even if what you say is dumb."

"They'll just figure it's you being you. Besides, I don't intend to say anything dumb." Zack was sounding sort of take-chargey, not like a high school kid at all. Even Harley looked surprised. "So the first thing I want you to do is go over to King Korndog and check on their progress over there. See what they're up to." He squinted at me. "You can do that, can't you?"

"I am trained in Criminal Justice procedures. What you are suggesting is a piece of cake to a pro."

"I'm not *suggesting,* Young Joe. If you're gonna be my assistant, you better start in taking orders."

Zack was being smartmouth, teasing me, luring me on so he could tell me to get lost and keep me out of the chocolate korndog loop. I resolved myself to outsmart him. "I will do as you say, Master," I went, bowing and smirking some, like in a joke.

Zack smacked his lips. Harley smacked his lips. "So, get to it."

I was dismissed, again. So I left and went up to my office, my dad's office, where even though Dad is over resting at the Jolly Times Rest Home, the office door is always open for business. We keep a ballpoint and a pad of paper on my desk for guys to write messages. And my phone has an answering machine on it that I have to re-program every time the power goes off (which it does all over Balona every time it rains). On the window it says in gold-painted letters, *Kenworth Kuhl Real Estate & Joseph Oliver Kuhl Private Investigations.*

I sat there in my leather chair which my Uncle Kosh bought for me and turned on my computer, which my Uncle Kosh also bought for me. I thought some good thoughts about my Uncle Kosh (really my Great-uncle Kosh) while the computer bonged and whistled. I played a solitaire game for a while, mostly losing.

Then I played a poker game, mostly losing to a dumb character in the game named "Riverboat Roger."

I was wondering to myself if I was accumulating too many unexcused absences from classes, when suddenly I got a visitor dinging the bell over the front door. It was Dirty Harry Runcible himself, the guy me and Zack had been discussing. Strange coincidence.

"Well, sir," I went. "How may I be of service?" I am always suave like this with potential customers since, if you aren't, guys will go to some other private eye. "Are you seeking the services of a top-flight private investigator?"

"If I was, kid, I'd get me Rowdy Brill or I'd do it myself."

Rowdy Brill is a real PI who works over in Delta City and is the dad of Brucie Brill who still owes me a dollar since we were sophomores at Big Baloney. I ignored Dirty Harry's ignorant answer. "Well, have a seat here, Mr. Runcible, and maybe I could steer you to a good house to buy or rent." I was being a good son, trying to keep my dad solvent, who isn't.

"No. I got me a nice room at Ms Francesca Poone's, y'know, and I'm all by myself nowdays, so I don't need much to keep me happy."

"Well, now, that's nice to hear." I was sucking up to the guy, which is the way you get ahead in real estate. Actually, it's the way you get ahead in any business, according to *How to Win Friends and Influence People*, a book I sort of read back in high school.

We sat looking at each other for a while, him munching on the wet stub of a dead cigar, me off and on glancing at my computer screen. There was an ad for a credit card blinking there, where all you had to do was click it and the card would be in the mail quick as a rabbit, no questions asked. Since I already am over my limit on four of those suckers at 22 percent interest each, I figured I'd better not try for another one.

"I hear there is something going on." Dirty Harry squinted his one good eye at me.

"Yeh? Something going on, you said?"

"A chocolate korndog."

I thought fast, the way my tradecraft Manual says you're supposed to do. "Well, there's a nice painting of one over in Mr. D. H. Carp's window."

"Yeh, sure. I seen it. What I mean is, I heard there was something else going on about it."

I decided to change the subject, a trope mentioned often in my Manual. "What's that pin in your lapel? Is that a sailor pin or a soldier? You a veteran?"

Mr. Dirty Harry Runcible sat up straight, took his cigar butt out of his mouth, wiped off his lapel button with his thumb, looked down at the button like it was his own prize hog at the Chaud County Fair. His working eye flashed with pride while the other eye sort of followed it later. "My button here shows I'm a member of the National Turkey Federation. I was a member of the King Turkey family, y'know. Course that's all over now, heh-heh."

"Well, now! I just guessed you must be a loyal member of that fine organization." I gave him a big smirk, showing clean teeth and a Holy Expression. "My dad worked over there a long time ago."

"Oh, sure. Kenworth Kuhl. A legend over there, y'know."

"I dit'n know. A legend?" Here was some good news I could finally take over there to Dad.

"Yeh, Kenworth. Ha ha ha. Talk about a screw-up. Been more'n 30 years since he got fired, and his antics are still recalled. He ever tell you about getting lost in the compost?"

I looked blank since I never heard the tale.

"Well, Kenworth wut'n of told you that one, I bet. You maybe don't know about the compost? Well, the feather pieces we don't use for pillow-fill, we compost, y'know. Dump 'em in a big hole we got dug in the delta down towards Fruitstand where the stink don't matter so much. Mix 'em up good with dirt, and they sort of rot in the ground. Later, we come back with a backhoe and sack up the rotted feathers for your garden. They do the same with stuff from over at King Korndog, y'know."

I didn't know. I decided to change the subject for strategic reasons. "I expect to belong to MI-6 soon as I get my PI certificate, and then I'll be off to England with connections."

He frowned. "So, you tryin' to sell me something, kid?"

"No, sir. You came in here on your own. I'm just being a gentleman, making conversation."

"Okay, I'll get to the point. I heard by the grapevine that you and that fat little redheaded kid are working up something in cahoots with Sammy Joe Sly. And it has something to do with that chocolate korndog."

"Your informant is incorrect, sir. Me and Zack are not in cahoots with Mr. Sam Joe Sly. Mr. Sam Joe Sly is doing his secret project all by himself, and we are doing ours all by ourselfs." Right then I figured maybe I had said too much, but Dirty Harry stayed quite suave.

"I been thinking. I been thinking about that chocolate idear."

"Well, the painting will do that. Even the idear is enough to start a guy drooling. My dad, for example…."

"I dit'n mean a chocolate korndog. I meant a chocolate *turkeylog*." Dirty Harry's face looked like he'd just won the Lotto. "You hear what I'm saying, boy? It'll transfix the industry. It'll destroy King Korndog!"

A chocolate turkeydog. I never heard the like. "Sounds sort of disgusting to me." I made my face disgusted, but still suave, unrevealing. "Besides, they don't have a bakery over there at the turkey factory. They cut'n come up with a chocolate turkeydog since they cut'n come up with the plain turkeydog in the first place."

"You don't have to. That's the beauty of our idear. And I dit'n say turkey*dog*, boy. I said turkey*log*. You don't use an actual weenie, just ground up turkey hamburger, and you wrap that up in a nice turkeylog baking mix that we'll start manufacturing as a sideline. It will come in a box, and you bake the thing yourself and then cover the whole thing with chocolate frosting. Kind of like a Ho-Ho, with turkey inside instead of whipcream."

"You mean like a chocolate frosted *burrito*."

"Yeh, that, too."

"Well, whatever. But why are you telling all this to me?"

"It's because you're going around with the fat little redheaded kid. Zack's his name?"

"Yeh. So?"

"He does what you say, everybody says. He follows you around. So, we believe little Zack's maybe got a patent application going, and we're concerned that it could get in the way of our turkeylog idear. You could maybe be helpful."

I noticed that Dirty Harry was saying "we" all of a sudden. He was not alone in his plotting. I decided to play him along. "You want me to influence Zack for something."

"Yep. We'll make it worth your while, money-wise."

"You'd pay *me* to influence Zack Burnross?"

"Yep. We'll pay you to slow down the patent app. Of course, it's all gotta be on the hush-and-hush."

"That might be possible, given the proper circumstances. But how's about Mr. Sam Joe Sly's Slydog project?"

"Slydog. Hah. That will get taken care of by other means. You don't need to think about that at all. In fact, just forget it."

I could feel my eyes getting beady, visions of sacks of cash, world trips, jeweled wristwatches, Willow Runcible in a thong at Ipanema, an Aston-Martin danced in my head. Mr. Dirty Harry Runcible's own eyes were now beady, too. He was sensing my interest and maybe was closing for the kill. He was thinking he could get my services cheap.

"You keep saying *we*. Who's we?"

He leaned forward and reached into his vest pocket, pulled out a white card. He handed it to me. It read: *Harry Runcible, Private Investigations.* Simple. Not a high-class card at all. Then it said his license number and phone, et cetera. Harry Runcible is a regular PI. Not only that, he was covert! An old guy nobody would suspect. You could have knocked me over with a turkey feather.

Unfortunately, he was talking about me influencing Zack, when the fact was, Zack was right then influencing me. Then I remembered how me and Zack had agreed that it would be useful for the Chocolate Korndog Project if Dirty Harry would say he ate a chocolate korndog every day so we could quote him in our advertising. On one hand, Dirty Harry is a turkey fan and is always claiming over his Frank's coffee that korndogs are bad for your health. On the other hand, Dirty Harry now wanted something from me.

I put on my poker face and commenced the negotiations.

Thirteen

⌘

I admit that twenty dollars is not much of a fee. It is not liable to lead to 19-jewel wristwatches and Willow Runcible in a thong, but if all I have to do is assure a guy you'll do something you probably will do anyway, then it's not all that big a deal.

I told Dirty Harry Runcible that for a small consideration I would do my best to advise Zack not to patent his chocolate korndog. How that connected with Dirty Harry and the Turkey Factory I couldn't figure out, but it didn't make any difference, and the twenty dollar bill that Dirty Harry was snapping between his fingers looked good, especially since I had a few debts that needed immediate attention.

One thing about a bill, though, you can always put the envelope it arrives in under something and sort of forget about it. What happens then, is the guys will simply send you another bill, which you can do the same thing to. You can work it that way for quite a while. Oh, they threaten not to sell you any more stuff. Big deal. You already got what you wanted.

Then they send you another letter. It tells you they are going to tell on you to a credit collector. Big deal. I've been reported to twenty or thirty credit collectors so far, and none of them ever got a dime out of me. This is the Balona Way. Works like a charm. New credit cards keep arriving for me in the mail every week.

I made the mistake one time of revealing my credit method to Cousin Nim. He *tsked* and wagged his head and said it wasn't the honorable thing to do.   So I never told him about any such thing again, him being so sensitive and all.

The one time it almost backfired was when a big hairy guy came to the house and told my ma he was going to put me in jail if I didn't pay my bill. Being bigger and hairier, my ma just threw him down the front steps and we never heard from him again. But then my ma said she would throw *me* down the front steps if I charged stuff without paying for it. "I can do that. You can't," she went.

Of course, she doesn't *have* to do it my way, since her Daddy Kon pays all her charge accounts automatically out of the old man's bank accounts, she says, a fact she never lets Dad forget.

Speaking of Dad, I went over and saw him, since I figured he was probably in the dumps from all the odors and sad sounds over at the Jolly Times Rest Home.

For recreation over there, the old folks sit in chairs or wheelchairs lined up in rows. They're all pointed at an old TV under the front window where you have to squint to see the picture because of the glare. There's a lot of drooling, too, but even though he is not exactly an old-folk, Dad was right at home with that first few days he was there. Now that his own drooling has sort of tapered off, he probably feels out of place.

Anyway, I sat on the bed in his room where he's now got three other guys in their own beds there, too. "How come you're not in a private room, Dad?"

"Well, your ma said it was too expensive, is all. Besides, I like the company." It is true that Dad likes company. His room mates are ancient and all of them seemed interested in our conversation, chiming in frequently, not always making any sense.

"How's the Secret Project going?" Dad went right away. Soon as he said that, the old guys had to chime in, wanting the skimmy on the Secret Project. I figured we might as well level with them, since nobody ever comes to visit them anyway so any secret information we give out at Jolly Times will stay right there in the room. I told Dad and the old guys about Dirty Harry's offer. I didn't mention my commission since, when I thought about it, I don't come off rich and famous.

"Well, Joey, uh, Joe, I been thinking about flavors, y'know. I mean, you can't have just chocolate. I mean, people get tired of everything right away. Just look at how the menus have to change at Peking Peek-Inn and TacoTime or else people won't come back. Guys got to have variety."

The old guys agreed. I agreed. Dad cheered right up. It looks like Jolly Times is the one place where guys agree with Dad, whether they can hear him or not.

"Besides, chocolate will constipate you," one old guy said. Then they talked between themselves for a while about constipation, laxatives, gas problems, varicose veins, et cetera, leaving me and Dad to converse among ourselves for a bit.

"You got old folks out there who want to take care of theirselfs so they don't die off at an early age. So they're the ones who will be interested in a high-fiber korndog and a fat-free korndog, and the korndog with glucosamine and gingko-biloba. I mean, just look at the magazine here." Dad pointed to an old-folks mag with a white-haired old lady with big boobs in an ad giving the eye to a white-haired old dude with abs like Sal Shaw's. The two of them were leering at each other while scarfing up pills.

"All those would be flavors of the chocolate korndog, Dad?"

"You got that right, son. And with the added coming attractions like that, you can soak 'em a pretty penny, too." Dad looked at me, worried like. "You think your ma will let me come home pretty soon? I really miss old Killer." I could see a tear starting to glint up in Dad's eye, so I looked away and pretended to listen to the old guys talking baseball.

Even though I don't much like baseball, since I could never get my bat to connect up with one, it is actually interesting about old guys talking baseball, specially if they are really old guys, like the old guys at Jolly Times. It's kind of like the way women talk about anything in a group. With women, each one talks about their own thing. They all talk about their own thing at the same time. Nobody seems to pay any attention to what the other lady is saying, but they're all talking a mile a minute and smiling.

The same with real old guys talking baseball. Each one was talking about a different game or player or season or year. All at the same time. And they seemed happy as crawfish in the Yulumne.

Then Dad happened to mention. "These friends of mine don't hear so good, y'know. If you want these fellows to understand what you're saying, you got to sort of shout. So if I want to have a conversation but am not looking for anybody to converse, I can mumble just about anything I want about anything, and everybody here is pretty agreeable. Is Killer getting his can of dogfood every day? You seen my magpie, maybe?"

Dad always asks about Killer's diet, and I tell him I'm taking care of it. Then he asks about his magpie, and I always have to sort of wag my head. I have never seen Dad's magpie. Or maybe once I did, after Dad had a Valley Brew and described the bird in considerable detail. Maybe I saw it then, at a distance.

I mentioned that the old guys at the Jolly Times Rest Home don't get many visitors. I forgot to mention Richie who bragged that him and Ricky do visit regularly whenever they need cash. They go into different Jolly Times rooms carrying flowers, supposedly for Grandpa Daddy Kon, and coming out with their pockets bulging with cash, rings, jewels, and stuff that obviously belongs in an old person's wallet or purse. That stuff probably ends up at the Delta City Fleamarket.

I was thinking to myself that maybe the next time Richie did something I could prove, I would confess him to Cod. After all, I am not my brother's keeper, the way Cousin Nim says you're supposed to be. I am not my cousin's keeper, either, but I decided I better report to Zack on my progress, show how enthusiastic I am about doing my master's business. I chuckled to myself at my humor.

I got a huge surprise when I got to Zack's house. Zack's ma, Aunt Pippa, was home instead of playing bridge with my ma or at a garden club meeting. She leered at me when I came in the side door to the kitchen. "You like a nice sangwidge, Joey?" She still calls me Joey, instead of Joe.

"Oh, well. All right." So I sat down and ate a weird sandwich which I didn't dare ask what was in it, since Aunt Pippa likes to give you gourmet stuff you don't want to know about. Tasted pretty good.

That wasn't the surprise, though. The surprise was, after I finished the glass of milk that came with the weird sandwich, she went, "Zacky's in the living room with his guest."

"What guest is that?" I wondered.

"Some young lady from San Francisco. I think she's from Davy Narsood. Zacky's not introducing me, though. He says I would get in the way." Aunt Pippa's eyes sort of teared up, reminding me of Dad. Zack is cruel to his ma. If I had a ma who fed me gourmet food every meal like Aunt Pippa, I would not be cruel to her. I would also weigh 200 pounds.

"Well, being in the project with Zack, I'll just mosey on in there and introduce myself."

"Oh, Joey. I don't know. Zacky might not want you to do that, y'know. He's a pretty masterful young man."

"He's my kid cousin." I didn't mention that Zack was also my Q, since Aunt Pippa is not a privy to that fact. So I swaggered on through the swinging door into the Burnross living room.

There was Zack, sitting back on a couch cushion, sipping from a cup. And there, sitting on a cushion at the other end of the couch, also sipping from a cup, was the most beautiful girl I have ever seen in my life. Prettier even than Willow Runcible. Maybe prettier than Millie Wong. I just stood there, my mouth hanging open with admiration.

Zack put down his cup, showing irritation on his face expression. I made a mental note to teach the young fellow how to disguise his emotions. "What do you want, Joe?" Not a welcome sound at all from the young high school student.

I decided to play along with Zack's game. "Just reporting back, Chief."

Zack looked surprised, then he smirked and waggled his head. "Well, come on in and meet somebody important. You may sit." He pointed for me to sit in an armchair across from the beautiful girl. She kept looking at me, admiringly, still sipping at her cup. She lashed her eyes at me over wide dark brown eyes in a heart-shaped face above very long legs and a short skirt.

"Hello there," I went, using my suave low voice, a real contrast to Zack's soprano. I leaned forward and pasted on a Holy Look.

"Meet Nadezhda Mussolini, Joe. Nadezhda represents Mr. Davy Narsood."

"No relation to either," said Nadezhda in a low sweet voice, licking her moist and pouty orange lips and still lashing her eyes at me again. I didn't understand what she meant about her *no relation* remark, but I nodded suavely and kept nodding, also glancing covertly at her nice thighs.

Ordinarily, I have erotic thoughts mostly about blondes and redheads, but there are brunettes, too, in my museum of passion, especially if they obviously respond to my own good looks, which Millie Wong unfortunately does not. At the moment, I was particularly glad I am tall and trim and handsome, where Zack is short and fat and ugly with tooth braces and smudgy glasses and too-long hair.

"Joe, I understand from Zachary that you are his assistant."

"Well, yeh. Sort of. For this project, since he....yeh. Sort of." Zack obviously had already established himself as top dog in his version of our relationship, so I decided to play along and see what might come of it.

"Joe's been out doing business for me this afternoon. How'd it go, Joe?"

"It went just fine, Chief." Zack's face expression glowed. I have discovered in my travels through life that guys like to be flattered, even if they don't believe it, and especially if it isn't true. I crinkled my eyes at Nadezhda, just to show her that I was teasing Zack a little. She crinkled back.

I decided that now was not the time to reveal about Dirty Harry and the Chocolate Turkeyloaf or about Harry's bribe or about me accepting it. I figured that Nadezhda was about to give us the news about Davy Narsood.

"So, Nadezhda," I went, with ultimate suave in my voice, "how's old Davy doing?"

"Mr. Narsood isn't old, Joe. And he doesn't like even being *thought* of as old. He's a vibrant man in the prime of his life, y'know." She uncrinkled her eyes. "But he told me about you."

I was flattered for a second, until I remembered my memory about flattery, and until Nadezhda went on.

"He told me to stay away from you."

We all three laughed up a storm, since I figured Nadezhda was joking me.

"Well, Nadezhda, it was me who briefed Davy on our plans for the Great Balona Chocolate Flavored Korndog Bakeoff idear." Zack face expression showed a glow from the way I described the Secret Project.

"Yes, Mr. Narsood mentioned that. He told me to let Zachary know that, as long as Joseph Kuhl isn't involved, Mr. Narsood would be happy to host the Bakeoff and produce one of his programs here in Balona, live."

"Wow!" I went, smirking and nodding and not registering the important part of that message right away. "He's actually coming to Balona. Wow!"

"You got to stay away, Joe, or Davy Narsood won't come here."

It registered. I could feel my face falling down like Patella's lip or Binky Swainhammer's belly. I felt crushed, depressed. It must have showed on my face. The tear probably helped, too.

"Oh, don't weep, Joe. I'll speak up for you. I know Mr. Narsood will forgive you if you just apologize. He's a great man with a great romantic forgiving heart as well as a wonderful talent and, unfortunately, a wife and eight children." It sounded like Nadezhda had some history there.

"Well, as long as you'll be here in Balona, too, I would say that everything will be all right." I gave her another sincere Holy Expression.

Zack finally offered me a cup of cold cocoa and the three of us had sort of a nice chat about how we might organize the bakeoff. Later he mentioned that Nadezhda had asked him if there was something wrong with my eyes. I plan to practice my Holy Expression in front of a mirror, work on it a little.

Fourteen

What we're trying to do now is work out the details of the Great Balona Flavored Chocolate Korndog Bakeoff and Carnival. First thing we decided to do was get some publicity. That meant we had to get Mr. Patrick Preene, Patella's grandpa, involved, since he owns the *Courier* and is Mrs. Shaw's boss. He could order Mrs. Shaw to write good stuff about our project. Me and Zack went to see him at his office.

"Well, boys, how's things?" he went, as you might expect.

"How's things, Mr. Preene?" we went, naturally.

Then he did a weird thing. He *told* us about things. "Well, boys, things're kinda slow around town, y'know. So, if you're looking for some free publicity, I don't know about that."

Me and Zack looked at each other. We were puzzled about how Mr. Preene knew our mission right away. Then Patella popped in, uninvited, and we figured that Patella was the guilty bigmouth.

"Hi, Grandpa," she twittered. "I bet you're talking about that big-deal Secret Project, huh!" She lashed her purple-framed eyes at me, even though she has proclaimed herself to be Zack's girlfriend.

I spoke right up. "We're not looking for free publicity for our selfs, Mr. Preene. We're trying to build up Balona so people won't laugh at us because we're from here. That's why we got Mr. Davy Narsood to come on over here and judge our contest live and on tape on the TV"

"Who?" Mr. Preene isn't a TV chef fan, I guessed.

"Mr. Davy Narsood is only the most world-famous TV chef in existence in the world today." Zack's voice was higher than usual, and louder, and his neck was getting red, a sure sign he was upset or hungry. "My bake-off will bring fame and glory—and business—to Balona, better'n the Sugarbeet Festival, probably."

"Well, we're just recovering from the Sugarbeet Festival, which I gave a lot of free publicity to, and where we actually lost money. You actually think folks around here will come out for something new so soon? My opinion is that Balona folks don't actually like new stuff." We started to get the impression that Mr. Preene was playing hard to get and was sort of baiting us to make us beg for publicity.

"Well, now, honk!" went Zack. Whenever Zack uses his special cussword, you right away get the distinct impression he's serious. "Mr. Preene," he continued, "you know for sure that Mr. Davy Narsood being here will attract Mr. Blip Wufser and his whole crew over here to cover the event." Mr. Blip Wufser is the famous ace newscaster from KDC-TV in Delta City. "And when Mr. Blip Wufser shows up, Mr. Buddy Swainhammer won't be far behind, them being big rivals—at least in Mr. Buddy Swainhammer's opinion." Zack took a deep breath, like he was about to continue.

Mr. Preene cut him off. "I heard that Buddy it'n interested at all in your secret project."

"Where'd you hear something like that?" Zack looked a dagger at Patella who glanced her eyes off of the ceiling. "That's a strictly temporary thing. Wait till Mr. Buddy Swainhammer hears that Blip Wufser is coming over here with his crew and all his equipment to cover Mr. Davy Narsood. Blip will probably show up in his new *Live Blipcopter*. Then you'll see a big crowd of media people rushing to Balona. Probably your big rival, Mr. Peavine, will show up to cover my secret event himself. You'll see."

Patella right away sucked up to her grandpa. "Mr. Peavine is no rival of Grandpa's. Grandpa's got no rivals, only colleagues and associates." Everybody knows that Mr. Preene considers his big rival to be Ted Peavine, Editor of the Delta City *Beacon*. Mr. Peavine lives in Balona but doesn't subscribe to the *Courier*, a fact which Patella says irritates and insults Mr. Preene.

"Son, somebody big-time shows up in Balona, we'll sure cover it. Otherwise, here's our rates." Mr. Preene waved his hand at a big sign on the wall that shows how much you have to pay *per line* to get any advertising into the *Courier*. Mr. Preene went back into his office, sat in his big leather high-back chair, and put his feet up on the desk. He was finished talking with us.

What a racket. If I wasn't already going into Law Enforcement or Secret Agent Work or Psychology or Professional

Poetry as a career, I would probably have to consider publishing, since it's obvious you can get rich quick there.

We decided to have a huddle and discuss strategy. That is, Zack and Patella decided to go on over to Mello Fello and have a pre-dinner pizza, and I had to invite myself along. "You got to pay for your own, Joe, since I got only two coupons." Zack always pays for his pizzas with the coupons he clips out of the *Beacon*.

"I'll just come along and watch you guys hog down your pizzas since I don't have any cash." I made my face expression sad so they would at least feel guilty about depriving an associate of nourishment.

We all three climbed into Patella's purple Barney which always smells like popcorn. I mentioned that fact and right away Patella got insulted and said if I couldn't stand the smell maybe I should walk, a mile and a half walk.

A fast thinker, I went, "I actually don't *mind* popcorn smell. It's just that it doesn't go with purple, y'know. Purple goes with grape juice or bubble gum, not popcorn."

Patella groused something I couldn't translate, but then she made Zack sit on the outside, me sitting in the middle. Then, while we drove over to Mello Fello, she rested her hand on my thigh, sort of casually, an act I couldn't do anything about without looking like it bothered me and making a big deal out of a friendly act. A sort of friendly act. Or an unthinking act. Maybe. This sneaky act of hers created a sort of spontaneous symptom, which I won't explain further in this family-type account. Out of the corner of my eye I noticed that Patella had a smirk on her face.

We got seated in Mello Fello right up front where Teddy Rimshot was throwing his pizza dough up in the air and making a big dramatic scene out of it. Teddy doesn't look very healthy to me. Sort of sunk-chested and pimply and pale. And he was coughing a lot. So I didn't feel all that left out when Zack and Patella ordered pizzas and milkshakes for themselves, not extending the hand of fellowship to me. Instead, they kept leering at each other about my obvious hunger pangs.

Mello Fello wasn't crowded, since it was really too late for lunch and too early to eat evening pizza. I sat there drumming my fingers on the table and looking around, also feeling sort of guilty that I hadn't yet revealed to Zack that I had that simple, reasonable talk with Dirty Harry Runcible. Zack would be suspicious of the twenty dollars I got from Dirty Harry. Zack would think I was actually trying to influence him, since I'm always trying to influence him.

Teddy came over with pizzas and milkshakes for Zack and Patella. I just had to sit there looking hungry and sad.

Between mouthfuls of pizza, Zack was holding his wallet so he could thumb through his many coupons for different stuff. He looked up at me every once in a while, like Scrooge thinking about giving Tiny Tim a coupon, too, but only *thinking* about it. Then I got an unpleasant surprise which turned out to be not too unpleasant.

It was Richie, usually an unpleasant surprise. There was this loud shouting and banging at the entrance and in came Richie and Ricky Placock. They swaggered right up to Teddy and gave their orders in loud voices.

Richie was wearing my old green sweat shirt and the tan pants they give you when you're locked up at Runcible Hall. Richie's pal Ricky was wearing his motorcycle jacket. Ricky is one of those guys who *looks* like a criminal. Hard to describe, except he slouches and looks sneaky. He's got black hair slicked back in a pony tail and a long skinny nose and black eyes and a pale face wih red lips like a girl. He never says much. Always leering. He does all sorts of crimes and misdemeanors. Of course, he never gets caught. Richie turned to our table.

"Hey, Joey, how's things?"

"How's things, Richie? You're out again already?"

"They cut'n hold me since I was totally innocent of all charges, and besides they cut'n prove anything. Hey, Humpty!" Richie always calls Zack *Humpty*, a name which Zack doesn't appreciate. Zack kept on looking at his pizza.

"Hey, Fats! How's things?" Richie poked Patella in the back of the head while she was taking a sip off of her milkshake. She ignored him, even though she could have made a smartmouth remark about Richie's obvious weight gains. Richie isn't as fat as my ma, but he'll be there soon, and he's no taller than Patella.

"How come you're not hogging down a pizza, Joey?"

"I dit'n feel hungry is why."

"Hey, Teddy, cook up a pepperoni with everything for my big brother here and put it on my order." Richie was actually buying me a pizza. My face smirked a wide smile, in spite of a sincere desire not to show any emotion at this largeness of my usually scrimpy little brother. "We would join your party, you guys, but Ricky here's got a proposition I got to listen to. You understand."

Richie sounded like a stockbroker or a banker, probably a trope he learned at Runcible Hall. He kept on standing next to our table while Teddy served me a nice large pizza which had extra cheese as well as lots of sausage. Smelled great. Zack and Patella had just about finished theirs. They looked at my pizza and frowned their faces. "We got to get going pretty soon, Zacky," went Patella, finishing up the last of her pizza while observing that I was biting on my very first slice.

Richie was still standing there. Ricky was sitting at the next table with their pizzas. "Hey, Joey. You want I should sprinkle some good dust on that pizza? Make you sparkle, bro!" Richie was talking about doping my pizza, right there in front of everybody. He laughed through his nose, and I thought about Ricky's plan for me to take the rap for some crime they will commit. "Just kidding, scouts!" he hollered.

Richie got kicked out of the Boy Scouts for some crime back when we had Scouts in Balona. That was before most of the parents figured they were too busy for such childish stuff. Besides, they heard that video games improved your eye-hand coordination. Every kid needs improved eye-hand coordination. This was a better excuse than most, so a lot of Balona dads got their kids video games instead of Boy Scouts. Besides, most Boy Scouts are noisy, smelly, unpredictable, and eat a lot. My dad got me a video game, but of course Richie broke it right away, so I was out Scouts and video games both.

Patella was wiping her lips with a paper napkin and looking at my pizza. "I guess you're doing some detective work or real estate for Dirty Harry Runcible," she mentioned.

"Who? I haven't read the book," I went, practically choking but thinking pretty fast. This was not how I wanted to disclose my trope to Zack. He was looking at me like I had committed a crime.

"Y'know. Mr. Harry Runcible, the turkey guy we all laugh at."

"Yeh, I know who he is. I don't laugh at him. Why do you laugh at him?"

"Well, the way he looks at you. You know."

"He dut'n look at me."

"He was looking at you just recently."

"Oh, yeh?"

"Yeh. I saw him go into your office. I was standing in the window at the *Courier*, and I saw him go in there. The reason being I had saw you go in earlier, and I was thinking about going over and saying hello, y'know."

"Oh, *that* Dirty Harry. Oh, yeh. Now I remember." I took a big couple of bites, filling up my face so I couldn't talk much.

"How come you're not answering the question, Joe? Patella's asting you a simple question here, and you're dancing around it like that old guy with the hat and the moonwalk on TV."

"It's a matter of professional discretion, Young Zack. A pro can't go around revealing clients. If he had a client, that is." I filled my face some more, smirking to myself about my quick thought. "I might reveal some of what transcribed there, but to my Q here only. Not in front of somebody who is so untrustworthy and bigmouth about secret stuff."

"Are you saying that I am untrustworthy and a bigmouth about secret stuff?"

"If the shoe fits...." (*If the shoe fits....* is a saying made up by my Uncle Peterbilt Kuhl, and means: If it walks like a duck and sounds like a duck, it is probably a duck.)

Patella trounced out in a huff, ducklike, and me and Zack had to run to catch up, me swallowing up all the rest of my pizza on the run.

I had committed myself in front of a witness to reveal my trope with Dirty Harry Runcible. I hoped Zack would take kindly to the information about the turkeylog and my secret assignment from Dirty Harry. It is tough when a guy has to perform as a double agent while suffering from heartburn.

Fifteen

The next thing we had to do, according to Zack, was get some sponsors. These are guys who will donate to the Organizing Fund. Zack mentioned several times that every festival, like the Sugarbeet Festival, has got to have sponsors to donate money to the organizers—in order to get the organizing done. There should be a little profit in it, too, for the organizers, but that fact doesn't always have to be advertised in a loud voice.

Zack figured the first people we should nail down would be Front Street merchants who will profit most from the huge inflocks of population that will show up for the Great First Annual Balona Flavored Chocolate Korndog Bakeoff, Festival, and Carnival. Zack also figured that the newest merchant was the one least likely to put up a lot of resistance.

"Who's that?" I went. "Who's the newest merchant? Claire?" I said that on account of how Claire restored the old Oliver and made it into the New Oliver, finally a clean-smelling movie house.

"No, Joe. Think, man. Who started a business here last year, where we had no such business before, except for Mr. D. H. Carp, who wasn't supposed to sell 'em?"

Right away I figured out Zack was talking about Mr. Hank Vibrissa, owner and operator of Henry's Pharmacy, the favorite target of that rat Richie and his evil companion, Ricky. "Yeh, Mr. Vibrissa ought to be ripe to donate." So me and Zack and Harley made our way up to Henry's Pharmacy where there was no customers at all. Mr. Vibrissa's got a jingle bell over the door, same as every place on Front Street. It jingled when we entered.

"Hey, boys! How's things?" went Mr. Vibrissa, a really hairy guy who caught onto Balona's language habits right away. Mr. Vibrissa's got a wife who's a doper who keeps running away to dope and gamble at Lake Tahoe, and Mr. Vibrissa has to close up shop and drive up and rescue her. He's also got a kid, little Zin

Vibrissa. She is a freshman at Big Baloney who is a doper wannabe, and an associate of my evil little brother.

"How's things, Mr. Vibrissa?" we went, all cheerful and friendly, since that's the way to make a sale, according to my dad, who told me all about it. Of course, Dad's last sale was about 17 months ago, but the good principles stay the same, he mentioned.

When you go into Mr. Hank Vibrissa's drug store he's usually talking to somebody. It's a wonder he ever gets anything done he talks so much. Most people when they're talking at work keep right on working as they talk. Not Mr. Vibrissa. When he talks, he talks. When he works, he works. Problem is, he likes to talk. So, when he's talking, he's stopped working, even when he's mixing up some medicine for a guy. It takes an hour to get a prescription filled. When he's talking, he's not looking at you, he's looking at the ceiling of his drug store or out the window at Front Street, and his hands have stopped doing what they were doing before he started talking.

Mr. D. H. Carp at his store is always looking straight at you with his pale eyes. Of course, that's why most Balona shoplifters do their best thing at Henry's Pharmacy.

Richie brags that when him and Ricky Placock go to Henry's Pharmacy to shoplift, one of them will engage Hank in conversation. Easy to do, since Mr. Vibrissa would rather stop working and talk to anybody than work. While Mr. Vibrissa is talking and looking at the ceiling or out onto Front Street, Richie or Ricky will be lifting the shop, so to speak. Some time when they get caught, they will probably find a way to hang the crime on me, like they are planning to do. I worry about that all the time.

But Mr. Vibrissa hasn't caught on to the shoplifting yet, even though lots of high school kids are seen going into his drug store during lunch time and right after school with empty pockets and bookbags. None of these young citizens ever actually buy stuff, but all of them come out with their pockets and bookbags bulging. It may be time to restore the counseling program at Balona High, where they don't have a counselor since they fired Mr. Keyshot to save the taxpayers money. This drugstore taxpayer whose money is saved may be losing more than he's saving in taxes.

I was thinking that Mr. Vibrissa's work behavior is sort of weird when it suddenly occurred that my dad is exactly the same way. He can't talk and do anything else at the same time. He can't even talk while chewing with his mouth full. That's why he's such a slow eater.

Carl at Carl's Shoe Repair is the same way. When he talks to a guy, he puts down whatever he is working on. When he stops talking, he picks up his work again. No wonder it takes weeks to get your shoes repaired over there.

Anyway, back to the proposition work. Zack was the first of us to speak about the donation, since it was his idea. Mr. Vibrissa beat him to it.

"I see you got a dog with you, young fellers," he went, giving Harley a hard look. "A pharmacy is probably not a good place for a dog to be, what with the purity of my product, eksedra."

Harley stopped in his tracks, quit smelling at the front door, where there probably was something good on the glass there to smell. Harley turned his head and looked over his shoulder at Mr. Vibrissa. Harley's blond eyebrows were frowning on his little black-haired face, and he turned and walked right to the back and sat down in front of where Mr. Vibrissa stood, just looked at him, cocking his head from one side to the other.

"You heard me, did you?" Mr. Vibrissa almost smiled—until *Harley nodded his head twice!* "Did he just nod his head in agreement with me, or do I need a drink?"

"Harley is a very smart and sensitive dog, Mr. Vibrissa. He's also very clean. He's insulted about your purity remark, I guess."

Mr. Vibrissa kept looking at Harley, and Harley kept looking back. Mr. Vibrissa had on his usual short-sleeve white smock, like a doctor. He's got curly black hair all over his arms, like fur. He's even got hair on his neck. You can see where he's got five o'clock shadow there where he's shaved his neck. After a while he went, "Well, I guess, under the circumstances I could make an exception." Harley nodded again—just once this time—and went back to smelling the front door. Mr. Vibrissa could hardly tear his eyeballs away from the little dog.

"So, how's Mrs. Vibrissa?" went Zack, right away softening up our client. "And how's little Zin?" he added, to rub it in, I guess.

"Uh, they're both just fine. Just fine." He looked out the window at Front Street and then up at the ceiling. "Yes. Fine." It was the kind of answer that told you that Mrs. Vibrissa and little Zin were not all that fine. So I guess Zack felt the iron was hot, so to speak.

"Well, Mr. Vibrissa, since you're a fine new citizen of Balona, and since you got a fine business here, we figured you will want to be a good citizen and support the Greater Balona First Annual Flavored Chocolate Korndog Bakeoff and Festival and Carnival." Zack was standing up straight for a change and had his hair sort of pushed back and you could see his eyes behind his glasses.

"What was that again?"

Zack repeated his whole speech, practically word for word the same.

"Never heard of it." Mr. Vibrissa turned to his work bench and started mixing something, his back to us.

"Well, no problem. We'll just scratch you off our huge long list of supporters and donators, and start up a list of guys who don't really support Balona." Zack sneaked a peek at me and probably winked his eye, which I couldn't see on account of the smudges on his glasses.

Mr. Vibrissa stopped mixing.

Zack repeated himself. "No problem, Mr. Vibrissa. See you around." And he turned around and pushed me towards the door.

"Well, now. Wait just a minute. Are you saying I'll be the only one on that list? The second list there?"

"We haven't even had to make up that list, so, yeh, sure, you'll have the honor of being up there all by yourself. We'll include your merchant name, not just your regular social citizen name, so it'll *read Mr. Henry Vibrissa, Proprietor of Hank's Pharmacy.* That's what we'll give the *Courier* when we submit the refused-to-donate list, y'know."

"Well, it's just that I never heard of it. What was it again?"

Zack repeated himself. Even in his high voice, he sounded pretty convincing. Even I considered becoming a donator/sponsor, if I had a few bucks to kick in. Then Zack went, "It'll be a big deal, bigger even than the Sugarbeet Festival, and of course it's deductible as a business expense. The hundred dollars, I mean."

"A *hundred* dollars? A business expense is still an expense you got to pay for. You're expecting a poor merchant to give over a hundred dollars? That's a lot."

"Well, that's what a lot of guys are donating. But you could donate $75 and get on the second string list, y'know."

"Oh." Mr. Vibrissa looked at the ceiling. "If I gave a hundred dollars, I would get on the first string list?"

"Oh, yeh. That would be guaranteed." Zack closed his eyes and smacked his lips.

"I'd need a receipt."

"Got your receipt right here." Zack pulled out a receipt book and his ballpoint. He held both up in a writing position. "Well, sir, which will it be? Second string or first?"

"Well. Well, I don't want to look bad on the list, do I. So, I guess. Well, yeh. Put me down for the first string. That gets me on the first string, does it?"

"Of course. Right up there with the other winners, sir." Zack didn't start writing. Him and Mr. Vibrissa just sort of looked at each other until Mr. Vibrissa reached into his cash register and pulled out a bunch of twenties. Then Zack started writing. "Give 'em to my assistant here," he mumbled, nodding his head in my direction. I stuck out my hand.

Mr. Vibrissa counted them off into my hand like he was saying goodbye to dear friends departing on the Greyhound.

"That'll be just fine." Zack zipped the receipt and gave it over with a flourish. "We thank you, sir, on behalf of the Greater Balona First Annual Flavored Chocolate Korndog Bakeoff, Festival, and Carnival. And we congratulate you for making the first string, sir!" Zack showed his tooth braces. Harley gave a short bark of appreciation. I worked up a Holy Look.

"Well, now, when's this thing supposed to take place?"

"I haven't decided that yet, but you'll be the first to know."

Mr. Vibrissa started looking at the ceiling. When we got outside and out of sight of Mr. Vibrissa we high-fived each other. Then right away Zack went, "Okay, you can be the banker." This was a surprise.

"But I'm the one with the first expenses, so I'll draw on the bank when I need to. The next donation we'll split according to a formula I already worked out." He sort of squinted his eyes and rubbed his chin. "Hmmm," he went.

"How come you're hmmmm-ing?"

"I'm considering who should be our next donator."

"Maybe Mr. Pezmyer. He's pretty rich."

"Mr. Pezmyer's the biggest grinch in town. Bigger grinch even than Mr. D. H. Carp. Dit'n you know that?"

"Well, sure, I knew that. It's just that we need to get more donations, and sooner or later we'll have to interview everybody."

"I notice you didn't do any interviewing."

"Well, I figured you had it in the bag right away, so I wut'n want to mess it up by saying something."

"A wise decision."

"So, if not Mr. Pezmyer or Mr. D. H. Carp, then who?"

"Who said not Mr. D. H. Carp? I dit'n say that. Let's go see Mr. D. H. Carp."

So we went down the street to try our luck there.

The store was empty of customers. Mr. Sackworth wasn't at his post, was probably in the toilet, as usual. Mr. D. H. Carp was reading a magazine at his desk, his feet up on the top drawer "Hey, boys," he went. "How's things?"

"How's things, Mr. Carp?" we went.

Then Zack went, "It's all yours, Joe."

"What? What?"

"Go to it, Joe. Make your pitch."

Zack had stabbed me in the back. I needed to go forth and rescue the situation. So I did.

"I hear you heard about the chocolate korndog, Mr. Carp."

"You know I did. I still got a few sitting in the cabinet there. So?"

"Then maybe you heard about the Balona Bakeoff Carnival."

Zack went, "The First Annual Greater Balona Flavored Chocolate Korndog Bakeoff, Festival, and Carnival."

"Nope. Never heard of it."

I strived on. "Well, it's gonna happen where the chocolate korndog gets celebrated."

"Oh, yeh."

Zack added, "And Davy Narsood is gonna do his TV show over here. It's all arranged. And Blip Wufser will do his news show, too. And Buddy Swainhammer. All those guys will be here for the Bakeoff, eksedra. We expect you will want to be part of the action."

"Oh, yeh? How so?"

"You will want to be one of the fine first-string partners."

"Sure. Put my name down. Buddy can introduce me to the crowd, then I'll introduce Davy whatsisname. There'll be a crowd, won't there?"

"A huge crowd. Your contribution will be only a hundred dollars."

"Put me down for ten. You can collect afterwards."

"Oh." we both went. That was it. Mr. D. H. Carp went back to his magazine, and we departed. We were both sort of quiet.

"It looks like you got to do some practicing, Joe. Well, I got to get on home and view the tape I made of Davy's show." Zack's got a video recorder up in his bedroom, of course, and he tapes programs he's too busy to turn on.

I get to be banker. I wondered how come Zack didn't grab the cash himself. I could feel the bills burning a hole in my pocket.

Sixteen

Now it's not only Zack and Mr. Sam Joe Sly who are working on the chocolate korndog. A whole bunch of Balona ladies have got the word that there is to be a bakeoff. Balona ladies are always competing against each other. Who's the richest, who's got the ugliest husband, whose husband can drink the most beer, who's got the smartest kid, et cetera.

Unless my ma is involved. Then usually everybody backs off, since Ma uses anything she can to win. Ma will eat chocolate korndogs, but she hasn't entered the chocolate korndog race since she thinks the whole idea is stupid because it requires kitchen work. So the rest of Balona ladies are trying out their own recipes. I heard talk at one of my ma's bridge games, where I was sitting on the landing, sort of doing my English homework.

"I tell you it wasn't all that bad," went Mrs. Shaw, wiping her mouth from the mini-pizza horse-derve she just ate in one bite. She was referring to Mr. Sam Joe Sly's chocolate korndog, the one she tried at Mr. D. H. Carp's Groceries & Sundries that time. "It had a sort of parsley flavor to it, but it was distinctly chocolaty, too."

"Ooo! I love chocolate," went Nancy Sporlodden, quivering her voice to make it dramatic. "I could eat chocolate all day and all night. Maybe I'll try to make one, too. My only worry is it will maybe make Kork fat, since he works out three hours a day to keep his abs fit." Right there was an example of a lady getting in her competitive licks, since there's nobody in Balona—probably not even Sal Shaw or Cousin Nim—who can beat Coach Kork's abs, which he will pull up his sweatshirt and show you any time.

Aunt Forey spoke right up. "Well, you don't have to make it like Sammy Joe Sly does his. I mean, his creation looks like a maple bar except for that little thing sticking out the end."

"That little masculine thing," went Mrs. Shaw.

The ladies all snicker.

Aunt Pippa: "That's the way Claire Preene painted it up."

THE CHOCOLATE KORNDOG

My ma commented: "That's the way Kenzy dreamed it."

"That's just one verjin," went Aunt Forey. "There's other verjins. I'll let you in on one of my newest."

"Newest. You mean you've done more than one?"

"I've done four already. Each one different. Anson ate 'em all. Talk about gas!"

My ma intruded about her brother Anson's appetite. "Anson would get gas from the *futzin* plate if he ate it fast enough."

"Well, that's true, Baps. But this latest one, now this is my best. I'm thinking maybe it's the one I'll bake up for the big bakeoff."

"Well, tell us, please." Mrs. Shaw had her notebook and fountain pen out, ready to copy down Aunt Forey's recipe.

"Well, what you do is, you make creampuff dough, see, and you make this creampuff and bake it up nice."

Nancy interrupted. "It won't look like a chocolate korndog if you stick it in a creampuff. The weenie will hang out both ends. And it won't look like Claire's painting."

"It dut'n have to look like Claire's painting. It has to look like *your* idear of a chocolate korndog. Anyways, pay attention here. I made my creampuffs long instead of round, see? I made me a whole panfull. Then you mix up your special sauce, but you leave out the ketchup and mustard, and instead mix up a little honey and some chocolate syrup with the peanut butter and you add some ground-up walnuts for the crunch, y'know. Maybe I shut'n tell you.

"Oh, well. Then you fry up your dogs. And since your puffs are finished, so you make a hole in one end of the baked-up puff and spoon in some special sauce. And then you stuff in your dog. And then you layer on your chocolate frosting. And then, ta dah, you got you a *special* chocolate creampuff-type korndog, see? I tell you my Anson can't get enough of 'em. Only thing is, I don't know if it'll qualify, without the corn in it, y'know."

There was a long silence from the players. You could hear the rain beating on the window and the wind blowing. Everybody was thinking about the special chocolate creampuff kornless dog. I was tasting it in my head. I could taste the combination of creampuff and peanut butter and chocolate. I was thinking, *this is like a giant Reecey Cup!* Then the weenie taste snuck into my head-taste. The creampuffdog was best without the weenie.

Mrs. Shaw broke the silence. "I think maybe it would be best without the masculine influence, without the weenie thing in it."

"I always suspected you was queer," went my ma. Everybody laughed except Mrs. Shaw.

"Well, the weenie taste is quite distinctive. It works against all the sweetness of the rest of the confection, dut'n it?"

"Sammy Joe Sly is making his weenies taste completely different, though."

"But why use a weenie at all?"

"Well, without the weenie, it wut'n be a korndog."

"Oh. Well."

"So, Forey. Also, without the corn part, it wut'n be a korndog either."

"Well, I figure I'll figure out a way to overhaul that problem."

"My Zacky is always figuring, y'know," Aunt Pippa bragged. "So he's got three or four new variations of his chocolate korndog over at the house right now. I'll get him to make up some for us and bring 'em over next time we play. When's that, Bapsie? When do we play again?"

"Well, how's about this afternoon?" My ma is always ready to nap, eat, drink, argue, or play bridge. Actually, these ladies don't really get much bridge playing in, but they do a might of talking and eating and drinking. They all agreed that they would continue their game after lunch and that Aunt Pippa would bring a box of Zack's korndogs along with her.

"They give gas, y'know," went my ma.

"We'll just make sure you don't get one, Baps," went Nancy Sporlodden joking, since Ma is bigger, stronger, and meaner than any of the rest.

"Your Zachary sure is a smart young man," went Mrs. Anna Trilbend. She sounded like she was sucking up to Aunt Pippa, for what reason I couldn't imagine.

"My Zacky is probably smarter than any kid his age."

"I bet he's not smarter than Jack Ordway," went Nancy.

"Oh, well, Jack is some older, y'know."

"Maybe a month."

"Well. He's a whole lot smarter than Joe."

"Joey is a *dum-shik* all right. I think I probably dropped him on his head when he was little." Everybody laughed. My ma had somehow stopped being her usual competitive self, when it came to bragging on me. I felt my stomach getting cold, along with my knees and bladder. "But Richie's a whole lot smarter than all of 'em put together, y'know."

Nobody said a word. You could just hear breathing. I could just imagine Mrs. Shaw *wanting* to say something, but holding it in.

My ma went on. "Richie's gonna be rich and famous when he gets a little older. He's got a lot of that good Chaud Blood in him, and that makes all the difference."

"I suppose Richie is all set to go to Harvard next year." This from Mrs. Shaw when I almost expected to hear it from Aunt Pippa about Zack.

"Richie don't need to go to college to get rich and famous."

"Well, you're right there, Bapsie. He's already famous." Aunt Forey, being Uncle Anson's wife who Uncle Anson brags to about all the criminals he's caught, is probably referring to how Richie's already got a criminal record. Famous for sure.

"What's all that racket, I wonder?" Aunt Forey went to the window, pressed her nose against the glass. "It's the fire brigade going east, in a big huge hurry. I wonder whose house is burnt down?"

People always say it that way, as if the house is already burnt down when the fire brigade gets to it. That's because everybody is a volunteer in the Balona Fire Brigade, and nobody moves very fast when there's a fire. A fire in Balona mostly degenerates into a beer bust since, on the way to a fire, the firefighters always stop the engine in front of Mr. D. H. Carp's Groceries & Sundries and pick up a few cases of Valley Brew to quench their thirsts.

"Well, let's go take us a look," went my ma. She always likes to go to fires, crunches her share of Valley Brew cans along with the fire fighters. Ma added, "Joey'll take us in his car. Go on out there and wait for me while I get my raincoat."

This was a surprise to me, since maybe Ma knew I was sitting on the landing all the time.

The ladies went out and got in my Yellow Peril, since nobody ever locks their car in Balona. My ma went out to the garage and got the garage raincoat that hangs there, along with the rubber boots I use to explore the dump in, and dad's golf hat.

I put on the yellow slicker and the fisherman's hat that Dad got when he was a member of the Delta City Slickers. We put on our rain stuff there in the garage. We didn't say anything to each other. Ma was busy in her thoughts, I guess. I was still thinking about her probably dropping me on my head when I was a baby. I wondered if maybe that accounted for me not studying much and not becoming valedictorian of Balona High. Thinking that way I started to feel better, since it's always good when things don't work out to have something to blame. Or somebody.

My Yellow Peril started right away, even though I haven't driven it for a while. I hoped it had some gas in it.

"Turn here," my ma went, giving orders as usual and, as usual, directing me in the wrong direction. Ma thinks of herself as a famous navigator.

"I think the fire must be over there," went Mrs. Trilbend from the middle seat. "Since that's where all the traffic is heading."

Ma insisted it was the other direction, so we drove around a while until I managed, little by little, to get us down to King Way where you could see smoke coming up through the wind and rain.

"Hey, it's the Kastle Keep," said Nancy, shouting from the back seat practically into my ear. "King Korndog is on fire!" Nancy's voice is not only loud, it's high and scratchy both. Made my ear itch.

The members of the Fire Brigate were standing around drinking beer and watching the smoke pour out of one of the buildings. Aunt Forey shouted out at one of the firefighters, "How come you're not in there fighting the fire?"

The firefighter took a pull on his beer can and went, "Well, Frank forgot the key to the hose lockers there. Just went home to find it. You better get that car off the middle of the street, kid." So I parked a little ways off, in front of old Mrs. Splinters's house, the house she gave to Mr. Burberry before she went off to Montana.

"Frank" is Mr. Frank Floom. He's the captain of the brigade. They have to keep the hoses locked up since Delta Doodle Dandies have been known to take the hoses out of the fire engine lockers and lay them out on Front Street, hooking the hoses up to the hydrants and spraying each other for fun. This sport usually happens in the summer, but they did it once around New Years, too.

"Is that the korndog bakery burning up, there?" Mrs. Trilbend was plucking at my elbow, leaning her boobs into me. She also lashed her eyes at me. In spite of all that distraction, I strived on.

I explained. "Naw, the bakery is over there. That's the lab, where they do experiments and stuff." It suddenly occurred that the King Korndog lab was where Mr. Sam Joe Sly has been doing all his experimenting with his chocolate Slydogs. It looked to me like maybe Mr. Sam Joe Sly's project was about to slow down.

Lots of Balonans were watching the smoke. No flames, just a whole lot of smoke. I saw Mr. Drumhandler, my old history teacher from Big Baloney. He was standing there with his mouth open, drawing with a pencil in a wet notebook. Richie and Ricky zoomed by on Ricky's motorcycle. Old Mrs. Crinkle under a purple umbrella came limping up to Ma who had already got herself a beer from the firefighter stash.

"I seen you from a block away, Bapsie. I thought you was Bena Splinters. I mean, your raincoat, y'know. Looks just like Bena's."

"This is Kenzy's raincoat. Too big for him so he keeps it in the garage." Ma doesn't usually explain anything to anybody, but Mrs. Crinkle is one of her bridge regulars. "You come on over this afternoon and we'll have us some of Forey's new chocolate korndogs."

"Well, okay, but I tell you, seeing that raincoat on a big fat woman really give me a start."

"I ain't fat. Just bold-looking. You need glasses."

The raincoat they were talking about was the raincoat that I found in a bag at the dump, so Ma was actually wrong. I didn't want to disturb the universe by telling her though. Besides, I was still thinking about being dropped on my head.

Mr. Frank Floom finally showed up with the key, and the firefighters took their axes and chopped down the front door. A King Korndog employee mentioned in a loud voice that since the door wasn't locked, it wasn't necessary to chop it down. But the firefighters were in no mood to argue and just trounced on in there, coughing and swearing a lot.

It was when they unlimbered the hose that the fun began. The employee shouted for all to hear, "No, no, it's just a smoke fire. Somebody just tossed a smoke bomb in here. Somebody was playing games. There's no need for water." But the firefighters were in a fire-fighting mood and so splashed the lab good. You could hear crashing and glass tinkling and firefighters laughing. It'll be a while before Mr. Sam Joe Sly experiments with his chocolate korndogs again.

Suddenly, at the front of the row of onlookers I spied a familiar figure leaning on his cane. When he saw me, he squinted his good eye at me under his black hat. He wagged his head, like I shouldn't recognize him. It was Dirty Harry Runcible, looking very suspicious.

Maybe the smoke bomb wasn't an accident!

Seventeen

I was sitting in the dark in my room, ponderating the fate of a guy who was dropped on his head as a child. I figured that fatal drop is why studying has never had a romantic appeal for me and watching movies on TV has. I always knew there was a reason Zack thinks faster than me. That head drop explains it all. I felt around my skull for evidence of holes, cracks, et cetera. Poor guy.

Since it was Sunday morning I thought briefly about going over to Tabernacle and getting cheered up by Pastor Nim who always will cheer you up. Of course, going to Tabernacle would mean putting on a shirt and pants and shoes. And Pastor Nim always makes a mouth if he sees you come into Tabernacle without a coat and tie. I decided to sit and think sad thoughts instead.

Then something fantastic happened! I got an actual phone call from Claire Preene. Some other guy might not think this is all that fantastic, but Claire is usually a very distant-type female, as far as I am concerned. A phone call from her is a big deal. It may be that in the back of her head she was considering the possibility that some day she will be in matrimonial matters with me. Actually, that is not likely, since she doesn't know it yet and would probably throw up if she did.

Anyway, she called me on the phone. "Who?" I went, when Ma hollered at me to hurry up and answer. I didn't believe it was Claire, naturally.

"Uh, yeh?" This was not a very suave beginning, but I was caught unawares, still thinking about being dropped on my head.

"Joseph? Is this you? You sound like you have a frog in your throat." This is the way Claire talks. She always sort of throws you off balance right away, especially if a guy has been sitting in a dark room, thinking sad thoughts. Patella does this throwing technique, too. My ma, also. I am beginning to wonder if it's a female trope.

"It's me. Is this you, Claire?" I had to be sort of smartmouth in order to show I wasn't on my knees ready to kiss her foot just because she was on the phone.

"Listen here, Joseph." Claire was ordering me right away. "I was talking to Fanny last night—Fanny Klimstroke, my popcorn lady?—and she is thinking about putting together a Balona recipe book. Don't you think that's a splendid idear?" *Splendid* is one of Jack Ordway's words he uses all the time, so you can see a definite influence creeping in there. Jack is a smart guy that his ma never dropped on his head.

"Yeh. Fanny. So?" I wasn't about to show I was too eager to hear what she had to say. You have to show your independence with women like Claire. Or Patella. Or my ma. With my ma, if you show you are too independent, she will lock you out of the house and make you sleep in the garage, which has happened a few times. But back to Claire.

"So, don't you think that's a splendid idear!" Claire wasn't asking this time. She was demanding that I agree.

For the sake of argument, I did. "Sure. Splendid idear. How come you called me about it, Claire?"

"Well, Zack's starting a Korndog Festival and you're his banker. I heard that from my lessee Mr. D. H. Carp. So this is another activity you could include in your agenda."

"Mr. D. H. Carp is your what?"

"My lessee. I lease the building to him."

"Oh. Well. Then you said I could include my what?"

"Your list of things to be included in the festival."

"Oh, yeh. I could include a recipe book." I didn't see how a recipe book would connect with the festival.

"Yes, you could. You get the recipes of all the entries and you have them printed up in a little book and you sell the book. Of course, you'd get the endorsement of Mr. Davy Narsood on the cover, too. Everybody knows him, and his endorsement would be a good ad. And maybe you could include a snapshot of each person who turns in a recipe. I bet a lot of people would buy it. And not only in Balona."

"Yeh, sounds like a great idear." I didn't sound enthusiastic, since I didn't think a lot of people would actually be interested in a book of Balona recipes. Except for Mr. Wong at Peking Peek-Inn and Mrs. Peralta who runs TacoTime, most Balona cooks cook up stuff that you wouldn't feed to your dog, in my opinion. Except Aunt Pippa could also be an exception, with her gourmet stuff that keeps Zack overweight. And Claire's ma who does stuff with marshmallows. And Jack Ordway's grandma who makes salty rice balls which are pretty tasty. And maybe Aunt Forey. Maybe a few others. "I'll think about it a while, and get back to you."

"Oh, don't get back to me, Joseph. Call up Mrs. Klimstroke. Tell her your good news."

"What good news is that?"

"That you will put her in charge of collecting the recipes, eksedra. You could even ask her to put the book together. As a matter of fact, I've already suggested that idear to her, so she's likely to be agreeable."

"She is."

"Oh, yes. And she's imaginative and she sews and typewrites, too, and her daughter Becky draws very nicely. Becky could do the book's page decorations. They could use my painting for the cover. I'll bet those ladies could put the whole project together themselves. I already suggested to Mr. Preene that he could print it. Of course, Fanny will need to get a cut of the profits. A generous cut. You might consider me, too, for giving you the idear."

"Profits from what?"

"From the chocolate korndog recipe book that gets sold, Joseph. The recipe book will have to cost something to buy. Dut'n that make sense?" Claire was sounding sort of impatient. In my travels down the road of life, I have discovered that women typically start getting impatient when guys don't leap up and agree with everything they say right away.

Of course, she now mentioned that it's supposed to be a *chocolate korndog recipe* book. Now that makes some difference. I was thinking at first it was only a regular recipe book which ladies at Tabernacle are always collecting and trading and making their families sick with. But this idea actually does make some sense. The memory then seeped in that Claire had already mentioned the idea to Mr. Preene and had included herself in the profits.

"Well, a flavored chocolate korndog recipe book might go over. Did I hear you mention yourself as one of the profiteers?"

"A modest percentage. Just a taste. After all, it was I who painted the inspiration for all the activity." Claire sounded like a fifty-year-old CEO. I had forgot about how she manages her own huge portfolio (which used to be my Great-uncle Oliver's) and how, when all the rich old guys in town lost their underpants in the big stock market crash, Claire actually *made* a bundle.

"Well, a taste of the profits might be possible. My dad inspired the painting, so probably he should get a taste, too."

"I have no argument with that, but all that should be drawn up in legitimate contract form. I'll ask my lawyer to get to work on it."

"Oh. Sure. Okay." Claire's lawyer is my Great-uncle Kosh, a guy who gives me all kinds of presents and who tells me he has faith in my brains, et cetera. Which sort of leads a guy to wonder if Uncle Kosh has got good sense. On the other hand, Uncle Kosh possibly doesn't know about the head-drop problem and would write up a good contract.

"We haven't seen you at Tabernacle for a long time, Joseph. As you are Zack's banker, I expect he believes you have a lot of ethics." Claire was hinting, since her dad used to be Pastor Preene before he died and she goes twice a week. But I didn't bite at her hook. "Well, that's all I had to mention, Joseph, so I'm off to Tabernacle. I'll expect a report now and then." Claire now sounded like Zack, with her *report* requirement.

"I'll give that my sincere consideration," I went in my suavest vocal tones. Then I started thinking about who would pay for this thing to get printed up in the first place. If Mr. Preene wouldn't do a little ad for free, he wouldn't print up a recipe book for nothing, either. But maybe Zack could talk him into it. Everybody seems to know I am the banker for this project. Maybe Claire expects the banker to fork over the cash to start off the recipe book. I thought it would be a good idea to wash up my ethics in public.

So I put on a shirt and a necktie and my leather bomber jacket and, since it wasn't raining, walked down First Avenue to Tabernacle where Cousin Nim's sign out front had this to say:

> *Whosoever desires to worship whatever deity*
> *with faith—using whatever name, form, and*
> *method—I make their faith steady in that very*
> *deity.*
>
> *—Bhagavad Gita*

Which Cousin Nim explains as meaning you're okay if you go to Tabernacle. But I got there after the service had started, which is not okay. Pastor Nim doesn't like for guys to come in late, so I stood out there in the foyer, listening to the singing and carrying on. After the offering when the ushers took the plates into the office to count the loot, I slipped into the back of the sanctuary and took a seat in a back pew.

Which was a mistake, since the back of the room is where teachers and preachers always look first to pick on guys. I was no exception. Pastor Nim gave me a big toothy smirk, nodding his head in my direction, and everybody turned around and looked at me.

"I am happy to see my young cousin Joseph Oliver Kuhl return to the fold after some absence," went Pastor Nim, a huge blond guy with two doctor degrees, a deep voice, no belly or wife, and a plastic foot from Vietnam where he was a U. S. Marine. "Welcome, Joe!" A bunch of guys turned around again and nodded their heads and said *Welcome, Joe!* I could feel my head turn red and sweat bust out on my chest and under my arms. I shuffled my feet and looked at the floor.

Then Pastor Nim went on, not about God or Krishna or Buddha or doing good or being kind to animals and your neighbor, stuff he often talks about, but instead about the First Annual Greater Balona Flavored Korndog Bakeoff Festival and Carnival.

This was a huge surprise to me, since he included a lot of Bakeoff Festival ideas for activities I never thought of or even heard of. Like roping off part of Front Street for dancing to the music of the Noble Korndog Jazz Band. And a raffle for a free rafting trip down the Yulumne when the water is high enough to raft on. And face-painting for kiddies by Becky Klimstroke. And five or six other things that sounded like a lot of fun. I wondered where all these ideas had come from.

"And if you're wondering where all these ideas have come from, here's a major part of the answer." And Pastor Nim pointed down to the front pew where Claire and her mom always sit. Next to Claire was somebody with dark hair whose face I couldn't see. "It's Ms Nadezhda Mussolini, assistant to Mr. Davy Narsood, who will be conducting his regular TV cooking show right here in Balona during the Festival. Thank you, Nadezhda, for your leadership!"

And Pastor Nim clapped his hands, so we all had to clap our hands for Nadezhda, me especially loud. Nadezhda blushed her cheek prettily but hardly turned her head.

Then I noticed the red-headed person sitting right next to Nadezhda. It was Zack. He could have sat next to his mother, but no, he chose to sit on the side of Aunt Pippa next to Nadezhda.

Well, I couldn't hardly blame him, even though he keeps saying he isn't affected by women.

Then we sang a hymn. Pastor Nim's religion isn't exactly what you would call traditional. His Tabernacle is called BoMFoG, which stands for Brotherhood of Man, Fatherhood of God. And we celebrate Christmas and the birthdays of a whole bunch of other religious guys. Weird as it is, Pastor Nim's way is respected by most of Balona because he is such a respectable guy.

After the service there is usually a buffet lunch where all the guys that show up for Tabernacle get to eat free. Of course, you're supposed to bring a dish of food and your own eating utensils. Being a single handsome guy has its advantages, so I just sort of hang around the tables looking sincerely at the food. Sooner or later some old lady will offer me a plate of something and a plastic spoon.

Today it was Claire's ma, the most beautiful mother in Balona. She's got long red hair and brown eyes and skin like a peeled peach without the fuzz. She always gives me a hug which always gives me a symptom. And I got my plate from her. "Sit here next to Nadezhda, Joseph," she went, lashing her eyes at me.

"So, Joseph," went Nadezhda, right away after we were all sitting down at the same table with her and Claire and Claire's ma and Zack and Aunt Pippa, and I had my mouth full. "Zack keeps mentioning how you're his banker. So how much money have you collected for the festival?"

I just about choked on my macaroni salad which had walnuts in it and pieces of chopped up apple and was pretty tasty. "Who said I collected any money?"

"Well, Zachary, of course."

"Well," I thought fast in spite of my head condition. "It will have to remain a confidential matter at the present time. To make sure everybody donerates his fair share is why. That's why." I took another big bite. I noticed Zack smirking to himself.

Zack went, "Joe's working on his presentation to our local merchants, where he can eventually make every magpie sing a pretty tune." Everybody chuckled at Zack's wit. I didn't.

I was sort of worried, since I had already used a few of the bills we got from Mr. Vibrissa to pay off some pressing debts. I would have to get out and sell the festival hard.

Eighteen

Patella's Patter
by Patella Euphella Sackworth

It seems like this columnist might be a favorite of famous TV star Mr. Davy Narsood since his picture by this columnist appeared in last week's *Courier* with a prize-winning story by this columnist. The prize will probably be awarded after this columnist submits the story to the prize committee over in Delta City.

But Mr. Davy Narsood sent this columnist an e-mail congratulating her on her fine picture and inviting her to cover his appearance at the First Annual Korndog Festival here to take place sometime early next month, which is just about two weeks off.

The handsome young man who has taken charge of the festival is Mr. Zachary Taylor Burnross, a senior at Balona High School, this columnist's fine Alma Mater. His assistant is said to be Mr. Joseph O. Kuhl, said to be a part-time student at Chaud County Community College, but Mr. Kuhl isn't saying much at this time.

The korndogs being produced throughout Balona are creating fine smells all over town. This columnist hopes that these sample baking creations are being sampled with cocoa, which goes with them best, as has been said, other opinions to the contrary.

As usual, it's hard to follow what Patella is saying in her columns, except that she feels she does a pretty good job. I noticed that she didn't get the Festival title named right, as she missed referring to it as the Flavored Chocolate Korndog Festival, and also missed the First Annual part.

Since I dipped a little into the Festival Bank, I have about $45 dollars left, in bills and small change. That's still a respectable amount, but I haven't shared with Zack that I had urgent needs that had to be taken care of. Zack is such a grinch that he would make a scene. So I had to think of some ways I could recover cash in a hurry. I thought first about getting Richie involved. Then I thought better of that thought. Richie would expect a cut. He would also find a way to advertise my encrouchment onto the Bank. I often wish I had a little brother like Zack's little brother who died at an early age.

Then I thought about Grandpa Daddy Kon, where my ma gets all her cash. But I realized right away that Ma just writes checks when she feels like it. She never even asks. Besides, Grandpa Daddy Kon looks at you like you're not even there. "Hey, Kosh!" he cackled last time I popped in to look at him. He was confusing me with his younger brother.

Which led me to thinking about Uncle Kosh. Uncle Kosh has mentioned that he is my lawyer. When a guy is having problems, what better person to go to than his lawyer? Providing the lawyer doesn't charge you. So I decided to go on over there and see him. I brushed my teeth and gargled for about ten minutes to make sure my breath was pure and nice. I squeezed the pimple on my chin and put a piece of tape over it so it looked less like a pimple and a little more like I had been in a manly fistfight. I put on my leather bomber jacket, a garment given me by Uncle Kosh and admired by all who see it.

At Uncle Kosh's house you have to pound on the door a while, since Mr. Medomaus, Uncle Kosh's valet, is a hundred and four years old (or so) and can't hear the door bell. I guess he can feel the pounding on the door through his slippers. Anyway, finally he came to the door and right away turned around and took me to the elevator.

Uncle Kosh's elevator is the only one in Balona. It goes from the basement all the way up to Uncle Kosh's tower, which he calls his *airy*. It is where Uncle Kosh has got his home office-pool hall-recreation center-study-sportsbar combination. It is a huge long room with leather-covered furniture and paintings of our old-time relatives giving you hard looks. He's got a new painting of my old Great-uncle Oliver now, too. Uncle Oliver's standing where he looks like he's hiding beside a window and has got pale blue eyes that follow you wherever you go. He's holding a smoking cigaret.

Uncle Kosh's airy has got TVs and a big billiards table and a big conference table with lights over it. Uncle Kosh has also got a nice brass telescope where he can watch birds on the delta or guys going into and coming out of Balona's HIR down on Seventh Avenue.

I once asked him why he was interested in the HIR (which is the way a polite Balona guy will refer to our House of Ill Repute). He mentioned that it's always a good thing to have information about town morale up your sleeve. Uncle Kosh was a judge over in Delta City for a long time and has certificates on the wall to prove it. He is my lawyer and doesn't charge me.

"Well, Joseph. How's things?"

"How's things, Uncle Kosh?"

"I hear you're banker for Zack Burnross. How did that happen?"

Uncle Kosh never asks a question he doesn't already know the answer to, so I was interested in how he was going to answer his own question.

I gave a smirk. "Well, maybe you can tell me?"

He smirked back and lit up a cigar, blowing the smoke at the ceiling. "I think maybe I can hazard a guess. He caught you napping?" Meaning I was standing there with my mouth open and Zack told Mr. Vibrissa to put the bills in my hand.

"Yeh. Napping. But it was a gesture in my faith."

"Well, perhaps. Zack's a good boy, but he was making sure if anything happened to the money you collect, it would be you and not Zack who would go to jail."

My knees and bladder started to freeze up right then, since Uncle Kosh seemed to have the story before I even confessed. "I wasn't going to touch it, but then some bills came up, y'know."

"And you've already touched the fund?"

"I've *sort of* touched it."

"Well, Joseph, you either touched it or you didn't."

"Oh. Well. Yeh, I touched it."

"How much do you have left out of the five hundred?"

"What five hundred?"

"I heard you've collected $500."

"Oh, no. We got a hundred-ten, if you count the ten Mr. D. H. Carp said we could collect after the festival."

"Ah. Well. The word is out that you have $500 in your Levi's all ready to support this new festival." Uncle Kosh looked at me keenly while he relighted his cigar. "Will you have a rootbeer to soothe your parched throat?" He always talks like that, sort of like Shakespeare or Judge Ordway or Cousin Nim. He went behind the bar to his fridge and got me a cold can of Hires, a beverage which I doubt anybody else up in his airy ever drinks. He popped it open and fizzed it into a tall clean glass. "No use getting your lip all frosty when we've got a nice glass right here."

I am not used to drinking my Hires out of a glass. The sensation almost brought a tear to my eyes. It was obvious that Uncle Kosh really likes me. Him and my dad. So, with all that good will staring at me, the only thing left was to make the pitch. I cleared my throat.

Uncle Kosh cut me off. "I tell you what. Instead of asking me to bail you out—bailouts are often signals of faulty thinking and acting—why don't I help you recapture your losses honorably?"

"Oh, yeh. Honorably." Honorably sounds like hard work.

"Honorably means I'll give you a job, and you can work until you make up your losses."

"Oh. Heh-heh. Yeh. That's great." I wasn't exfoliating good vibrations. I remembered something. "I already got a job, Uncle Kosh. I work at Mr. D. H. Carp's, y'know."

"Well, I know that, Joseph. I'm thinking of after school and Sundays and evenings."

"Oh. All those?"

"Well, unless you can tell me how you can put your various expertises to work, you'll be doing minimum-wage jobs around here." He waved his hand, showing his office area. "Of course, that will take quite a bit of time."

"And I'm a student, y'know."

"Yes. I hope you're still a student. You still attend classes over there, do you?"

"Oh, yeh. I'm more or less a faithful attender over there. Yeh."

"Mm-hm. Well, let's think of things you might do around here that will help you regain status honorably." He sat in his big leather chair and pulled on his cigar. Smoke puffed out from under his gray mustache. I don't like tobacco smoke smell, but Uncle Kosh's cigars don't smell as cigarry as, say Uncle Oak Runcible's cigars, which smell a lot like the Balona Dump.

I thought maybe I could put some of my expertises to work and not break my back at the same time. "Maybe you could dictate stuff to me and I could write it down in shorthand. I learned shorthand back at Big Baloney."

"Good idea, Joseph. How rapidly can you write shorthand?"

"Well, I don't exactly know. A while."

"A while. Well, let's try you out." And Uncle Kosh gave me a pencil and a pad of paper and started dictating. I started writing shorthand. He was talking not too fast, and I was writing a mile a minute. After a while he stopped, raised his shaggy gray eyebrows. "Got it?"

"Well, yeh. Sort of."

"So, read it back, please. Let's see how you did."

"Well, I'm an ace at writing it. Only I'm not such an ace at reading it, y'know."

"That's okay, Joseph. Let's hear what you got."

"Well. Well." I looked at my notes. It was the head-drop thing all over again. I couldn't make out what I had written there. "I got transferred out of shorthand in the middle of the semester, back then, y'know."

"Uh-huh."

"Society Thrust kept taking her shoe off and sticking her toes under my shirt and tickling me in the back like that, and also saying spicy stuff in a low voice. Kind of distracted me from my shorthand studies, y'know."

"Uh-huh."

I mentioned the main problem to Uncle Kosh. "My ma dropped me on my head when I was little, y'know."

"Joe, Joe, Joe. We were all dropped on our heads by our mothers. That's the Balona way." Uncle Kosh was trying to collapse my head-drop defense. He was a lawyer all right. "So, how's your window-washing arm?"

"I got to wash windows?" I have never enjoyed washing windows.

"I have lots to wash. They seem to get dusty or streaky or spotty rather often, so there'll be plenty of work."

I looked at Uncle Kosh's windows. They didn't look dirty to me. Maybe it would be easier washing these windows than trying to decipher my shorthand.

"Then you could help Mr. Medomaus with the washing machine. At his age it's increasingly difficult for him to dash about up here and down there. You could perform as his assistant. And you could dust up here and sweep up and generally keep the place tidy. As long as you didn't disturb the papers on my desk."

That sounded a lot better. I could watch TV while I labored.

"Of course, you wouldn't be able to watch TV while you were working, but I have a nice library of classical CDs here, and you could sweep and dust and wash windows in time to Bach and his friends." He gave me a sharp look. Not a hard look, but sharp. "You do want to resolve this financial problem of yours honorably, don't you?"

"Oh, yeh. Sure I do. Sure. Thanks, Uncle Kosh. I don't know what I'd do without you."

"Well, good! You can start right now. Just report down to Mr. Medomaus, tell him you're his new part-time assistant, and grab a broom. Start on the front stoop. Get it nice and clean. And then come on up here and we'll talk some more about how you can keep honorable books for your korndog project."

"Oh. Yeh, well, I got to study tonight."

"Sure. Plenty of time to study after dinner, right? Right now, it's the broom and the stoop." He crinkled his eyes at me and nodded his head. "Good man!" he went.

How could I say no?

Nineteen

We were shooting the breeze over at Zack's. Nadezhda was combing Harley on her lap, using her own comb, where he was lashing his eyes at her over his shoulder. Harley is a real spoiled little dog. I was wishing that it was me sitting on her lap, her combing my hair. Instead, I was sitting in Zack's dad's cigar-smelly leather chair. Balona is full of old guys who smoke cigars.

"So, Nadezhda," I went, using my suavest tones, "how come you're driving over here all the time? Is Davy afraid we're gonna screw something up?"

Nadezhda frowned out her pretty lips. "Mr. Narsood just wants to make sure that any enterprise with which he is involved is well organized, and that he is center-stage at all times. Of course, he doesn't say that last part. I just put that in because it's my job."

"You must stay pretty busy."

"Oh, indeed. Of course, Mr. Narsood has four other assistants, each of us lining up locations and organizing the rubes." She blushed prettily. "Oops, sorry! I mean, that's an expression our producer uses. Among others." She frowned her nose prettily and you got the impression that her producer regularly uses swinish language around the office.

"Well, you don't have to worry your pretty head, Nadezhda. That's a pretty name—Nadezhda—since we got everything pretty well organized at this end." I stretched out my legs so my clean ankles showed.

Zack explained to Nadezhda's prettily raised eyebrows. "Joe dut'n believe in wearing socks, even in winter when it's cold, since they just get dirty and smelly and somebody's always got to wash 'em, he says."

"I see," went Nadezhda, nodding her head. My trope evidently made sense to that sensible and beautiful young woman. "In that, Joe is much like certain other young men noticeable in San Francisco and Hollywood." She pushed Harley off of her lap and put away her comb. "Now that you've mentioned it, what *have* you organized?"

I looked at Zack. Zack looked at the ceiling. Zack is getting habits a lot like his dad, what with ceiling-watching, lip-smacking, mumbling, and other quaint habits of his. I waited for Zack to answer. Zack didn't answer. Nadezhda kept looking at me.

"Well, Nadezhda. We got a lot of good idears, some of which you already know about."

"I know about the ideas I have presented and you folks are supposed to act on—if you approve, and so forth."

Zack intruded. "We approve of your idears, Nadezhda. What we got to do now is give each guy a job to do, like be in charge of bingo, that sort of thing."

"I'd say that's a beginning. What is important right now is that you establish a date that is satisfactory to both Mr. Narsood and the weather."

"The who?"

"Mr. Narsood needs to work in the open air. Or perhaps under an awning, but without rain. Rain clogs his sinuses and he feels he doesn't present well if he has to blow his nose all the time, especially while he is cooking on camera." Nadezhda raised her pretty eyebrows and squinched her eyes at us. Then she looked worried. "Also, Mr. Narsood says he's not been sleeping well since he visited Balona. Some big woman he saw when he was here in Balona, he says, has disturbed his hormones."

Harley climbed up on the couch again and sat and gazed at her. I felt like going over there, pushing Harley aside, and snuggling up to her. A guy dropped on his head as a child—even a guy noticeable in San Francisco and Hollywood—has certain unfelt needs that need regular feeling.

"I'll get us a good accurate dry date right now." And Zack took us all up to his room where I followed behind Nadezhda and thus got a nice view of her regions. Zack got on the Internet and pulled down the weather report for the next few weeks. "Here's the best date possible," he went, drawing a circle around his choice and showing it to Nadezhda, who was sitting on his bed. I was sitting in the window seat where Harley usually sits. Harley was crouched next to Nadezhda. I felt like going over there, pushing Harley aside, and confessing my feelings to Nadezhda.

"A Saturday. You believe a Saturday is the best choice."

"Sure. Everybody's out of school."

"Mr. Narsood would have to tape a Saturday show since he doesn't work on Saturdays or Sundays. He likes to work live. Saturdays and Sundays are the days he communes with nature."

"Well, you cut'n find more nature to commune with than Balona."

"I'll mention that to Mr. Narsood. Everybody's out of school, you said. So, you expect many school children to be baking chocolate korndogs for the festival competition."

We sat there thinking about that. Probably not too many Balona kids will be baking flavored chocolate korndogs.

"We could try to get the schools involved, except they're all crazy to make a hundred on those tests, and everybody over there is practicing arithmetic all day, since that's where Balona kids flunk. That and English."

"Speak for yourself, Joey. I get A's in math and English both."

Nadezhda snickered inside her pretty head, probably about Zack with his nose to the grindstone. "Well, if not the schools, you could get the mothers and other homemakers of Balona involved. I think they're the ones who will do the baking anyway, aren't they! Ah, and we mustn't forget the same-sex couples."

"What same-sex couples are those?"

"Ah. Well. This is Balona. For a moment I forgot. You wouldn't have same-sex couples."

Right away Zack goes, "Sure we have. There's old Mr. Bertie Fandango and Mr. Connie Ratched. That's a same-sex couple. But I think they only bake up fruitcakes nowdays." Both me and Zack broke up over that while Nadezhda frowned her pretty eyebrows at us, being in the media and more political correct than us.

"And there's Mr. Keyshot and Lamont, they're both guys."

"Well, honk, Joe, Lamont's a dog. What a stretch! That dut'n make an actual couple."

"What I was meaning to communicate was that it's important you don't leave any constituency out, y'know?" Nadezhda sounded like she was running an election for Congress.

Zack then showed off his schedule poster where he's printed the activities he thought up and Nadezhda contributed and made a chart. On this chart are places where Zack can write the names of the guys who will be in charge. "This is a big job, y'know," he went.

"Of course. Mr. Narsood believes that for any program to be a good program, it takes a lot of jobs well done, all working together."

I went, "You said Davy's got five other assistants. Are they all as pretty as you?" Nadezhda blushed her pretty complexion.

"Well, four others, actually, and it's true they're all women. Mr. Narsood likes to keep women around him, whether or not they meet the criterion of Hollywood-type beauty. Women inspire him, he says." There was a tear gathering in the corner of her beautiful olive-colored eye. "He is somewhat temperamental, as you will discover. But he's a great man, and I wish it were I who inspired him." She sighed. "But there's somebody else inspires him more at the moment, so I'll just have to wait my turn and try to put on a little weight."

"Oh," went Zack, "that's probably Mrs. Narsood."

"Each of the five ex-Mrs. Narsoods has at least one child. One of them has two. But they're all too busy with maternal duties to provide the proper inspiration for Mr. Narsood. Besides, they're all in different locations, like in different cities and states."

This sounded very strange. A tall slim beautiful woman waiting her turn to inspire Mr. Davy Narsood. I wondered what you had to do to inspire that temperamental guy besides gain weight. I decided it might be political correct not to ask.

Zack strived on. "Well, there's one more big favor you could do, Nadezhda. You could go over to the *Courier* and tell Mr. Patrick Preene to play up the festival big. We can't get to first base with him. He wants money just to say the word festival. Maybe you could tell him that Mr. Davy Narsood would feature him on the TV show. Maybe Mr. Preene could wear a chef hat and stand next to Mr. Davy Narsood, and fry up something on air."

"I think that might constitute a bribe, don't you?"

"Yeh, sure, of course," me and Zack both said.

Nadezhda laughed a pretty laugh. "Ha ha ha! I'll do my best with Mr. Preene. I believe he has a columnist who does the social life of Balona?"

"Oh, yeh. Mrs. Shaw."

I had to contribute some intelligence here. "Patella, too."

"Patella? The young woman who wrote the confusing piece about Mr. Narsood? And took the picture that was printed? The picture cut off Mr. Narsood's legs. He was concerned about presenting only part of himself to his public. He likes to think of himself as larger than life. But about this Patella. I don't know. I got the impression from the writing that she is not particularly competent. Mr. Narsood requires that those who write about him be competent to do so. Does this Patella do a regular column?"

"Whenever she's not busy she writes one up. She's Mr. Preene's granddaughter."

"Ah! Ah! I see. Well, I'll have a private chat with her then, and a regular chat with Mr. Preene, and maybe an interview with Mrs. Shaw." Nadezhda was writing stuff on her tiny little hand-held computer.

"Does that thing really work?" I asked.

"I couldn't do my job without it." She pushed some buttons. "It's telling me I must be off."

So she was gone in a whiff of flower smell. Harley was the one quickest to follow her downstairs where she reached down and scratched him behnd the ears just before she left through Zack's front door.

We could hear her Jag vrooming as it turned the corner of First Avenue and proceeded towards Front Street. She was on her way to fix it with Mr. Preene.

"Well, Joe," went Zack, "here's a list of guys we could ask if they want to do stuff. After they say yes, we make a big deal over it and let everybody know they're in charge of that thing. So if it dut'n get done, everybody will know who to point at and nag. That's how Mr. Croon does it over at Big Baloney. It works for him." Zack watches guys and zones in on their tradecraft. He handed me the list. "Here, you take these guys and I'll take these."

I reminded Zack that he was a great salesman and would probably make Chief Justice of the Supreme Court on account of those skills. I then mentioned that I had some incredibly crucial homework to get to and, besides, I had to wipe the fog off of Uncle Kosh's airy windows right then. I took off before Zack could make up a smartmouth answer about how I wasn't carrying my share of the organization load.

Besides, I was telling myself, after Nadezhda gets through with bribing Mr. Preene, and Mr. Preene prints up stuff about the festival, guys all over town would be begging us to be part of the organization. Probably would be begging us to donate to the expenses fund, too. That reminded me of window washing, so I took off for home, reminding myself that I should probably get over to Uncle Kosh's in the near future.

We didn't have to wait long. Mr. Preene got the message right away and Mrs. Shaw's column the next morning showed that Nadezhda got Mrs. Shaw nicely bribed, too.

Bellona's Balona
By Bellona Shaw

The Man Who Came to Dinner is coming to Balona! This columnist has discovered that The Man is not only coming to dinner, he will prepare dinner!

Of course, The Man is Mr. Davy Narsood, the world famous chef of TV fame. Mr. Narsood has consented to perform not only his regular TV cooking show right here from Balona, he will also serve as Master of Ceremonies for the new korndog bakeoff festival that is now being organized by several local people.

Our publisher, Mr. Patrick Preene, has been invited to serve as Mr. Narsood's assistant during his broadcast on nation-wide TV, and this columnist will interview Mr. Narsood on air, during the broadcast.

Always the leader of community benefit enterprises, Mr. Preene has prepared a list of festival tasks that will require executives. Elsewhere on this page are directions as to how our citizens may sign up for those positions.

This korndog festival should become another one of those marvelous civic opportunities Balona is noted for.

Mrs. Shaw had got some of it right, only Mr. Preene is taking all the credit, and my name and Zack's name wasn't even mentioned. And she got the name of the festival wrong. And she didn't tell the date or any details. Well, I figure maybe Patella will now clean it up with her own column.

Twenty

Zack got up from his desk where he was studying his English vocabulary list again and I was looking at a magazine, thinking about going on home and studying my own English vocabulary words. Also thinking a few passing erotic thoughts about Nadezhda. "Well, honk! I forgot again," Zack went. "I got to wear that dang thing more."

He traipsed to his walk-in closet where he's got all kinds of rich-kid stuff stored in labeled boxes and sitting on shelves. Like his giant-size candy-apple-red motorcycle helmet he used to wear to school, getting ready to own a Harley (which he now owns a dog version of). "I wore that helmet for dramatic effect," he would say. And up there next to the helmet sits his leaking Burberry Box, a beautiful thing, now consoled to darkness because of a minor glitch of construction.

Zack pulled his foam neckbrace off of the shelf and snapped it around his neck. He usually wears it *to practice my behavior*, he says. When I ask him, *What behavior is that?* He goes, *Whiplash behavior*.

"Well, fooey," I went.

"What fooey?"

"Nothing to do around here." So I took off and went home and went up to my room, originally intending to do some studying and get an A in English where I flunked last semester. But instead I sat in the dark, cogitating about how some guys have a lot of extra brains and can think fast and can do all kinds of stuff without thinking. Where other guys, guys who were dropped on their head as kids, for example, those guys always come in second.

I wondered if my dad was dropped on his head. Uncle Kosh said something about all of us in Balona have been dropped that way. But I think Uncle Kosh was making a metaphor. Something like that. Thinking about a metaphor, I was reminded that Dad often sits in his chair and looks at the carpet. He will sit and look that way even in the dark, after my ma has turned off the TV. For a long time I wondered what he was thinking about during those times. I thought to myself, *Maybe he thinks the same kind of sad thoughts I think about when I'm sitting in the dark, looking at the carpet*. So, back a few weeks ago when Ma and Mrs. Earwick were gone on their holiday to Hawaii, I asked him.

"Say, Dad, when you're sitting there in the dark, what are you thinking about?"

"Sitting where?"

"Sitting right there where you're sitting, but in the dark, after Ma has turned off the TV and gone to pour herself another drink. What are you thinking about then?"

"Your ma it'n here, Joey, uh, Joe. Her and Mrs. Earwick went off without us to Hawaii just to have a good time. We're all by ourselfs here."

"I know, Dad." Dad sometimes forgets that I know stuff. "What I was wondering was, what were you thinking about?"

"Not thinking anything. Just sitting. You don't have to be thinking when you're sitting. You can just be, well, *sitting*." Dad sounded a little testy. Maybe Uncle Kosh wasn't saying a metaphor after all. Or maybe Dad didn't want to tell me what he was actually thinking. Maybe he was thinking evil thoughts, the kind that sometimes creep into my head. Or sad thoughts.

I don't want to tell people about my sad thoughts—about Bobby Varnish, for example. When we were about fourteen or so, me and Bobby went swimming in the Yulumne, and Bobby drowned. I think about that sometimes. How, if I hadn't bragged about how I was a better swimmer than him, he wouldn't have jumped in and hit his head. How, if I was a faster thinker, maybe I could have saved him. Stuff like that.

On the other hand, I'm not naturally a sad guy. After I have sat thinking my sad thoughts for a while, I will go and try and find something tasty to eat, always a challenge in my house, especially if Mrs. Earwick has gone off to Hawaii, the way she did with Ma. Of course, both Mrs. Earwick and Ma are back home now, but even so, there's nothing good to eat in the house. So I go back over to Zack's, where either Zack or Aunt Pippa has always just cooked up something succulent.

"Back again, Joey?" went Aunt Pippa when I dragged it into her kitchen. "How'd you like a nice something I just cooked up?" I sat at the kitchen table and ate something gooey and sort of sweet with a crust on it. "It's a pasty pie, the kind they bake up over in

Cornwall. You like it?" It's hard to say you don't like something somebody just cooked up for you and is standing over you looking like you better like it. What you do is, you fill it up with conversation, even with your mouth full. "Where's Cornwall?"

"Cornwall? I think it's between Delaware and New Jersey. How's it taste, huh?"

"It tastes, uh, interesting." That's always a good thing to say, but only if you have a thoughtful expression on your face and a smile.

"It's the turnips in there. Sometimes I make it without the turnips, but this time I used turnips. And a couple mashed-up raspberries, for sweetness. Makes it taste interesting, don't you think?"

I already said so, so I just chewed up some more and looked like I was appreciating the food. I thought about a chocolate korndog, since it was time for dessert. "You tried your hand at a chocolate korndog yet, A'nt Pippa?"

"Oh, my no. That's Zacky's territory. I wut'n dare bake up one of those, long as he's around to criticize. He's so cruel with his criticism." Aunt Pippa sounded suddenly sad. There was a sob in her tone. It is true that Zack is cruel to his parents. If I tried to be cruel to my ma, she wouldn't allow it. In our house, it's her who is cruel to us.

"Well, everybody in Balona is supposed to try his hand at baking up a chocolate korndog, so I'll tell Zack he better let you do it, too."

There was a tear in the corner of her eye. "Oh, good." She lowered her voice. "Well, just between you and I, Joey?" She waited, her eyebrows way up.

"Yeh?"

"Actually, I did bake up a few samples of my own, if you won't tell Zacky."

"Hey, I'm in training to be a secret agent, A'nt Pippa. You cut'n drag it out of me with a D-9." A D-9 is a huge tractor that anybody around Balona would know about, so that is why I used that trope.

Aunt Pippa opened a drawer and took out a tray covered with wax paper. When she moved the wax paper you could see the things right there. They looked just like Claire's redaction of my dad's dream. "Wow," I went. "You got 'em looking right anyways."

"Oh, you have to taste one. Even my Kenworth likes 'em." Her Kenworth is Zack's dad. Kenworth is a popular name around Balona, with maybe a dozen guys with that name. If you holler, "Kenworth, call for Kenworth," at the New Oliver, four or five guys will get up and come to the lobby. (Never mind how I know.)

"So, where is Uncle Kenworth?"

"He's napping, of course." Uncle Kenworth Burnross does a lot of napping.

"I bet I win the bakeoff!"

"I thought you said Zack wut'n let you."

"I thought you said you would fix it with Zack."

"Oh, yeh."

She zapped two of her creations in the microwave so their *ganache* sagged a little bit. She set the dogs before me and gave me a fork. I dug in. "Hey!" I went. "This is really good. What did you do to the dog to make it all taste so good?"

"That's my secret. I'm not going to tell anybody, or the secret will get out and people will steal it and use it on their own."

"I'm pretty confidential."

"You go ahead and eat then, and stay confidential."

I did, but I kept thinking that Aunt Pippa's creation will win the bakeoff for sure. "You will probably get featured on Mr. Davy Narsood's program with this. It's that good."

Aunt Pippa's face expression glowed. There wasn't a tear in her eye. She suddenly started to look crafty. Her eyes narrowed. "Is Bapsie planning to enter?"

"Hey, everybody knows my ma dut'n cook or bake, either one."

"Well, I don't know about that. The other day she was telling us that we dit'n have a chance, since she was entering the bakeoff, and her entry would win the grand prize."

"What grand prize is that?"

"Well, the grand prize Zacky is planning. I don't know what it is. I thought you would know. Maybe it's getting crowned by Mr. Davy Narsood on national TV? You think maybe that's it? Oh, I can hardly wait. Bapsie dut'n have a chance." Aunt Pippa sounded like Captain Jean-Luc Picard promising to beat up on evil.

Walking home again, I was thinking about Mr. Preene taking over. Everybody is supposed to sign up over at the *Courier* if they want an executive position in the bakeoff. Every Balona guy over four years old wants an executive position, especially if there's no work involved in the job. I called up Patella. She says there's been a line of guys signing up for different jobs.

"Where'd he get the different jobs?" I went, meaning who figured out for Mr. Preene what needs to be done to get a nice festival off of the ground.

"Oh, it was Mr. Davy Narsood's assistant's list, the long skinny drink of water with the polluting Jag and the pointed chin, the one you can see her underpants even when she's standing up, that one." Patella always manages to get in some critical remarks about other women.

I decided to defend Nadezhda. "She's got a big job and probably makes a lot of money. And she talks like she's got a lot of education."

"She looks like she belongs over at the HIR house."

Patella always has to have the last word, that particular word meaning a popular place among Balona guys. I figured I might as well leave it alone, since she would just answer back, and I wouldn't be able to think up a smartmouth answer quick enough. "Mr. Preene took over Nadezhda's list?"

"I guess. Dit'n you read Bellona's column? That's what guys are signing up for." Well, that was a relief. Me and Zack don't have to do anything except collect fees. Then Patella added, "Grandpa figured there ought to be some fees, so he's collecting the fees, too."

"Oh." It suddenly occurred that maybe our druggist Mr. Vibrissa might have been overcharged if he signed up. "Did you happen to see Mr. Hank Vibrissa's name on the list?"

"Oh, I saw Mr. Vibrissa himself. In fact, he was one of the very first to sign up. He and Grandpa were having some sort of an argument about something, but I was too busy to listen in on it."

Too bad. Patella is usually not too busy to listen in on gossip, but when it means something to a guy, she's "too busy." Maybe Mr. Vibrissa mentioned that he'd already paid his fee.

I felt in my Levi's to see if I still had some of that fee left, since now that I'm making some extra money working for Uncle Kosh, I felt it was natural that I could dip into the fee money for personal expenses, now and then. Feeling in my pocket, I discovered some money-feeling feel on my fingertips, so I felt better that there was some left.

I decided to find out for myself, not wait to discover it in Mrs. Shaw's column, if my ma was going to enter the bakeoff. These things you have to do diplomanically. I tried to figure the most diplomanic way to approach the subject, but I couldn't think of one, so I trounced on in headfirst.

"So, Ma, I hear you're gonna enter the chocolate korndog bakeoff."

"Of course I'm gonna enter the bakeoff. I'm gonna win, too. I hear you get a crown if you win and Davy Narsood himself puts it on you and gives you a big juicy kiss on national TV. Yeh, I need another crown."

My ma's most glorious day was the day she won Korndog Kween at Big Baloney back in days of yore. She got to wear the Krown to class for the rest of the year, until she sat on it and crushed it up. She has wanted another crown since then.

"I never heard about the crown part, but I guess it's possible. You got a secret recipe?"

"I should tell you? I'd tell Richie, but I wut'n tell you. You'd right away go over and tell Pippa. Sure I got a secret recipe. I been thinking about it all week. But it's secret. It's so good it'll blow Davy away. It'll get me the crown for sure!"

Twenty-one

My ma was actually TV-watching something besides her usual soaps. "Is that Davy Narsood you're watching, Ma?"

"What's it look like? Sesame Street?" I could tell from how she didn't swear at me that Ma was in her light-hearted mood.

Davy was stirring something up and looking right at the camera while making his comments. He had on his white chef's hat angled on his head, and a stripey red-and-white apron. You could see the black hair on his arms and a gold wristwatch. No wedding ring. I notice stuff like this because of my training in tradecraft and Criminal Justice.

"This is one good-looking guy," went my ma after taking a sip on her cooling beverage and leaning forward. She crunched on her ice and passed a little gas. "Lookit that nice wristwatch. I wonder is he tall."

"He's pretty tall. Got a big chest and curly hair, as you can see. More fat than tall."

"He don't look fat. He looks nourished. Fit. Maybe Hawaiian. Maybe Narsood is a Hawaiian name. Hmmmm." At the commercial, she didn't turn to look at me where I was standing in the kitchen door. "I guess you actually talked to him, to Davy there?"

"Yeh. Me and Zack. Over at Peking Peek-Inn. Mostly me, since I was the one clued him in about the festival. Mr. Wong, too."

Davy was back on, waving a knife. "His eyes burn right into you while he's cutting stuff up. Lookit that. He don't even look where he's cutting. Takes a nerve."

"That's TV, Ma. He's a pro chef, and everybody's eyes burn into you on TV."

"I mean, they burn into *me*, you *dum-shik*. I think I'm in love."

Now this was not only an unusual thing for my ma to say. It was the most unusual thing I *ever* heard her say. (Except maybe back a long time ago when she was accusing Mr. Putzi Purge to Dad about poor dead gay Mr. Purge's supposed crimes and misdemeanors.) So I figured it was another of her jokes. Mostly when she imitates guys she can break you up, she's so right on. But she also does joke some, now and then. So I went, "Well, you'll get a chance to tell him when he gets here for his program."

"I will do that. I will declare my passion while I'm presenting my korndog for the grand prize." Ma was showing her humor again. Maybe it was humor, except she sounded serious.

"Well, I haven't seen *that* yet, Ma. When are you gonna practice baking it up?"

"Who needs practice? I got it locked. Me and Sammy Joe." Then she turned and gave me a look that just about froze my liver. "You don't tell anybody that, hear? Me and Sammy Joe are going in together, only it'll be under my name, since I'm the brains behind it, and the dog is his."

When I say Ma's got a look. I should say she's got *A Look*. Since she's got one blue eye and one green eye, when she gives you A Look, it sort of shrivels a guy.

Liver frozen, I strived on. "Mr. Sam Joe Sly's lab was ruined by the fire brigade, Ma. He dut'n have the stuff to do the job any more, I bet, so maybe you're out of luck."

"It's not luck, *dum-shik*. It's brains." She went back to ogling Davy on his TV screen and wouldn't say another word to me. Over the sound of the TV, I could hear her nose whistling from her breathing.

I got to remembering how Dad every once in a while mentions how back in days of yore when him and Ma and all of them were young, he would sit around Frank's Soupe de Jour when it was just Sam's Diner before it was Frank's.

Dad would drink coffee with Mr. Sam Joe Sly and Cousin Nim and discuss stuff and eat danish. That was in olden times, before the korndog became so popular. They would talk about school and girls and money and girls. And the future. Sometimes they would talk about Ma, since she was as loud then as she is now, Dad says.

Mr. Sam Joe Sly liked Ma in those days. Took her out on dates, but I guess Dad liked her better. Dad says that when they were drinking coffee and eating danish they didn't talk much about the war that was going on over in Vietnam. But when they did talk war-talk, Cousin Nim was patriotic and said he would go in the service (which he did). Dad said he would go if he had to (which he finally did). Mr. Sam Joe Sly said nobody could make him go (which they never did).

Nowdays guys either ignore or don't talk much about the war going on, except the war is a different war this time. It seems there's always a war for kids to ignore or not to talk about or sign up for. If I ever qualify for MI-6, I will probably get to be in a war, except my war will include fancy cars, good food, martinis shaken and not stirred, and women with long legs and big boobs.

Speaking of which, Nadezhda showed up at the *Courier* one morning and wanted the list from Mr. Preene, Patella says.

"How come?" went Mr. Preene, according to Patella.

"I need to make personal contact with each to see that each person is fulfilling his or her obligation satisfactorily."

"Well, lady, this is Balona. We fulfill our obligations."

"Then there should be no problem, Mr. Preene. The list, please."

Nadezhda got her list. Mr. Preene mumbled a little, but later confessed to Patella that he felt better when Nadezhda went away with it, since she took a burden off of his back. I know what he meant. If he actually said it, and if Patella wasn't making it all up just to show how determined a woman can be. So Nadezhda is sort of taking over the organization of the festival.

Of course, Mr. Preene still gets to keep the entry-fee money he collected. Nobody has seen a list of how much that is, or how he is going to divvy it up.

I was thinking about going over there and demanding a Freedom of Information Act about it. Then I thought about it for a while. I figured if I did that, he would right away ask me about Mr. Vibrissa's account. And there's a slight problem there, what with me having some more immediate expenses and Uncle Kosh not paying me much yet. Of course, I haven't done much to get paid for over at Uncle Kosh's yet, so I haven't put the arm on him for back pay.

Things all get very complicated for a guy when you get into the world of business. That's something Dad keeps saying. Now I understand.

Things also get complicated when a guy's ma starts talking about how she's in love. A guy gets a queasy feeling.

When stuff gets complicated and queasy, I usually go over to Mr. Keyshot's place, and he checks me out to see if I'm okay.

Since Mr. Keyshot used to be a counselor over at Big Baloney, he sort of knows what he's doing. He's pretty long-winded, but he's cheap, being that he accepts my tutoring in tradecraft as payment for his counseling.

You'd think a guy who counsels people would be a goldmine of information for a guy who is engaged in studying Criminal Justice and International Espionage tradecraft. But even though Mr. Keyshot talks a lot, mostly it's about stuff he's just read or seen on public TV, not about his clients. Disappointing but understandable, since if he blabbed about his clients to a guy who was not absolutely discreet, nobody would come back for seconds. I have told him several times that I am absolutely discreet, but he just smirks and nods his head or scratches Lamont's ears or looks at the ceiling.

So, feeling sort of depressed-feeling and concerned about the head-drop thing and the maternal passion thing, I went over there where he's got his home office up above Mr. D. H. Carp's Groceries & Sundries. I tromped up the stairs sort of whistling Mr. Burberry's tune softly to myself, trying to get myself to think about world peace, et cetera. I knocked on the door, and Mr. Keyshot answered himself. He had a surprised look on his face.

"Well, Joseph. I expected you would be in class this morning, and when I heard whistling, I thought to myself, 'Ah, Mr. Burberry must have returned.'"

Mr. Burberry is famous as a whistler even though his whistling style has sort of a wide vibrato. Mr. Burberry even did a whistle concert up on the stage at the Sugarbeet Festival, only no one could hear, since I guess his lips were dry while the Delta Doodle Dandies were at the same time engaged in their Valley Brew chug-a-lug contest. I was feeling depressed, not interested in Mr. Burberry. But when Mr. Keyshot said he thought I was Mr. Burberry, maybe he had revealed that Mr. Burberry is Mr. Keyshot's client. You find stuff out by putting other stuff together. That is the Criminal Justice Way.

Anyway, I went on in and sat down, and Mr. Keyshot fixed us a cup of tea, which I don't especially like but drink anyway to show how suave I am. It isn't bad if you put sugar in it, and better yet if you add milk, which I did.

"So, Joseph, how's things?"

"Well, how's things, Mr. Keyshot?"

"Well, I asked first!" Mr. Keyshot crinkled his eyes. "Isn't that right, Lamont!" Lamont is Mr. Keyshot's old black dog with a gray mustache who sleeps all the time in a box at Mr. Keyshot's feet, right next to his chair. Lamont didn't open his eyes, but sort of groaned and thumped his tail once.

I had thought I might confess to Mr. Keyshot that I was in love with Nadezhda, but then I thought it would sound silly, since last time I was here, I confessed to Mr. Keyshot that I was in love with Willow Runcible. He would think I was not a faithful guy. So I changed the reason I went to see him. Actually, the first thing popped out before I could stop myself.

"Well, I think maybe I'll get arrested."

"Mm-hm. Arrested." Mr. Keyshot nodded his head and slurped at his tea, like it was a common thing for Joseph Oliver Kuhl to get arrested.

"I mean, I am not hot to go to jail, but I think maybe I probably will, if something dut'n happen."

"You think you will probably go to jail." Mr. Keyshot usually repeats what you just said. I guess he wants to be sure you know he's listening. Back at Big Baloney, guys sometimes said he would fall asleep when he was counseling them, and this repeating trope is sure a way that makes sure he's not falling asleep.

"I mean, I spent some of the money I am supposed to be banker for. For the Korndog Festival."

"Ah. The First Annual Balona Flavored Chocolate Korndog Bakeoff, Festival, and Carnival."

"Wow. That's the first time I've heard anybody besides Pastor Nim say it right. Even Zack dut'n say it right all the time."

Mr. Keyshort sort of smirked. "I read the *Courier*, where To Be Accurate is their motto." He frowned over his cup. "But you did spend some money."

"I did. But I'm gonna pay it back."

"Well. That solves that problem, doesn't it?"

"I guess." My depression lifted up. Talking to your counselor helps a guy, for sure. But I still had feelings of depression. "I still got feelings of depression, though."

"Feelings of depression. Have anything to do with Willow Runcible."

"Who?"

"The girl of your dreams, Willow Runcible."

I could feel my face getting pink. "Well, not exactly Willow. It's Nadezhda."

"Ah, Willow's changed her name. One beautiful name to another. You can pick them, Joseph! Nadezhda. Know what it means?" He right away told me. "As you may well know, in Russian, it means *hope*. I like that. I believe in hope. As you may well know, some of the diminutives are Nadya and Nadyenka. You might call her one of those some time. Surprise her, y'know. So Willow's got a new name. Well, that's interesting. Willow's a lovely name. I wonder why she changed it."

I decided I wouldn't confuse things by telling Mr. Keyshot about how I no longer think a lot about Willow, but now have passionate feelings for Nadezhda Mussolini. He would just laugh or *tsk* or wag his head and go *Joe-Joe-Joe,* like Cousin Nim and Uncle Kosh.

Mr. Keyshot has got hair that is getting grayer and grayer. His temples are mostly white. He's got brown eyes, and he looks at you like he likes you. He was in the Marine Corps in Vietnam, like Cousin Nim. He knew Cousin Nim over there and they got wounded at the same time, the second time for Cousin Nim. Mr. Keyshot once told me he settled in Balona because Cousin Nim is here.

"You seen your Cousin Nim lately, Joseph? I'll be he'd like to talk with you about your depressed feeling. He's a great person to counsel with, I've found." Mr. Keyshot has now revealed to me that Cousin Nim is his counselor, a fact I already figured out, since Mr. Keyshot is always over there at Tabernacle when he's not in his office.

"Well, I went to Tabernacle and saw him, and he saw me." Then I let the other thing slip out. "I think my ma is in love with Davy Narsood."

"Ah," Mr. Keyshot went. "Well, that happens. As you may know, women are complicated creatures. Sometimes they have interesting fantasies. Perhaps in that they are not very different from us men, eh?" He twinkled at me.

"You think it's not a big deal."

"I think many women must be in love with a TV personality. That doesn't mean it's going to go any farther than looking at the TV set."

"I guess you're right." I guess he's right. Besides, my ma likes to joke.

Twenty-two

A lot more people are talking about entering the flavored chocolate korndog bakeoff. Frank Backhouse has signed up, even though he's famous for preferring his own Franksburgers. In fact, guys around here suspect that Frank will present two offerings at the bakeoff, one of them a sort of korndog which would make you sick if you ate it, and the other a regular Franksburger. Cod would eat both, probably, and not get sick, and ask for more.

I had been following Nadezhda around all morning, where she went from person to person listed on her paper and gave them assignments and ordered them around, me standing in the background, watching for terrorists.

"Why are you following me, Joseph?" Her question wasn't rude really, but it was actually sort of pointed. "Aren't you a student at that little school over in Delta City? Shouldn't you be attending classes over there right now?"

"I got sort of leave to follow you around and provide you with some official Balona security. And that little school over there, like you say, is actually a big school. It's Chaud County Community College and it's got a couple thousand guys go there and a huge parking lot."

Actually, I was cutting classes in order to protect Nadezhda, but that's a good as excuse as any when I use it on Mr. Dainty, my Criminal Justice teacher. It's no good at all for Doctor Fardel, but I've just about resigned to spend another year in English anyway, so missing a few classes is not going to cause my world to collapse. Besides, I get to associate with beautiful Nadezhda. We had finally stopped in front of Junior Trilbend's house.

She went, "I'd just as soon you didn't follow me around, Joseph. I can't imagine anything unpleasant happening to me in this little town." She laughed prettily in her little nose.

"Well, I just consider it my duty," I went, giving her a Holy Look. Unfortunately, since it was a foggy morning, she was all bundled up and her feminine charms didn't bulge out much, being sort of covered by a raincoat slung over her shoulders and a scarf around her neck. She was also wearing long pants and boots that did not emphasize her nether charms.

Nadezhda has been staying for a few days with the Preenes, where she's got the bedroom Patella's ma had when she was a kid. I got to admit that, since Patella's ma is a cousin of mine, then so is Patella sort of a shirttail relative, too. I should remind Patella of that next time she's hinting about getting married to a "home town boy."

"How d'you like your wheels?" I went, referring to Nadezhda's Jag, a low red thing that's got a nicely defective muffler that makes a lot of noise.

She didn't twinkle her answer. "I'm still paying for it, an arm every month, and then a leg every other month." She meant that her car cost her a lot.

"That's why I'm jogging around after you, instead of driving my own fine car, what with the cost of gas, eksedra."

"Your running behind my car looks like I've lost something and you're trying to get it to me. Maybe you could carry a cleft stick and make it look official."

"What? Well, that's just about right, since I been trying to convince you that I am a fine candidate for romance." I almost strangled to hear that leaking out of me. I could feel my face burning with heat, not from running.

She ignored my passionate outburst. "Well, remember, I'm here on Mr. Davy Narsood's business, not monkey business." Then the sun broke out from her face when she smiled with all her pretty teeth showing. No tooth braces.

"How old are you, anyways? You about nineteen?"

"It's not polite, Joseph, to inquire about such things. But thank you for the nice compliment." Maybe she's a little more than nineteen.

"Well, this is Balona. You're not supposed to be polite. You're supposed to ast straight out. Besides, I'm in private-eye training."

"Oh, really." She sounded like she didn't believe I was an honest student of Criminal Justice. She started to walk up to Junior Trilbend's front door.

"That's Junior Trilbend's house. He's not gonna help us."

"This is the address of Mr. Fragonard Trilbend, Joseph. Mr. Trilbend has volunteered to be a significant part of the festival.

He's already donated a considerable sum, and I am going to make sure he's committed to some personal involvement. She reached out for the doorbell button.

"I wut'n do that, if I was you. Mr. Trilbend's got a new house up on the West Levee Road. This here is his mean kid's house. Junior Trilbend is a bad actor, a big, smelly bad actor, Nadezhda."

She smirked and pushed the button. "Go away, Joseph."

You could smell the beer smell as soon as he opened the door, even before he pushed open the screen door, like the smell that comes out of Ned's Sportsbar when you walk by. Old beer mixed with cigaret smell and foot.

"Hey, baby!" went Junior Trilbend. Junior is six-four and has muscles behind the flab over his belly. He almost beat Sal Shaw for the Valley Crown in heavyweight wrestling when we were all seniors at Big Baloney. Now he hangs around the house, steals dogs and sells them at the Delta City fleamarket, and drinks beer with his buddy Bobby R. Langsam. Sometimes he works at King Korndog, but mostly he just sort of hangs out.

Junior gave Nadezhda a big leer. "You come right on in!"

"Are you Mr. Fragonard Trilbend, sir?"

"Yeh, that's me, sweetlips. C'mon in."

"That's *Junior* Trilbend," I went, correcting Junior's version. "His name's the same as his dad's because that's why he's called Junior."

"You signed up with Mr. Preene?"

"Hey, did I? Uh, sure I did. Get lost, Joey. I got me a fine chick here. Now, c'mon in." Junior opened the door wider and stepped forward. Nadezhda stepped backward.

"I think I've made a small mistake. Sorry," she went and started to turn around. She had realized that I was giving her the straight scoop and that Junior was not a legitimate target of her affections.

But Junior wouldn't hear of she taking off on him. He didn't even look at me, but he reached out and grabbed Nadezhda by the arm.

Wow! Was that a mistake. I can't explain how it happened, because it happened so fast, and I was just standing there with my mouth hanging open. But next thing I knew, Nadezhda had Junior on his face on his front porch, her boot on the back of his neck and a growl coming out of her pretty lips.

"Ow!" went Junior, and made a few other sounds, groaning. "Hey, I dit'n mean nothing."

"You try anything else and I'll neutralize your manhood, boy." Nadezhda was talking in a strange voice that came out of her chest, and she was also rocking forward on her boot a little bit.

"Ow! I was just being friendly."

"You heard me, did you. worm?"

"Ow! Yes, ma'am."

Junior's attack was over. Me and Nadezhda walked back to her car while Junior stayed right where he was, on his hands and knees, not even looking our way.

"I think it's lunch time, Joseph. Since you're my protector, I guess you deserve a free lunch. Follow me." She didn't invite me in to sit beside her on the genuine leather seats, maybe because of the result of my running all morning and working up a nice sweat.

So I jogged after her where she parked in front of Frank's. I must say she didn't drive as fast as before and I got close enough to read the decal in her rear window. *United States Marine Corps*, it said.

Seated in our Frank's booth, I interrogated her about her background. "Hey, Nadezhda," I went, "Where'd you learn your tradecraft."

"Marine Corps. And my second husband was a Marine D.I. We used to work out together."

"D.I.?"

"Drill instructor."

"What was that you did to Junior Trilbend?"

"Gung-fu, aikido, meanness."

"Wow. I saw some of that stuff on the TV. But what's the meanness part?"

"It's the personal part a woman learns best, if she's been kicked around some." Nadezhda squinted her beautiful camouflage-colored eyes, reminding me of my ma's mean look.

Maybe, I thought, Nadezhda is not nineteen, after all. She may be some older. "I guess you been married."

"Oh, yes. Yes." She looked at the table. "But I'm not married now and I'm eternally hopeful about men, y'know. Especially big dark men with curly hair."

I gave her a Holy Look out from under my straight blond hair to show that I was hopeful, too.

"You shouldn't do that with your eyes, Joseph. May I be frank?"

"I'm Frank," went Frank, trying to lean strategically over Nadezhda, the way extra tall guys will do over girls with extensive boobs. "And what'll ya, y'know, have?"

We ordered Franksburgers, since Frank's korndogs have tasted sort of weird lately, like they had something strange in them. Mr. Sam Joe Sly was probably throwing his chocolate korndog mistakes into the chopper hopper. Or maybe he was running out of first class beef and substituting mystery meat again, like my dad always accuses.

I was interested in Nadezhda's frank remark. "You said about frank?"

"I was going to say, about your eyes. You have nice eyes, Joseph."

That was nice to hear, since it was a long time since anybody ever said that to me. I think Patella said that once when we were in seventh grade and she wanted to soften me up and invite me to Sadie Hawkins, back in the days when we had Sadie Hawkins dances, when it was sort of a new thing for girls to ask guys. So I went to Nadezhda, "Well, that's nice to hear."

"Yes, you have. And it's a shame to ruin them when you bulge them out like that."

"Like what? Bulge 'em out? I bulge out my eyes?" She was not interpreting my Holy Look as a Holy Look. She was figuring it was some kind of twitch. "Oh, well, it's only a trope I use to make me look sincere." Oops. It escaped me without even thinking what I was saying.

"Well, it doesn't look sincere, Joseph. It looks stupid. I wish you'd stop doing it."

I felt like she had slapped me on the face. I could feel my face turn red right where she slapped me. But just then Frank plonked the Franksburgers down in front of us and I sort of forgot the pain for the moment.

"Hey, Frank," I went. "Can we have some special korndog sauce to use on the Franksburgers?"

"It's reserved for the korndogs. My Franksburgers don't need the special korndog sauce."

After I argued a while, and Nadezhda backed me up, saying she wanted to try it, too, Frank bad-moodedly banged a saucer full of special korndog sauce down on the table in front of us. I slopped it into my Franksburger, and so did Nadezhda. We each took our bite.

"My! This is a fine condiment. I wonder what's in it."

So I made a big deal out of giving her chapter and verse about what Balona special secret korndog sauce might be made of.

"I'll be Mr. Narsood will be interested."

"Well, you can't reveal it, since it's a Balona secret. Kind of like Homeland Security."

"Oh, now! Nobody would mind."

"Oh, no. Everybody would mind. If guys got wind of the idear that Davy was gonna blow the national whistle on the Balona special secret korndog sauce, the festival would be off. Nobody would show up for Davy's show. It would start raining. Cod would arrest Davy and put him in the back room in chains. Believe me, you don't want to tell Davy about this. I made a sort of slip-up there in telling you, but you don't have to make a bigger mistake and tell Davy!" I could feel my voice getting higher and my face getting redder.

"Okay, okay. Just a thought." Nadezhda chewed on her burger and didn't say any more, but she had a suspicious, sort of sneaky, look on her pretty face.

Me looking at her that way with her mouth full, she began to look sort of older. Considerably older all of a sudden.

I wondered if I could trust her.

I also worried a little if she would pick up the bill for the Franksburgers, since all I had in my pocket was money that really belonged to Mr. Vibrissa.

Twenty-three

Balona fog doesn't come rolling in through the Golden Gate on little flat feet, the way it does over in The City. It is just here when you wake up in the morning. Then it sort of hangs around all morning, causing your hair and T-shirt to sag, promotes wrecks on the Interstate, and general gloomy feelings in poetic guys dropped on their head as a child. Then, about noon, the sun pops through and before you know it, you've got rain or clouds or it's clear. Either way, it's cold this time of year.

I have been writing poetry in hopes of bringing up my English grade, even though Doctor Fardel says I'm supposed to do the work she assigns instead of my own creative offerings. I spent most of yesterday afternoon thinking about an argument to convince her, when I should have been either in class over at C4 or else doing stuff at Uncle Kosh's.

While writing poetry it occurred that probably Mr. Davy Narsood will send somebody over to Balona to set up his kitchen. I wondered what Balona person had signed up to supervise that job. So I called up Patella to find out.

"I don't know stuff like that, Joey. I know that there's a lot going on over in Hannibal Chaud's Funerals parking lot that isn't a funeral. But right now I am getting ready to go to class, which is something you ought to be getting ready for, too."

"I am engaged in thoughtful pursuits, like writing a poem, one that will probably make me famous some day."

"I would like to hear it."

"I would read it to you, except I haven't finished it yet, and it dut'n have the right scansion yet."

"What's that?"

"That's what we poets use as a word to describe how a poem feels."

"Oh. Well, when you finish it, you could read it to me at any hour. Right now, I got to get going. Uh, you want a lift over to C4?" Patella probably feels guilty for being generally rude to me.

"I have to think some thoughts right now. But I would also like to find out about who's handling Mr. Davy Narsood's festival kitchen."

"You should ast Grandpa. 'Bye." She hung up on me. Just like a woman, thinking of her own needs before a dear friend's. If I was a dear friend.

So I called up Mr. Patrick Preene. "Hi, there, Mr. Preene," I went in my most joyful tones. "This is Joseph Oliver Kuhl with a question."

"Oh-oh," he went, not sounding joyful in return. "Hank Vibrissa tells me you collected his support fee for the festival. That right?"

"Well, I, uh, had that honor to bestow on Mr. Vibrissa. Yes, I did." It is always the best policy to tell the truth, especially when you have no choice.

"When you gonna bring it over so I can put it in the safe over here and write it in the book?"

"Very soon, Mr. Preene. I was thinking about that just the other day. I said to myself…."

"Well, just do it. We got people putting the site together right this minute and needing some cash to do it with."

"Putting it together already? Well, that's exactly what I was calling you about." No use to let a good phone call go to waste.

"So, now we know, don't we!"

Mr. Preene sounded a little sarcastic but I strived on. "But I was also wondering a question, which was, who has the honor of preparing Mr. Davy Narsood's festival kitchen."

"I thought you would know that, if you knew anything."

"How come's that?"

"Well, your fat little cousin signed up for it. Paid the fee and everything. Zachary T. Burnross it says right here on the sign-up sheet. He's gonna be the executive in charge of Mr. Davy Narsood's festival kitchen. Of course, probably Mr. Narsood has his own staff and little Zack will be out his fee." Mr. Preene snickered in his nose.

"Well, yes, of course. I knew all that. But…." Zack just wants to get an advantage with Davy so his chocolate korndog entry wins the grand prize. But I couldn't think of anything else to say to Mr. Preene, so I just hung up without having to go into when I would go over there and give Mr. Preene the cash from Mr. Hank Vibrissa.

THE CHOCOLATE KORNDOG

My ma does the same thing, so I must have learned the trope by what scientists call *pediculosis*, an inherited thing. Right in the middle of a conversation, even in the middle of a word, she will get bored and hang up. "Saves a lot of hot air," she explains. You can always blame the telephone company, a bunch of guys that are famous for making a lot of mistakes anyway.

I had to wait until noon to see Zack and chew him out for him going off and doing something secretly, when we are supposed to be blood-related. I walked over to Big Baloney past where Bootsie Dwindle and the Flag Fems were twirling their flags in time to the Noble Korndog Band dragging their feet across the wet lawn. Maybe they were getting ready to perform at the Chocolate Korndog Festival.

I stood on the sidewalk outside the front door of the school where all kinds of kids were coming out, the girls all giving me admiring glances. I had worn my brown leather bomber jacket to heighten the expected effect. I whipped out my comb and did a job on my hair which had sagged down some.

"Hey, Joey!" Now there was a sound I had not heard for a while. It was way up high on the scale, like a squeak. It was Society Thrust, who is now a senior, like Zack. Society is the daughter of Superintendent Thrust, a guy who does not hold me in high repute, but who I stay out of the way of.

Society always wears a Balona Noble Korndog cheerleader's sweater, even though she never got elected a cheerleader. Nobody dares call her on it since her dad is so mean, so she strives on. Society gave me a hug, an act which drew the envious stares of her classmates. "How come you're over here on the schoolgrounds, where it's illegal for a non-student to be?" she squealed.

"I am an alumni of this institution and a voter, and I got a right to be here."

"Not according to Daddy. But I wut'n tell. I would tell you about what's in my competition chocolate korndog, but I gotta go get some lunch with my buds." And she was off in a convertible that pulled up behind us, not with her buds, but with a bunch of big hairy guys who looked like football players.

Balona kids who don't eat the korndogs offered in the cafeteria go over to TacoTime and pig-out there. Of course, some do go shoplifting at Hank's Pharmacy. Or they drive out to Mello Fello for a pizza. Or a few go to Peking Peek-Inn, only Mr. Wong won't stand for any big noise in his place and will pick you up by the back of your neck and throw you out if you give him any lip.

So even Society, a girl that brags that she never does anything to help her ma by sweeping, cooking, baking, or even making her own bed, is going to enter the festival. This could mean we will be overwhelmed by entries from other Balona princesses. I wonder how Davy will handle that. I'm glad I'm not in charge. I'm glad it's going to be on Zack's back and not on mine.

I thought I would catch Zack on his way home for lunch, where he goes every day to watch *The Young and the Ruthless* and also to set up his machine to catch Mr. Davy Narsood on tape. I waited and waited, but still no Zack came out. I decided to go on in and find him. I got stopped in the hall.

"You do not belong here, Joseph," went Mr. Drumhandler, my old history teacher. "I am on duty here for Mr. Croon, and he made it clear that ex-students were not welcome on campus. So, you better turn right around and go." Mr. Drumhandler looks like a squirrel without the fur and never did like me.

But I am a forgiving man, so I smirked at him and nodded my head and went, "Understandable, sir. I fully agree. But I am here only to find my young cousin, Zachary Burnross."

"Well, I saw you out there fondling young Miss Thrust."

"Well, it was her fondling me."

"I should call Mr. Croon. Better yet, I should call Doctor Thrust, except he's back in the kitchen working on his chocolate korndog."

"Doctor Thrust is going to enter the competition?"

"I believe he's one of a number of us, yes."

"You said us. You mean you're gonna enter, too?"

"I am considering it, yes. Now, you better go, Joseph."

"Uh. What about Zack? I mean, I came to talk to Zack."

"Young Zachary gave up his lunch to coach Doctor Thrust on some baking techniques, I believe. Zachary is accommodating in that way, as you may well know."

Mr. Drumhandler sort of spits on you when he talks, so I backed off a little, not only from the spit, but from the surprise of the information I was getting. "Well, in that case, maybe I better go on back there and supervise my cousin, before he gives away some secrets of the competition."

"I think you need to leave now, Joseph. Or perhaps I should call Constable Cod Gosling. He may be able to convince you more quickly than I."

I left then, more depressed than usual, but I right away forgave Zack. I figured that Zack was sucking up to Doctor Thrust for a good recommendation to Oxford, a reasonable thing to do.

I made my way up First Avenue to Front Street where I gazed my eye south and saw a lot of activity in the distance. Usually there isn't any activity in the distance, except for a fire or a flood, neither of which we have had downtown lately. I decided to go see.

Patella was right for a change. Uncle Hannibal's parking lot was a honeycomb of activity. We always use his parking lot for city stuff since Uncle Hannibal can just put off having a funeral until the celebration is over. He's got a big fridge in his shop where he can keep any customers he needs to delay.

Uncle Hannibal also has a huge oven back there. I got the idea that we could have guys bring their unbaked korndogs right up to the back room over there and get them baked up all at the same time. Sort of a quality control idea. I ran the idea by Uncle Kosh, but he wasn't keen on it, said Uncle Hannibal was sort of a grinch about loaning out his oven for non-commercial purposes. He told me to forget the idea, but it still sounds good to me. It's a shame people aren't more generous and helpful for civic stuff.

Actually there were some guys who should have been at their own work, instead doing their civic thing, putting up booths all around the edge of the parking lot. It looked suspiciously like we were about to witness another Sugarbeet Festival since the booths look pretty much the same. The hollering and swearing were the same, and the guys working were the same.

This is another thing I have noticed about life. It's usually the same guys who do all the work, whatever it is that needs to be done. It's also the same guys who supervise the guys doing the work. It's also the same guys who stand around in the shade watching, smoking, eating, criticizing, and otherwise doing nothing. Then, after everything is built up, it's also the same guys who come by in the middle of the night and try to trash whatever the other guys have built up. It's all like a play where the same characters enter and exit over and over again.

Richie is one of those that comes by in the middle of the night. Him and Ricky each wear twin holsters on their belts for the spray paint cans which they graffiti stuff with. They wear these when they're not wearing their police get-ups. My ma says Richie carries spray paint cans around because he's artistic. But it was too early for Richie and Ricky. They always wait till something's been finished, and somebody's proud of it, before they trash it.

One of the supervisors was obviously in charge, since she had a big white sheet of paper and was unrolling it for a bunch of guys to look at. And then she was pointing. Of course it was Nadezhda, telling guys where to set up their booths.

"Hey, Nadezhda," I went, all cheerful and complimentary.

She was engaged in reading her chart, so she didn't exactly beam at me. "Yes, Joseph. You're here to help, are you? Good. I think that group over there can use all the assistance they can get." She was pointing to a group of old ladies from Kute Kurls and Nails who were trying to hammer nails but mostly missing their targets.

"Well, I'd be happy to help, but I'm on an important mission right now."

She frowned her pretty eyebrows. "Well, then. Just stay out of the way."

"How come Mr. Runcible is putting up a booth there? He dut'n even like korndogs."

"Over there with the black hat? He's paid his fee and is entitled to set up a booth. And he's doing so, as you can see. Mr. Davy Narsood couldn't care less if Mr. Harry Runcible doesn't like korndogs. Mr. Narsood will be concentrating on doing the best show he can produce. And I'm concerned only that it looks good and that all of it is focused on Mr. Narsood, not on Harry Runcible."

"Okay, okay. I just ast is all." Nadezhda even knew Dirty Harry's first name. She is on the ball, as we say in Balona.

Dirty Harry was supervising some guys putting up his booth. He wouldn't look at me when I interrogated him as to how come he was putting up a booth in korndog country.

But he did remark out of the corner of his mouth. "You got your fee, kid. Just keep your mouth shut and keep up your end of the bargain. Don't worry about our booth and our product. You'll see when the time comes." He turned away, then turned back again, squinted his good eye, sneered his lip, and growled, "Make my day."

Dirty Harry sounded sinister all right.

Twenty-four

░

The day dawned bright and early. (I read that in some book, but when you read it out loud it sounds sort of dumb, since every day dawns early, if not bright) Anyway, it was Saturday and not bright. It was foggy as usual, and I got up early for a change, since it was a work-at-Mr. D. H. Carp's-day, not a school day.

I had a leisurely breakfast of graham crackers with mayonnaise, a pickle, and a Hires. The kind of breakfast that livens up your taste bugs, if not warms you. Ma was still in bed. Richie was still in bed, since he didn't get home until a few minutes before I got up. Dad was still over at the Jolly Times Rest Home, but was talking about signing himself out, since he discovered he could do that.

"I'm thinking about signing myself out, now that I can do that," he mentioned the other day.

"How come you didn't do it before, Dad?"

"Well, it's shameful me being here in the first place, so having to admit it was the reason. But in the second place, it's pretty comfortable, which is sort of shameful, too. And the tapioca pudding is pretty good. But I miss Killer. So, probably I'll sign myself out pretty soon. Only don't tell your ma. She wut'n like it, her not being totally in charge of everything."

"She wut'n like it, you coming home without she knowing about it, would she?"

"Well, Joey, uh, Joe, we'll see, I guess. Maybe sooner or later."

So, that's where we left it, him checking for fleas under his sheet.

Up on Front Street, Uncle Hannibal's parking lot honeycomb had a lot more bees working in it which, as Doctor Fardel keeps telling us, is a metaphor. Practically overnight, the whole place already looked better than the Sugarbeet Festival. Part of it was because somebody had put up crepe paper streamers and colored plastic pennants all over the street. There was a huge banner across Front Street hung on a rope stretching from the roof of Mr. D. H. Carp's Groceries and Sundries across the street to the roof of Kute Kurls and Nails.   It said *Chocolate Korndog Festival.* Nothing about First Annual or Flavored. At least it was painted in red so you could see it.

The *Courier* that came out this morning had a huge black headline saying, "Korndog Festival Today!" And also missing the chocolate part. Hopefully guys will show up for the festival today instead of going to Delta City to the mall over there to do their shopping.

I had been worrying that Ma would march over and bust whoever it was that was judging the entries in the bake-off, since she couldn't possibly bake up anything winnable. So I asked Nadezhda during that sort of romantic luncheon we had. "Who's gonna judge all the chocolate flavored korndogs?"

"Oh, don't worry about that. We have a committee of tasters who will winnow out the best to present to Mr. Narsood. After all, he must be the final arbiter."

"Who's on the committee? Could I be on the committee?"

"The committee is already selected, Joseph. You have special sauce on your chin. Right there." She pointed. I wiped. She handed me a paper napkin to wipe off the back of my hand with. She is definitely older than nineteen.

"Who selected the committee? I mean, is that a big secret?"

"Some of the town fathers are on the committee."

"Well, who selected *them*?"

"They did, Joseph."

That figured, since this is Balona. But I had to get my two cents in. "Well, if it's town fathers, my dad ought to be one, since he's a father who imagined the chocolate korndog in the first place."

"You mean Mr. Kenworth O. Kuhl, of course. Well, his name was presented and he was actually considered. Briefly. But it was also mentioned that Mr. Kuhl is out of circulation, so his spot was taken by another."

So I never did find out who was going to do the tasting.

I was standing there at the parking lot, watching the activity, wondering who might treat me to a mid-morning snack, when a familiar white van pulled up and blocked the driveway. It was the KDC-TV van used by Mr. Blip Wufser, ace newscaster. Mr. Wufser didn't have his whole team with him, only his driver.

"Hey, Mr. Wufser!" I went, like one of his favorite fans, but he only raised his eyebrow and one side of his upper lip, looked the other way. Finally he deigned to speak.

"What time's the festivities begin, boy?"

"Right before lunch there's gonna be sort of a carnival start up where you can eat regular korndogs and get your face painted, eksedra."

Mr. Blip Wufser snorted through his nose. "I mean, when is the big wheel chef gonna show up?"

As this was something I did not know, I made up my answer out of my imagination. "Well, sir, probably pretty soon, since Mr. Davy Narsood is famous for being on time, eksedra."

"Is he going on air live or on tape, d'you know?"

I didn't know which, but it's not wise in Balona to give the impression you don't know something. Guys will point at you and laugh. So what you do is you give a sharp answer. "I believe so, sir."

Mr. Blip Wufser is short, has got a sandy-colored beard and mustache, and a loud voice. He said a rude word. He spied Nadezhda who was ordering somebody around across the lot. "There's somebody who looks like she's in charge of something." He left me standing there without a word of excuse. Rude fellow. So I followed along to discover stuff, the way the Manual suggests you do.

Nadezhda was standing under a huge green portable awning. A monster yellow truck was parked behind the awning, and cables and wires snaked out of the truck to lights on tall stands. A big stove was set up in the middle under the awning. Over the awning, on the top of the truck, you could see a satellite dish, more impressive-looking than the puny one on top of Blip Wufser's van. A long table was beside the stove, and folding chairs were opened up facing the stove and table. You got the impression that there would be a star appearing close by.

Guys with tools were moving back and forth from the truck to the awning, setting up huge TV cameras and cables and equipment. They were wearing blue jackets with a big yellow "Davy Narsood" printed on the back in big letters, like the FBI ready to storm a doper den. Of course, Nadezhda was the one giving the orders. I took a place of observation nearby, so I could see and hear all the transactions that would transact.

"Hello, there!" went Blip Wufser to Nadezhda. His tone was all public-relationsy. "I'll bet you're Davy's advance man."

Nadezhda gave Blip Wufser a busy look that softened up right away when she looked behind him at his TV truck with the big logo on the side. "I'm Mr. Narsood's assistant, sir. You're with the local media." She stood up straight and showed her teeth.

"Blip Wufser of Blip Wufser and the News, KDC-TV, known as the media giant of these parts, Miss…?"

"Nadezhda Mussolini."

"Mussolini! Ha ha ha. That's rich! Oh, it's for real? I mean, that's your actual name. Mussolini. Well, it's a well-known name anyways. Yes. Well." Blip sort of faded out since Nadezhda was giving him her hard look again. "Anyways, I figure you guys can use all the air time publicity you can get, right? So, I'll expect some space here."

"Mr. Davy Narsood's on-camera team will arrive with him and will take the necessary shot-spots, Mr. Wufser. Mr. Narsood will be live, networked nation-wide. So, any shots you'll want of Mr. Narsood during his broadcast will have to be of the entire setup, at a distance." She gave more orders to the guys who were plugging in cables. Mr. Blip Wufser stood there, his belly sort of sagging, not in charge at all.

Nadezhda looked at Blip Wufser out of the corner of her eye. Then she looked at me. "Joseph," she went, "you could get Mr. Wufser a copy of this morning's *Courier*. It has the schedule for the day right on the front page. That should help him decide what, if anything, he wants to cover." She turned to Blip Wufser and gave him a very quick smile. "Cover from a distance." Then she disappeared into the back of the big truck.

"How's about that, kid? You do that for me, will'ya?" Blip actually smirked at me. So, being a polite kind of a guy, I searched far and wide for a *Courier*. Which I found a whole huge stack of at Mr. D. H. Carp's Groceries & Sundries, right in front on the rack where passersby regularly steal copies. So I stole one, too, and took it back to Mr. Blip Wufser, who grabbed it away from me without even saying thanks.

I stood next to the van while Blip and his driver discussed the agenda for the afternoon. "See, here, Ralph. Here at 2:00 o'clock is where the fat guy starts his broadcast. That's when I'll arrive in the Blipcopter. *At a distance.* Hah! Those studio nerds don't know about our lenses. We'll see then who gets the headlines."

THE CHOCOLATE KORNDOG

Mr. Blip Wufser has a famous new helicopter which he shows up in whenever there's a huge fire or accident, parking his airship right in the middle of the street. He then interviews guys right there on the ground, blood and all. He's even won a prize for being "on the spot." "Ralph," he went, sounding all serious now, "I want you to use the van radio here giving me the exact cues, so I make it a timely entrance. Hear me?" Ralph nodded his head, so I guess he heard Blip who was practically shouting.

Mr. Blip Wufser is going to upstage Mr. Davy Narsood for the sake of getting national coverage. He is not planning to pay any attention at all to the Flavored Chocolate Korndog Festival itself. Mr. Wufser is interested in his own glory. How un-suave.

I stepped out of the shadows and confronted Blip Wufser. "Say, Mr. Wufser, have you ever tasted a chocolate korndog?"

"Can't say as I have. Sounds disgusting."

I was astounded that Mr. Blip Wufser would come over here to Balona to the Chocolate Korndog Festival and not have heard about the Chocolate Korndog. I started to walk away, since my position at Mr. D. H. Carp's Groceries & Sundries beckoned.

"Hey, kid. She said your name's *Joseph?* Don't I know you from somewhere?"

"Well, I watch *Blip Wufser and the News*." Actually, I don't watch *Blip Wufser and the News*, but this kind of a fib is sort of a social comfort device. I could tell it worked since Blip's face expression sort of softened up and he waggled his head.

"No, no. You're a fan, of course—most folks are, y'know. But I've seen you somewhere before. You're not just out of jail, are you?" He was using his Good Blip voice.

"Probably you seen me over at Chaud County Community College where I'm a straight-A student of Criminal Justice." I did exaggerate that a little.

"Straight-A student. Yeh. Possibly." Blip had a look on his face that almost had him identifying me as the guy whose boat he landed on when he crashed his old helicopter on Third Avenue during the last Balona flood. Then he gave me a hard look, meaning that whatever he remembered, it probably wouldn't be a good memory. He went on in his Bad Blip voice, "I never forget a face. It'll come back."

"Look who's here, Boss," went Ralph, pointing at a skinny guy with red suspenders and no jacket gimping his way across the lot.

"Hey, Buddy!" went Blip Wufser, like he was hailing a good friend.

"Hey, yourself," went Buddy Swainhammer, his tape recorder strapped across his shoulder and covering his chest. The recorder, a big silver-colored box with little wheels on the front and a microphone hanging from it, is a real old one, Buddy brags, but it does the job—*like its owner,* he always says. "I see yer playing it safe today, Blip."

"How's that, old timer?" Blip is famous for trying to insult Buddy.

"Yer not driving that heliocopter. Safety first, I guess, eh?" Buddy is famous for teasing Blip about Blip always crashing his helicopters, or at least crashing one once.

"Well, at least I'll be on the evening TV news with something important."

"Well, I'll come on the radio after you and comment on your failure."

They went on like this for a while, Buddy putting his recorder down and snapping his famous red suspenders, which to show everybody is the reason he never wears a jacket, even on a cold morning.

I started to angle my way across the street, resigned to going to work finally. The beeping and hollering next to me caused me to leap out of the way, just in time to avoid getting knocked down by stupid Ricky Placock's motorcycle vrooming by. Richie on the back and him were both wearing their white police helmets and black sweatshirts and pants. Richie hollered something I couldn't understand.

"You ought to be in school!" I yelled after them. Then I recalled how it was Saturday and the day of the Greater Balona First Annual Flavored Chocolate Korndog Bakeoff Festival and Carnival. Being Saturday, a guy wouldn't have to learn anything today.

Twenty-five

The festival started up right before noon, with kids from Mr. Rimshot's art class at Big Baloney along with Becky Klimstroke painting the faces of littler kids. I thought about doffering my green apron and going over to have my face painted. Earlier, I had mentioned that great advertising idea to Mr. D. H. Carp but Mr. Carp thought that my painted face would scare the old ladies who shop here, so he nixed it. Actually, the old ladies who shop here don't usually shop here on Saturdays. They shop over in Delta City. But that's another story.

Standing near the front door a guy can get a good look at Uncle Hannibal's parking lot, the front part, anyway. Ralph, Mr. Blip Wufser's driver, had come back again from Delta City and parked his white van right outside the store. He was reading a paperback book and smoking a cigaret. He had his feet up on the seat. A real informal guy.

A stream of people—mostly women—carrying covered dishes kept coming by and turning into the lot. Obviously bringing flavored chocolate korndogs to be windowed. Nobody seemed to be coming out. I decided that since no customers showed up in the store for twenty minutes, I had a need to go over there and check out what was happening. Maybe even get an experimental taste or two. So, since Mr. Carp was across the street judging anyway and Mr. Sackworth probably was in the toilet taking a nap, I finally doffered my green apron, put on my leather bomber jacket, and slipped out the front door.

Mr. Davy Narsood wasn't due for a while, but the Flag Fems from Big Baloney were already prancing around on Front Street, twirling their flags, drawing a crowd, but probably just practicing for when Mr. Davy Narsood actually would appear and they could show off big time. Pieces of the Noble Korndog Band started showing up, too, mostly trumpets and drums, which practicing attracted a lot of little kids on skate boards and guys who usually hang out at Frings Bowls on Saturdays.

Did I say the weather was fine? Well, it wasn't exactly fine, but at least it wasn't raining. Cloudy. Sort of cold. Leather bomber jacket weather.

Richie and Ricky raced by in their police mode again, buzzing the Flag Fems formation and making the girls all squeal and drop their flags. Bootsie Dwindle who throws up her baton instead of a flag dropped the baton and hollered something after those guys. Probably something rude. Then she pointed at her dropped baton and started to cry and throw up her breakfast, tropes she usually does under most circumstances. Mrs. Langsam had to go over and strive to give her a hug, watching her own shoes at the same time.

I started thinking about Richie and about what I could do to take him down a peg or two. I have been trying to take Zack down a peg or two for quite a while and have never got to the first peg. I think Zack is probably smarter than Richie, no matter what my ma says, so I'm thinking maybe I have a chance at Richie, anyway.

Richie is crooked. No question about it. He's mean to little animals. He would be mean to Killer, too, a nice gentle old dog, maybe a little smelly and home to lots of fleas. Except Killer runs to get behind Dad when Richie is around. When Dad is not around, like nowadays, Killer stays far away from Richie.

Richie swipes good stuff from me. The only reason he doesn't swipe my good leather bomber jacket and wear it himself is he can't get it out from under my mattress, which is where I store it when I'm sleeping. Otherwise, Richie would sneak in and swipe it, not only to keep him warm, but just for fun and to be mean.

Richie is fat and has got a lot more pimples than I ever had. He's got one blue eye and one green eye, like my ma, and that gives him a great weird look. He's also got Ma's round red nose and what she calls *bee-stung* lips.

Richie never brushes his teeth the way I do after every meal. He is also dirty and doesn't wash his hands after he goes to the bathroom, the way you're taught in kindergarten. I'm always washing my hands. He chews with his mouth open. Of course, that's a Balona way to chew, so I can't fault him too much for that. Because he's dirty, he smells pretty ripe most of the time, so I don't like it when he wears my sweats.

I'm sure it was Richie swiped my Burberry Box and trashed it.

So what I have discovered is, that I don't much like my own brother. I mentioned that fact to Mr. Keyshot one time, and Mr. Keyshot went "Hm." Just "hm."

I went, "Well, it'n that awful? Not to like your own little brother?"

"Well, I don't much like him either, Joseph. I can actually see some of the reasons you don't like him. So, no, I don't think it's awful. In fact, I think it shows a rather mature judgment."

"Oh," I went, feeling better right away about the *mature judgment* part, but wondering about a counselor who would agree with a guy who admitted not liking his own brother. But then I figured it was okay, since everybody knows that Richie is bad news and that Mr. Keyshot is weird.

Thinking of Mr. Keyshot must have had a vibration effect on that guy himself, because suddenly there he was, standing next to me on the sidewalk. He had his dog Lamont on a leash, a thing Lamont doesn't like, says Mr. Keyshot who knows how Lamont thinks and feels. "Lamont is my bud," Mr. Keyshot always says.

"Are you gonna go over there and get your face painted, Mr. Keyshot?"

"I gave up painting my face some years ago," he went. As we stood there watching the goings-on across the street, I thought about that for a while and figured out that Mr. Keyshot was talking about painting his face when he was a marine over in Vietnam.

"Oh. Yeh," I finally went. "I wonder why women still do it."

"Well, gilding the lily not only decorates, it also disguises. As for the why, Joseph, the heart of a woman is incomprehensible."

"Yeh." I agreed, since you couldn't argue about that, especially when you didn't know what *gilding* means, and was not about to ask, since you'd get a long-winded answer.

"But perhaps they feel it *necessary* to disguise themselves, do you suppose?" Mr. Keyshot always has to have a theory about stuff. And he always has to tell you his opinion or ask you yours.

"Yeh. Well, my ma sure needs to disguise herself."

"I won't argue the point, Joseph." I think when he said that, Mr. Keyshot dissed my ma, but I am too polite to call him out. Also, I said it first.

"I think Richie is going to do something evil and try to hang it on me."

"Has he said so?"

"Sort of. I overheard him and Ricky. Plotting."

"As you may well know, forewarned is forearmed." He looked at my face. "It means if you have knowledge that

155

something is likely to happen, you are better off because you can be prepared for the eventuality."

I have discovered as I trod the primrose path of life that telling somebody your troubles always makes you feel better, especially if you get told what to do—and if what you get told agrees with what you already decided. However, Mr. Keyshot didn't tell me what to do to forearm myself. So I didn't feel all that much better.

"Lamont, let's be off to observe the Flagwomen of Balona more closely." Mr. Keyshot's description of the Flag Fems makes them sound like something out of a hero TV cartoon. The two of them took off down Front Street. Guys say that a man and his dog often look alike. Mr. Keyshot doesn't look like Lamont, the dog being black and no more than two feet high. But watching them walk away, I noticed that both Mr. Keyshot and Lamont have the same limp.

Suddenly, there was Zack standing in line with a covered dish in his hand. "Hey, Zack!" I hollered. Zack didn't look. Instead, he kept on talking to Mrs. Applehanger, also in line. I decided to cross the street and check out his korndog.

"Hey, Zack," I went.

"You can't cut in line there," Doctor Thrust hollered.

"I'm not cutting in. I'm just checking out a korndog here." Even after my graceful explanation there was still grousing and mumbling. Some of the grousing and mumbling was from Patella, farther back in the line.

"I don't want to uncover my product, Joe, since exposing it to the cold air might damage the *ganache* or something."

"Oooh! I bet you used Davy's *ganache* recipe, did you, Zachary?" Mrs. Applehanger bobbed her head like she was almost ready to peek under the cover on Zack's dish, but since she had both hands busy with her own dish, she didn't.

"Well, I used it to begin with, Mrs. Applehanger. But then I sort of improved on it."

They both ignored me, preferring to talk about their dumb *ganaches*. So I went, "Well, I guess I'll just go back across the street and observe the scene again."

They continued to ignore me, so I re-crossed the street and stood leaning against Mr. Carp's front door, observing the scene. When a guy is ignored, it's a feeling hard to describe. But it didn't last all that long, since the Noble Korndog Band struck up a fine loud tune, mostly together, and marched by.

What they do for every festival is, they march by and when they get down past Frings Bowls they turn around smartly and march back, playing all the while. Old Mr. Langsam, the band director, staggers alongside the band, hollering at them to stay in line, stay in tune, stay up with the rest, et cetera. After a couple turns, the Flag Fems get out in front of the band, flinging and twirling their flags, and that is quite a sight. Guys come out of all the buildings on Front Street to watch.

When I was back at Big Baloney I was in the band for a while, but as a percussionist I couldn't stand the long waits between beats of the drum, so I intruded a few beats of my own along the way. Mr. Langsam isn't a patient guy, or much of an appreciator of performance art, so I got kicked out. "Joseph is too creative for his own good," was the reason.

Mr. Keyshot transferred me into shorthand, sort of a tribute to my impatience, he said. As mentioned before, that didn't last too long, either. A creative guy has a rough hoad to roe, as Cod would say!

I thought about what might be happening right now if I had deigned to enter the flavored chocolate korndog race. The judges would be arguing about which of my entries ought to get the grand prize. Probably I would win either with my *roughage-added* korndog (suggested by my dad) or my *vitamin-E-enriched* model (suggested by Uncle Kosh). I would become a star on the cover of national magazines, a photo there showing me in my leather bomber jacket, gazing at the camera, my mouth open, about to munch on one of my prize-winning flavored chocolate korndogs.

I would make a million dollars in international contracts and marketing my prize-winning recipes. However, when it came down to actually baking something, at the last minute I decided it was too much of a hassle for a guy engaged in college-level homework.

Thinking more about recipes in general and wondering about where my ma was with Mr. Sam Joe Sly's Slydog entry, I also wondered if Mrs. Klimstroke had done anything with the recipe book Claire was harping on. I decided to go over and search the booths for evidence.

I couldn't find recipe books of any kind among the food booths and the souvenir booths, so I hollered at Becky Klimstroke, busy painting kid faces. Becky is what Patella calls "a large girl" with yellow braids and pink cheeks spread out over a stool that was too small for her. "Hey, Becky," I went. "Is your ma selling her recipe book?"

"It's being printed up right now over at the *Courier*," went Becky, not even bothering to look away from her little face. "Mr. Preene has decided to give the book away as a premium to subscribers of the paper."

So, somebody actually followed up on Claire's idea. Then it occurred that guys usually follow up on Claire's ideas, especially if they are Claire's employees or relatives. I have decided that women with money are dangerous creatures. On the other hand, that sort of danger is strangely attractive to a guy with adventure in his blood.

Next to the huge green awning, some guys were putting up a green tent. When Balona guys do this sort of work they usually swear a lot. These guys were quiet, a strange phenomenon to observe. This tent was round, like an Arab circus tent, not like the tent our Boy Scout leader Mr. Frank Prulapse used to put up in days of yore when we went on camping trips out on the delta.

The tent we carried out there for Mr. Prulapse, while we slept on the ground and he slept on an air mattress on a cot, was just barely tall enough for him to stand up in. This big green tent was tall enough for maybe a giraffe to stand up in. The guys took a sledge hammer and pounded iron stakes down into Uncle Hannibal's asphalt and tied the tent down with ropes all around.

Then they brought a carpet out of the truck and put it in the tent. Followed by a king-size bed. And a dresser with mirror. And what looked like portable closets. "What is all this?" I said to one of the guys.

"It's Mr. Davy Narsood's traveling relaxation station," the guy said in a quiet voice, like he was describing a holy cathedral in a foreign country. "Don't you dare go in there," he added, frowning his face.

Since I couldn't legally investigate more in this area, I decided to try to observe the actual judging. So I sneaked behind the booths over to Uncle Hannibal's back yard where they had another big awning stretched out over a long table. The judges were busy figuring out which of the entries were good enough to be considered by Mr. Davy Narsood as champion material.

I drew nearer.

Twenty-six

Mrs. Applehanger was complaining, a trope she usually does when she isn't ornitharoling. "Aren't you going to taste my entry? You should give it a taste right now, not let it sit out in the cold like those." She pointed at all the entries sitting next to each other on one end of the table, some of them still steaming in the chilly termperature.

"We got to enter and number the contestants first, Anna," went Mr. Pezmyer, one of the judges. "Then we'll start in cutting 'em up. This'll be number 41. Move aside, Anna. Next!"

Sophie, from Kute Kurls & Nails, wrote *41* on a card and taped it to Mrs. Applehanger's pan.

Mrs. Applehanger frowned her expression. "Forty-one! I'm only 39!" Then she tittered, whistled a short birdcall, and everybody in line and all the judges laughed up a storm, since Mrs. Applehanger is easily a hundred years old, or thereabouts. "Oh, well," she went.

Zack pushed his way forward and presented his goods. "This one's gonna take the grand prize," he announced. Zack was number 42. "I dit'n realize there would be so many." He looked behind him and saw another ten or so people still in line, Patella and Doctor Thrust included. "Wow," he went. "My win will be even more significant!" Zack has got plenty of self-confidence.

After they took his entry fee, Zack joined me at the sidelines, him ogling his entry to see that nobody messed with it, I guess.

"How much did you have to cough up?"

"A fiver." Which meant Zack had to pay five dollars to enter. Times about fifty entries, that meant the judges got to split up about, more than, more than a hundred dollars.

"You seen my ma?"

"I haven't seen A'nt Bapsie all day, but I know her entry is right there on the table. It's *Number 1* there. Everybody in line was talking about how she was taking advantage of weak-headed old Mr. Pezmyer , since he is scared of her."

Mrs. Applehanger was still hanging around, too, and joined our group of watchers, sort of clucking to herself, chicken-wise. "Bapsie got Mr. Pezmyer to bring her entry and enter it. I don't know if that's fair, but it's Bapsie and there's no use arguing it, since arguing with either a judge or Bapsie never got anybody anywhere in Balona."

Some of the entries were covered and some were uncovered. They were all sitting in the tin pans Mr. Preene sold at the *Courier* and made you put your stuff in, so the confections all looked pretty much alike, except for the really weird ones. And you could see some weird stuff there with the uncovered ones. One looked like a french roll with five little Vienna weenies sticking straight up out of the chocolate frosting like little smokestacks on a boat. Another one had what looked like fat little garlic sausages sticking out of both ends. Most of the rest of them, including Zack's, looked a lot like Claire's painting.

"Eeeeeew!" I went, even though as a suave guy I try not to becry stuff. "What is *that!*" *That* was a linguiça sticking way out of both ends of a folded-over tortilla, chocolate goo over the top of it, a little lettuce peeking out of the side. "Hey, I bet that's Mrs. Peralta's. A chocolate tacodog, wow!" Mrs. Peralta is Mr. Peralta's wife who runs TacoTime where you get your Mexican food in Balona. Mr. Peralta teaches Spanish over at Big Baloney and claims to be a seventh-generation California Mexican. "As you may well know," I went, "Mr. Peralta's wife is Portuguese, and that's why the linguiça, I bet."

"Weird!" went Zack, in agreement. "But takes all kinds, as you may well know," he added, smirking for some reason.

"You boys get away from here." My Uncle Hannibal was leaning over the table, doing the arranging of the entries. Obviously a judge, too.

"I'm an entrant." Zack sort of squealed his response.

"I don't care if you're an exit. Beat it. We got serious work to do here."

He didn't say it to Mrs. Applehanger, who just sort of stayed there and leered at him, whistling sort of a twitter, like a quail. We moved away, noticing that the judges also included Mr. Carp, Uncle Ned, Constable Cod, and Carl from Carl's Shoe Repair. With that many judges, it shouldn't take much time to window the best entries.

I didn't see Dirty Harry in line and I didn't see anything that looked like a turkeylog, either. Maybe he had something up his sleeve. Something criminal.

Me and Zack walked around looking at stuff. I watched Zack get his face painted, but I pleaded professional ethnics to keep my cheeks plain.

Then *he* arrived.

First there was a lot of hornblowing from out on Front Street. Then this huge white stretch limo pulled up into the lot, continuing the hornblowing and scattering a bunch of little kids who were lined up for face painting and french fried sugarbeets, a Balona delicacy that actually sort of sags greasily after you re-heat them out of the freezer, but you eat anyway because of Balonism.

Then, a bunch of guys from the green awning rushed forward to try to be first to open the car door. Then the door was opened. Then out stepped Mr. Davy Narsood in a blue suit with a red necktie.

By that time, quite a crowd had moved forward to see what was what, including all the judges and what was left of the line. Everybody applauded the great man. I noticed Richie in his cop outfit back there where the judging table was. He had his visor down, so I couldn't see whether he had a sneaky expression or not. Him being there was sneaky enough, since everybody was watching Davy and had their backs turned to whatever Richie was doing back there. When I looked back, Richie was gone. I thought for a brief second or two that maybe Richie was going to "dust" the entries, the way he was going to "dust" my pizza. No, he wouldn't do that. Not even Richie would do that. Would he?

Mr. Davy Narsood doffered his hat and coat to his chauffeur. Nadezhda stepped forward and handed him a floppy white chef hat and his trademark apron, red and white striped, which he put on right there in Uncle Hannibal's parking lot. He did all this action in a slow way, like a great thing was about to happen. Then he waved his arm grandly like a TV politician and stepped into his green tent where Nadezhda had held the flap open for him. Then Nadezhda went in, too, and the flap closed.

That was that for a while, I guessed. But me and Zack and a bunch of others, including some judges, stood there watching the flap for any significant sign of life. It got strangely quiet. Pretty soon Nadezhda came out with her clipboard and went back to the truck guys, probably cleaning up the details before Davy's big show.

"Hey, Nadezhda," I went. "When is Davy gonna come out and do his thing?"

"Everything is on-schedule. Mr. Narsood is recovering from the trip. He needs to compose himself, rest his throat, and so forth. Right now he's resting, so please keep your voices down."

"How come he put on his chef's hat and his apron then?"

"Mr. Narsood always needs to make his entrance appropriate, so that you are all sure that it's Mr. Davy Narsood you're seeing in front of you. That's just his way, you see." She smirked sweetly, her lips sort of puckered, turned her back on us, and went back to her tasks.

"I wonder how the judges are going to judge," I went, sort of to myself.

Zack said, "I think they're gonna cut a piece off of every entry and try it out."

"There won't be any left for Davy to window out, if those guys eat them all up."

"Don't worry about it, Joe. I'm gonna win anyhow."

"Say, where's Harley?"

"He's out looking for lost dogs. He doesn't much like crowds, as you may well know. Too much noise for sensitive ears. When he finds a lost dog, he'll report back to me, and I'll notify Mr. Preene who will notify Cod."

Zack's got it all worked out so that he will go to the owner first and collect a small reward. "What does Harley get out of this?"

"Well, of course, he gets the feeling of a job well done." Zack looked at me sort of funny and wagged his head like I was the champion dunce of Balona for not already knowing how Harley feels.

It sounded to me like Harley gets the short end of the lost-dog stick, but I decide not to make an issue of it since Zack is looking pretty proud of himself, having a smart dog like that.

But just then there was a big uproar from the judges. "Where's the numbers?" somebody was hollering. "Who's got the numbers?"

Another voice: "How're we supposed to tell whose is whose if we don't got numbers to look at here?"

Another: "Only number left is number one. That's Bapsie's."

Somebody, some rat, had gone back to the judges table during Davy's entrance and swiped the identification numbers from all but one of the entries. I had a sneaking suspicion who it might have been. But then, I had no proof, so what could I do? Besides, the one left had my own ma's number, so she would probably be the one to win.

Right away Zack went in a loud voice, "I can identify mine. Gang way!" And he ran over and started messing with the entries, moving the pans around.

Uncle Hannibal and Mr. Pezmyer both shrieked at Zack. "You get away from here, bunny. We got to figure out what to do about this." Uncle Hannibal probably called Zack *bunny* on account of how Zack had got his nose and cheeks painted, with whiskers, et cetera. A red-headed bunny with glasses.

"Y'know, Hannibal," went Carl, "they all look alike, these korndogs."

"Except these few, and they're not really korndogs. Look here, I mean, a tortilla isn't a korndog."

Mr. Peralta spoke right up, "It's a corn tortilla. Nobody said it had to be anything particular, only that it had to be baked and be part corn and have a sausage. You got a nice huge sausage there. Also a nice chocolate salsa on top, and a little chopped cheese and lettuce thrown in for esthetic effect." Mr. Peralta smirked, a sort of victory smirk. You could tell he expected to win.

The judges all grumbled to themselves. You could tell they didn't believe Mr. Peralta about the genuinity of the tacodog.

"It looks *foreign* to me," went Mr. Pezmyer, giving Mr. Peralta a hard look.

Mr. Peralta turned dark red and frowned his face. "The tortilla is native to this continent," he went. "Tell me where weenies come from, eh?"

"Well, you got a huge linguiça there. I supposed that it'n a foreign thing." Mr. D. H. Carp smacked his lips like Uncle Kenworth Burnross.

"Well, the basic tacodog meets all the published specifications."

"Well, let's get on with it, boys. How we gonna settle who's entered and who it'n?" Uncle Hannibal was determined to solve the problem, that was sure.

"Well, we got only one actually registered there. Number One there." Mr. Pezmyer pointed at Ma's entry.

"Well, my wife's entry is entered. I paid the fee and you gave it a number, and you were just criticizing it. You people know whose entry it is." Mr. Peralta wasn't about to give up.

"Mine is that one there, with the sparkly *ganache* you could see if you lifted up the wax paper. Mine's the only one with genuine wax paper over it, see?" Zack wouldn't give up, either.

"Mine here is better than all of those disgusting things," went Patella, still standing there with her pan in her hand.

"Well, you haven't paid your fee, so you're not entered," went Uncle Hannibal. "And I declare the entries over with and done."

"Hear, hear!" All the judges nodded their heads.

The ten or so guys in line all grumbled and groaned and complained. Doctor Thrust said something about suing the town.

"We got enough trouble without more entries." Mr. D. H. Carp said. "Besides, I got an idear."

Everybody perked up their ears for the idea of Mr. D. H. Carp which would solve the problem.

"Since this is Balona, and since any product of Balona has got to be superior and good and wholesome, eksedra, even those that dit'n get registered, I say we declare all the pans a tie."

Silence. Everybody was thinking this was either the greatest idea ever thought or it was the dumbest thing ever.

Mr. Pezmyer spoke out first. "Except Number One there, the one with the number. We could present that one to Mr. Davy Narsood as representative."

"We could also present the chocolate tacodog as an interesting variation," went Mr. Peralta.

"We could present my orange flavored chocolate korndog as representing the best *ganache*." Zack wasn't about to give up, either. He was really hollering in his high voice. And definitely making an impression, bunny-face or not.

"All right, all right," went the judges, trying to shut Zack up.

There were questions from ignorant guys in the crowd about what *ganache* was, and Zack had to give a brief lecture. "As you may well know...." He began, and went on from there until guys started to grumble and tell him to knock it off.

What I learned from all this was, you can't hang back and be a modest guy in Balona. If you want to get ahead, you got to holler.

So, since everybody was now declared a winner, nobody was still really mad, except Doctor Thrust who is mad irregardless.

Nobody's entry had been tasted, either. But my ma's entry was declared representative. Being the worst cook in Balona, she was probably also the worst baker. On the other hand, she herself said her entry wasn't really hers. It was Mr. Sam Joe Sly's Slydog that would be presented to Mr. Davy Narsood, along with the tacodog and Zack's special orange *ganache* dog.

Twenty-seven

As the time for Mr. Davy Narsood's broadcast crept up upon us standing there in Uncle Hannibal's parking lot, it looked like Nadezhda had got everything shipshape. She had clapped her hands and got all our attention—not an easy thing to do in Balona. She told us that we should clap our own hands like crazy when Mr. Davy Narsood made his appearance.

Then we were supposed to watch her, and when she held up a white cardboard we should clap some more. Also, we should laugh at Mr. Davy Narsood's jokes. She would laugh, and that would give us a clue about when we should laugh, too. There would be a "warm-up," where Mr. Davy Narsood would come out and look over the entries that had been placed on the table next to his stove. He would make some comments, and then the broadcast itself would begin.

But it didn't quite work out quite that way.

I was by this time standing farther back by the face-painting booth so I could see what was going on in the street, as well as up front. I figured that from the side I could get into Blip Wufser's pictures when he showed up, as well as Mr. Davy Narsood's cameras when they turned to show Davy's crowd to the TV viewers. I couldn't do anything about my ma's peccadildoes which I didn't know were about to happen. In fact, I wouldn't have done anything about it anyway, since my ma is well known as a sort of force of nature you can't do anything about.

So speaking of which, it was my ma, Bapsie Chaud-Kuhl who showed up just as Nadezhda was finishing up her speech and was just standing there with her white cardboard looking pretty and smirking. Ma came barreling up from back of Uncle Hannibal's place, barefoot as usual and wearing her new purple muumuu, but with her face colored up. Her eyebrows were dark and heavy—not Groucho style, but heavier than usual. And her mouth was all red. Gross looking. It looked to me like she planned to get on TV. She ordinarily sits around a lot, but when she wants to move, she can move fast. She was moving fast.

She went up to the table and grabbed her *Number 1* pan and plowed her way through the seated audience till she was standing across from Mr. Davy Narsood's tent flap. "You gotcher winner here! Come on out of there, you great big handsome hunk!" she went. "Come out and lem'me give you a taste of something you won't forget!" When Ma hollers, she can really bust your eardrums. Mr. Davy Narsood was camera-ready, his face painted sort of orange when he opened his flap and came out, his cap and apron right on straight.

"Only ten minutes to air time, Mr. Narsood," yelled a guy from the back of the stove.

Mr. Davy Narsood stood there with his mouth open. My ma posed there, six-foot-two, 240 pounds, *Number 1* clutched tight.

"Wha! The woman in my dream. A Junoesque confection in lavender. A veritable queen!" gasped Davy, probably referring to Ma in her muumuu, not to the chocolate korndog in her pan. "Quick. Come inside!" And he held the flap open for Ma. They both disappeared into the tent, and the flap closed.

This created a sensation. Of course, anybody in Balona might have expected Ma to be so bold. But not that Mr. Davy Narsood would be so reckless.

But the two of them weren't in the tent more than three minutes—just time for Davy to sample *Number 1*—when he came staggering out of the tent, his mouth full. "My God!" he went leaning over, gasping for breath, his face pale and all twisted up, coughing into his huge white hanky which he's usually got stuffed into his sleeve to wipe the sweat off of his face with. "That was, was, was *horrible!*"

Everybody thought he was referring to the *Number 1* until Ma appeared, too, and explained to the crowd: "Well, I was just being relaxed and natural. A natural person." Her face expression showed she felt offended, insulted, and misunderstood by Davy's reaction to her naturalness. But we all figured out right away she'd had not only given Mr. Davy Narsood a sample of *Number 1* to chew on, but she had also blessed him with one of her special natural gas tributes, maybe by accident.

Anyway, that experience seemed to ruin Mr. Narsood's appetite for whatever else he might have been preparing himself for.

Davy and Ma were still standing there, her with her pan in her hand, him gasping heavily with his cheek still pooched out with chocolate Slydog. Suddenly you could hear the Noble Korndog band start up on Front Street. By this time all the trombones had showed up, so you could really hear what sounded not like *The Star Spangled Banner,* but sort of like the Big Baloney *Alma Mater,* which all us old grads naturally stood up for when we heard it. It always starts with a big fanfare and drumrolls, which almost brought a tear to my eye from sentiment, remembering my days in band back then.

Nobody who went to Big Baloney ever learned the words to our old school anthem, but whenever you hear the first stirring bars of it, you're supposed to stand up and sort of groan and move your mouth so it *looks* like you know the words. The words sound a lot like

> *O, orrono blah glohrono*
> *Blah ohso glo moe foble*
> *Groh blah-la oh, mo flugel so*
> *Blah o Balona glo*

Even guys ancient as Uncle Hannibal stood up and groaned out the song, in Uncle Hannibal's case possibly because it sounds more like funeral music than rock. Uncle Hannibal was obviously not remembering the words, either, which made us younger guys feel a lot better. Uncle Hannibal and Mr. D. H. Carp and all them are Big Baloney Old Grads, too, of course. Everybody came in loud on the last couple of lines and looked around, obviously pleased with themselves.

The same guy who had hollered, "Ten minutes!" now hollered, "Five minutes, Mr. Narsood. Places, please." He also moved behind us—everybody watching all this, of course—and put up his hand palm out, trying to stop the entry into the parking lot of the Flag Fems and the Noble Korndog Band, that probably being the intention of Mr. Langsam whose knees were going up and down, showing the Flag Fems how they should prance their stuff.

Being obedient Balonans, they did stop out on the street, marching in place, Mr. Langsam keeping his knees high, the drums beating, the bones blowing, not all stopping at the same time. But then came another sound which, to us in the know, meant that we were all in for a usual experience in an unusual way.

We were in for it more than anybody expected, since it was another turkey run. This time, however, the turkeys didn't take their usual route down Front Street to Airport Way and then back by King Way to Eighth Avenue. No, probably freaked out by Mr. Langsam and the Flag Fems mostly blocking their usual path, along with the drums, and all the other noise and color, the turkeys made a hard right and swept into the parking lot.

Understand, when the turkeys make their run, it's not just a few, it's hundreds. And they're going fast and noisy. And you can stand there and put your hand up and holler, "Stop," like Mr. Narsood's brave guy did, but that's not going to stop a group of determined turkeys who figure they got the right of way. And the guy didn't stop them. They were good-size birds, so they just knocked him down and ran him over. And they found their way through and around the booths and face-painted and french-fried sugarbeet-eating kids, through the audience and Mr. Davy Narsood's setup and staff and his truck and awning and tent.

They were gone in a minute, leaving only a few floating feathers and a strange hot smell. In the silence, since the band all had shut off their blowing and drumming and prancing, and since nobody said a word because of surprise, you could hear the gobbling proceeding east on Third Avenue.

"All *right!*" went some kid with a high voice, maybe Richie, meaning this was a fun thing. "All *right!*" went somebody else, and pretty soon we had the audience and all the guys applauding. This festival was turning out to be pretty good.

"One minute," shouted Mr. Davy Narsood's man, who had picked himself up and dusted himself off. "One minute to air time!"

Davy had recovered by now and, even though he looked like he was still in shock, he took his place behind the stove and licked his lips and cleared his throat. You could hear the recorded music that Davy uses as his theme song playing in the background. The bright lights came on, all pointing at Davy. Everything was ready for broadcast.

The director, a skinny guy with no hair on top but a pony tail in back, held up his hand and counted his fingers: *Five, four, three, two, one*, and he pointed at Mr. Davy Narsood who suddenly showed all his teeth and started to say something.

I don't know if Davy ever finished what he started to say, because right then you could hear only the loud *whump-whump-whump* sound that means a helicopter is right overhead. It was Blip Wufser, making good his threat to upstage Mr. Davy Narsood.

Blip Wufser's helicopter—the Blip Wufsercopter—usually will land right in the middle of a street, and you are always sure he is going to get tangled up in telephone wires, but he never does. Or never did, except once, when he almost did and crashed his old Blipcopter down on Third Avenue, Balona. Also landing on my Love Boat and trashing it. But that is another story which, as you may well know, was told in my famous book, *Spring Break*.

This time, I guess Blip was looking to land in the street, since the parking lot was pretty full of booths and people, sort of landing hazards for a helicopter.

I could hear Blip hollering over his helicopter radio at Ralph, sitting in the KDC-TV van across the street. I wandered over there to get a better listen.

"Okay, Mr. Wufser, if you'll hang on and sort of hover up there for a while, I'll get these kids out of the street." Ralph started to walk away from his van. The radio crackled again.

"No, no, Ralph. There's a heliport right across from you."

"What? There's no heliport anywhere in Balona, Mr. Wufser. That's the funeral parlor over there."

"No, Abe here is an experienced pilot. He says it looks like a *kosher* heliport to him. Got the target all painted up and ready for us. Great camera angles from there, too. Won't need to worry about interference from the rubes for a change."

Just then I noticed Richie standing in the street with his white helmet on, his visor down, making his traffic cop signals. He was pointing with his left arm straight and moving his right hand over it, up and down. He was giving Blip Wufser the signal to land on Uncle Hannibal's roof.

"Well, maybe it looks like a heliport," yelled Ralph into his radio, "but you don't see any stairs or ladders down from there, do you?"

"You are getting kind of insubordination sounding, Ralph. I guess you don't value your employment with me." Blip was sounding really snotty. "For your information, since apparently you don't pay attention to necessary details, there's a cop down there, just a ways from where you are, giving us the landing signal, so we're going in, and that's that." Blip sounded just like he might have smacked his lips after he said that, like Uncle Kenworth Burnross. And Zack.

"Hey, Mr. Wufser, that's not a traffic cop. That's a kid."

"You're fired, Ralph."

Making a lot of noise, the Blip Wufsercopter came straight down and landed on Uncle Hannibal's roof, right on top of the new Balona red, white, and blue advertising bullseye that Junior Trilbend and Bobby R. Langsam had painted up there. The landing created quite a sensation, not only because of the sound of the motor which was pretty loud, but also because of the huge tearing and groaning and splintering sounds from the roof giving way.

And then the helicopter just sort of disappeared, chugging and sagging its way down into Uncle Hannibal's funeral parlor, not remaining on the roof the way you might expect a helicopter to do. Since Uncle Hannibal's building is a one-storey job, you could see the rotor rotoring for a while. You could then hear Mr. Blip Wufser saying discouraging words in a loud voice.

You could hear Uncle Hannibal saying clearly words children shouldn't hear.

You could hear Mr. Davy Narsood shouting to his camera operators, "Did you get it? Did you get the crash?" Showman that he is, I guess Davy was more interested in getting a news flash on the air than in getting our flavored chocolate korndog winners identified, et cetera.

At least Uncle Hannibal's place didn't explode right away, the way you might expect. But then somebody went, in a pretty loud voice so everybody in the lot could hear, "Oh-oh, I bet the turkeys are on the way back!" And everybody who had been crowding closer to Uncle Hannibal's place to see if maybe they could get a look at a patch of blood or a body part cleared away from the middle of the lot to make room for the return of the turkeys.

But those birds had other plans, returning their traditional way, up Eighth Avenue and then making their regular S-pattern to end up at their Green Door, considerably slowed down and only loud enough to be heard if you listened for them.

Everybody was agreeing that, with the celebrities and all the surprises, it was turning out to be a pretty fun festival.

Twenty-eight

Of course, the festival wasn't over just because we'd had a turkey run, a helicopter crash, and a surprise appearance by Bapsie Kuhl. It occurred that Mr. Davy Narsood was broadcasting on a Saturday, a day he "never broadcasts on" and "communes with nature on," according to Nadezhda. So, maybe he was actually taping his program, rather than doing it live, the way everybody had thought. In that case, he had a lot more latitude, and the show could go on any way fate took it.

But the Blipcopter's crash did change the agenda some. Guys in the audience, and even Mr. Davy Narsood himself, were now paying attention to a piece of the helicopter rotor sticking up out of Uncle Hannibal's place, maybe hoping to see somebody do a chin-up on it. Maybe somebody would climb out over the wall. Maybe it would be Blip Wufser himself. You could recognize his famous voice making noises in sort of a muffled tone.

Maybe there would be a huge explosion and fire. That often happens when helicopters crash on TV. Everybody was hopeful, in a nice way, naturally, that the explosion wouldn't be *too* huge.

Maybe I mentioned before that most guys in Balona have got a cell phone. You can hear the things burbling and peebling at all hours in all places. Guys driving down the street or walking on the sidewalk are always talking into their phone. So as soon as Blip Wufser's helicopter made its unusual landing, guys were calling 9-1-1, and reporting the event or telling their wife or their friend or their cousin in Lodi. I myself unclipped my cellphone and punched in some numbers, only for the suave effect, of course.

What was Davy doing during all this excitement? He was standing behind his stove, arms crossed over his chest, looking either like he was awfully hungry or awfully disgusted. Or maybe both. His camera people were pointing their cameras at the latest disaster, not at Davy.

Anyway, it wasn't all that long until the Balona Volunteer Fire Brigade engine and firefighters showed up, blowing both their airhorn and their siren. They had obviously forgot that blowing both those things at the same time is the Balona Earthquake Signal. The idea being if you didn't already know there was an earthquake going on, the horn and the siren both going should clue you in, even if you were fast asleep. What you did after that was supposed to be up to you. Hold tight onto something, probably.

Anyway, the fire engine and the shouting firefighters succeeded in scattering the Noble Korndog flutes and clarinets and scratching a number of parked-car fenders. The firefighters were on hand so quick probably because their regular beer supply was almost across the street from the festival.

The volunteers began right away shouting orders at each other. As you may well know, the Balona Brigade has a boss and an assistant boss for any fire specialization you can name. There's a wheelmaster, a pumpmaster, a laddermaster, a hosemaster, and of course a beermaster. It was the laddermaster who shouted the directions to get the long ladder up to Uncle Hannibal's roof. And then Chief Frank Floom himself scrambled up to the roof and then right away tripped and disappeared through the roof and down into Uncle Hannibal's reception room. You could hear Mr. Floom shouting something truly rude.

Patella had her camera and was flashing pictures of Uncle Hannibal's wall where Mr. Floom vanished and you could just see a piece of blade hanging over the top. Patella flashed five or six shots. "Hey, Patella," I went. "You're gonna get just a picture of the wall from so close. You need to get up on the ladder there." I was being artistically helpful, but Patella didn't move back at all.

"I'm expecting Mr. Floom to show himself up there pretty soon, and I'll catch him with a surprised expression on his face. So that's why I'm flashing the pictures from here, if you want to know." Being as how Uncle Hannibal's wall is about twelve feet high, I then mentioned to Patella that Mr. Floom was only about five-foot-eight and didn't have suction cups on his hands and feet and so probably would not appear for her artistry.

But all that didn't matter, since pretty soon Mr. Floom and Blip Wufser and his pilot Abe did all come marching out of Uncle Hannibal's front door, seemingly none the worst for wear, except considerably wet. Since the hosemaster and his crew had got up on the ladder and were spraying the whole scene with a lot of water—just in case, they said. They were also squirting each other and laughing a lot, tropes that Uncle Hannibal kept shouting at for them to quit. By that time, Patella's camera was out of film. Patella said a discouraging word, too.

"I bet you got some great wall pictures," I mentioned, but Patella huffed off toward the *Courier* office, not even waiting for the Davy Narsood Show to continue. Which it did, pretty soon.

All this time, Cod had sat on one of the folding chairs in front of Davy, eating out of a huge bag of popcorn. Mostly he had his eyes fixed on the big TV monitor up above Davy, so the audience could see what was being broadcast. The screen was still blank. Cod isn't usually bothered by turkey runs or helicopter crashes, but I wish he had seen Richie do his execrable signaling trope that stimulated the crash. Richie gets away with everything.

But then my wish came true, since here came ex-assistant Ralph along with dripping Blip himself, and with Richie held by the collar, Richie hollering all the way. "Here you go, Officer," went Ralph at Cod. "Here's the guy who made Mr. Wufser land his helicopter up there. He's dressed like a cop and made signals for those guys to land up there. He's the one. Do your duty, Officer!" And he shoved Richie so that Richie almost fell into Cod's popcorn bag, squealing and sniveling all the while.

"That's the truth, Officer," went Blip. "That kid there. Now I see it's a kid. Before, up there, I thought it was a regular cop."

Cod just looked sort of interested. Not real interested. "More paperwork. You got any proof?"

Blip hollered, "We seen him with our own eyes, my pilot and me. And my loyal assistant Ralph here did, too." Ralph was re-hired on the spot, I guess.

Ralph looked over at me. "And that kid saw it, too, since he was standing right across from me. You seen it, huh, kid?"

I nodded my head sadly. Poor Richie. Poor fat, pimply little Burberry Box thief. Poor guy. Runcible Hall for him again.

"Well," went Richie, "Joey there made me do it. It was all his idear!"

Everybody looked at me as if I was a criminal, not exactly a new look, but a shock anyway.

"Yeh," went Ricky Placock, off of his motorcycle for a change and speaking up for a change. "Yeh, it was Joey Kuhl went over and whispered in his ear and told poor Richie to do it. And Richie it'n too bright, y'know, so he went and did it. I seen that myself." Ricky smirked his wet girl's lips and snickered.

Then my ma horned in, from where she had been sitting in the front row of chairs, depressed looking but waiting for Mr. Davy Narsood to begin his show. "Richie cut'n of done it by himself, that good boy. It was Joey for sure egged him on." My own ma was accusing me of the terrible crime.

"*Ma!*" I went, shocked. Shocked.

But a loud voice from up front stopped all that. It was Mr. Davy Narsood. He went, "I have no particular regard for that young man, that Joseph Kuhl, since he got me into this *mess* over here on false pretenses in the first place. But I've been watching this whole spectacle from my vantage point here—standing right here all the while—and I saw it all. Joseph Kuhl was standing over there..." and Davy pointed accurately, "...and the little fat boy in the helmet was over there with the other young fellow and his motorcycle..." and Davy pointed at Ricky. "And it was the little fat boy in the white helmet that made the signal and was laughing about it and carrying on like some vandal. Joseph Kuhl was not involved."

Mr. Davy Narsood had saved me from the pokey. A fine fellow. In doing that he had created another sincere fan in me. On the spot I decided to take up cooking, at least as a hobby.

"Well, I oughta take 'em all three in, since they're always doing something bad." Cod was including me in this trio of evildoers. "But since I dit'n see none of this, I'll have to put off doing anything for now. Besides, I want to see this show by my favorite tef of all chimes, Mr. Navy Darsood." Cod grabbed up another handful of popcorn. Around a mouthful he went, "Hey, Bapsie! I'm puttin' Richie in your charge for now, whilst I think about doing something about this mess to Uncle Hannibal's place."

"Mr. Narsood, one minute?" The bald guy with the pony tail was asking Mr. Davy Narsood if he wanted to start all over again.

"Why not!" went Davy, and straightened up his chef hat and brushed off his apron.

I guess Mr. Langsam took all that as a cue for the Noble Korndog band to start up again, and we all jumped out of our skins when the drums started the fanfare behind us, and we could recognize our Alma Mater tune again. All of us, including the firefighters who weren't still spraying each other, leaped to our feet and stood at attention, even Cod. We all groaned our great school song again.

Unfortunately, Mr. Davy Narsood's theme song which uses guitars and banjos and flutes, but no singing, was starting over again at the same time, so what you heard was sort of mixed up, but Davy kept on showing his teeth through it all. All the music stopped at the same time, and Davy began his broadcast. Or his tape, whatever.

"You might ask," he began, "what's famous about Balona, California? And you might answer, 'the Sugarbeet Festival, the Yulumne River, and korndogs.' And you'd be right. But the little town on the delta has other industries and other charms. Among them, King Turkey, one of the proud new sponsors of our show, products we appreciate for their purity and wonderful taste and astounding versatility."

Davy had the three chocolate korndog samples on his table. And beside them was a plain white box I hadn't seen before. Talking all the time, Davy cut little pieces off of the korndogs and the tacodog, chewed on them, raised up his eyes like he was thinking about the flavors, and went, "Well, about flavored chocolate korndogs now. These are the most interesting. This one, marked Number One has the taste you might expect of a korndog, and the added piquancy of some mysterious spices, all addressed by a competent chocolate frosting."

"Yeh! That's mine! That's Bapsie Chaud-Kuhl's!" Mr. Davy Narsood smiled sort of faintly on one side of his face.

"This one," and Davy cut off a piece of the tacodog, chewed on it, threw his eyes up again, thinking. "Hmmm. Yes. The flavor of the chocolate does lend an air of mystery to the taco. Notice how the cubes of cheese would add a lubricant to the otherwise harshly chewy quality of the sausage and its cover. Quite interesting."

"Olé!" went Mr. Peralta. Mr. Davy Narsood smirked with his lips.

"Now for this one," and Davy cut a hunk off of Zack's entry, chewed at it, *hmmmm'd,* and nodded his head. "Interesting bit of orange and peanut enhancement to the chocolate. *Very* nice accoutrements."

"All *right!*" hollered Zack. Everybody laughed. Mr. Davy Narsood smirked at Zack.

"Of course, the strong meat flavors of the sausage clashes with the chocolate in all the entries. The chocolate flavored korndog seems to me to be a wonderfully creative idea—and a miserable product that should be consigned to the trashcan." He took the three samples and dropped them into his trashcan, right up there on his set. *Klunk, plonk, plorp.*

There was a huge gasp from everybody, and then dead silence. Even Cod's popcorn crunching stopped for a minute while he processed the information Davy just passed on to us. Then Davy continued.

"But here is something that might save the day." He opened the white box, turned down the sides all around. Everybody strained to see. The camera zoomed in, and we all stretched our necks up to look at the monitor to see better what Davy had there.

"As you can see, it's a rolled confection, covered in a nice *ganache.* I slice it open and discover a center surrounded by a..." he tasted. "Ahhh. Whipped cream." He sliced another piece and chewed on it. "Mmmmm. A spongey, somewhat corn-flavored roll, chocolate covered, around a filling of whipped cream, and within the whipped cream a center of tender flavorful King Turkey breast. Ladies and gentlemen, I have the pleasure of introducing to you for the very first time a wonderful new product of our sponsor, the King Turkey people of Balona, California. A creation that you will be able to prepare for yourself, a product whose makings will be available everywhere in just a few weeks: The King Turkeylog!"

In the silence you could hear Mr. Dirty Harry Runcible back there, snickering in triumph. "Heh heh heh," he went.

A recorded trumpet fanfare blared out of the speakers on each side of Davy's stove. The camera zoomed in closer, showing the turkeylog in living color—actually mostly brown and white—then moved up to show a smirking log-eating Davy Narsood, his eyes closed in delight, whipped cream on his lip, his cheeks pooched out with turkeylog.

Mr. Davy Narsood had stabbed us in the back. He had turned our Chocolate Korndog Festival into a national celebration of a King Turkeylog festival.

Nadezhda held up her white piece of cardboard and showed her teeth, meaning we were supposed to clap like crazy. Nobody clapped. We just sat there, all of us giving Mr. Davy Narsood our hardest looks.

Mr. Narsood clapped his own hands once. "Let's wrap up and get out of this burg," he went. And his guys started to tear down his stuff and trundle it into the big yellow truck. We all just sat there.

"Where's my crown?" went my ma. It took all of Cod's weight to hold her as Davy and Nadezhda got in his limo and took off.

Twenty-nine

Suckered and diverted by Mr. Dirty Harry Runcible, for a measley twenty bucks. The fellow growled at me out of the corner of his lip. "Don't worry about the patent deal, kid. We was never really interested in that." He just wanted to make sure nobody was paying attention to the turkeylog idea, which nobody was in the first place. I had to admit, though, that his tradecraft was superb. To outfox a guy trained both in Criminal Justice and by UITS (Universal Intelligence Training School—Pronounce it "Wits!"), it had to be.

Anyway, at first everybody in Balona laughed at the King Turkeylog. Everybody preferred flavored chocolate korndogs for a while. Maybe fifty variations showed up in kitchens around town. Frank and Mr. D. H. Carp both reported dips in their over-the-counter sales of regular korndogs for a couple of weeks. Everybody was saying they *liked* the "strong meat taste" in the chocolate korndog. But then, nature took its course, and folks returned to their natural habit of eating good old King Korndogs, even though sometimes the good old korndogs have an unusual taste. Maybe we got used to the chocolate entrancements.

Mr. Sam Joe Sly, when interviewed by Mrs. Bellona Shaw for her *Courier* column went, "Chocolate? Oh, ha ha ha. I was having fun is all." So you got the idea that King Korndog Inkorporated was not going into production of the Slydog. But Mr. Sam Joe Sly offered to buy Claire's painting. "Sentimental reasons," he said. But he offered Claire only ten dollars, so she's got the painting hanging in her bedroom. "Better than a diet pill," she says.

I mentioned my dad would truly appreciate having it, and Claire said she'd think about that. Then she waited with her eyebrows up, probably for me to offer her money for it. But all I had was nine dollars, left over from Mr. Vibrissa's hundred. So I'm staying away from Hank's Drugs for a while.

Also, within the very next week, Mr. D. H. Carp was selling King Turkey turkeylog ready-mix. Those guys must have been getting ready to sell it for weeks anyway. The mix comes in a red box with separate plastic packages of log mix, chocolate frosting, and imitation whip cream you're supposed to add water and whip up yourself. All you need is to buy some King Turkey, bake the mix, stuff it, whipcream it, roll it up, and smear chocolate on it. I had some at Zack's, where Aunt Pippa serves it often.

"It's easy," she went when quizzed.

"It's tasty," Zack went.

I agreed. It's not so bad, if you don't think about it. Sort of a chewy turkey Twinky, you might say.

Mrs. Peralta has got a big hit on her hands over at TacoTime, selling more TacoDogs at lunch time than she can ever get made. Kids at Big Baloney are agitating to have them on the menu in the cafeteria.

It was fun watching the giant crane they brought in to lift the Blipcopter out of Uncle Hannibal's funeral parlor. The old guys who hang out at Frank's Soupe de Jour and Frings Bowls brought folding canvas deck chairs and sat on the sidewalk across the street in the fog and watched. There's a whole story there about how the crane company which is headquartered over in Fruitstand had to bring the parts over on a huge truck and put the thing together in Uncle Hannibal's parking lot, making quite a few more holes in the asphalt there. And then how the cables broke a few times while hoisting.

Uncle Hannibal didn't show much good humor about it, either. Except he bragged to Uncle Kosh how he was going to remodel his place with all the insurance money he's getting. He says he's going to double the size of his green and red neon sign and put it up on the roof, "so you can see it all the way from Delta City," he says, "and so it will be in the way of any passing helicopter looking to park on my roof." He's also planning to put a double-decker underground parking garage where his parking lot is. One thing about Balona, we sure know how to milk insurance companies.

Patella still isn't speaking to me directly except to complain about my advice. "It was your fault my snapshots dit'n turn out," she wailed. I reminded her about how she should have climbed up on the ladder a ways, but she claimed it wouldn't have been ladylike. I decided not to make a smartmouth comment about that.

THE CHOCOLATE KORNDOG

However, Patella does leave presents for me on the front porch. Like today she left her "formula" for cocoa that you're supposed to drink with your korndog. It calls for lots of sugar and "a little whipcream on top." She pinned the formula onto the first page of our *Courier,* with a heart and an arrow and my name drawn up in the corner. So maybe she is angling for romance again.

Ma has been depressed lately, sitting in Dad's chair in the dark and looking at the carpet. It's the first time I know of that she didn't get her own way. She is probably suffering, thinking about the crown she almost won. Since she doesn't like to suffer alone, she's left Dad at the Jolly Times. But maybe he'll check himself out one of these days. Spring is just around the corner.

Actually, nobody got an actual crown out of the festival. Or a prize, either. Mr. Preene just put a list in the *Courier* of all the guys who were part of the flavored chocolate korndog contest. He made a big deal about how they were all prizewinners. So nobody yet has asked about what the prizes are. Maybe some time he'll just split up all the fees and give the money out as prize money. That's Zack's version of Mr. Preene's probable idea.

But, then again, maybe the prize money will just sort of disappear. Mr. Preene keeps mentioning how expensive it was to promote the festival in the *Courier.* Fees that disappear is a Balona tradition, so nobody is liable to complain, since everybody figures next time maybe he will get to be the fee collector.

Richie is still loose, hanging around, cutting school, doing crimes with Ricky. Richie claimed he wasn't really signaling the Blipcopter to land on Uncle Hannibal's roof. He says he was just doing exercises on the sidewalk there in order to lose weight, since he planned to pig out on flavored chocolate korndogs later. Cod thought that was a pretty good excuse, Cod himself being about three-hundred pounds overweight.

Ma and Zack each have been looking at the TV for Davy's show about Balona but so far no luck. Maybe he'll air it so we can't see it here. Maybe it will go out overseas somewhere. Maybe he will scrap the whole production. Probably he made a mint selling his pictures of Blip Wufser's crash.

Speaking of which again, Buddy Swainhammer just won't let go of that bone, mentioning Blip's crash on every one of Buddy's broadcasts, Zack says.

Patella says her grandpa got a "nice thank-you letter from that skinny one with the underpants showing," meaning Nadezhda, of course. Maybe Nadezhda thinks nice thoughts about me. On the other hand, she's probably too old for me to waste time on her, especially what with she being married already a few times. And also she having erotic thoughts about Mr. Davy Narsood. But it's unusual in Balona for anybody to get a thank-you letter for anything. In fact, I don't even know what a thank-you letter is.

What I do know is I'm going to have to take this semester over again, since those guys over on the faculty at C4 do not have any sympathy for a guy whose great-uncle had a helicopter fall into his funeral parlor, therefore causing the guy to forget to do his homework out of grief. Even Mr. Dainty, my Criminal Justice teacher, looked at me with sort of a snort when I told him about my plight.

"If you're gonna talk the talk, you gotta walk the walk," he went. I wrote that down in my notebook, planning to use it on both Zack and Richie, whenever possible. I still have to take those guys down a peg or two. Ω

Stockton, California 2002

More Balona Books

Besides **A Chocolate Korndog,** Jonathan Pearce's other published "Balona Books" to date include

—from Infinity Publishing
(http://www.BuyBooksontheWeb.com)
call toll-free 1-877-BUYBOOK :

The Balona Klongs: A Demi-mystery Caper
Finding Dad: A Quasi-mystery Adventure
Focusing the Private Eye: A Mysterious Term Paper
One Brick Shy: A Hemi-semi-demi Mystery Adventure
Spring Break: A Wet Adventure
A Cuisine of Leftovers:
Stories and Sketches of Eminent Balonans
Thing with Feathers: A Different Romance
Heavier than Air:
Riches to Burn in Balona
The Far Side of the Moon:
A California Story
The Burberry Style:
An Enigma-wrapped Mystery
and
—from 1stBooks Library
(http://www.1stbooks.com):
call toll-free 1-800-839-8640

John-Browne's Body & Sole: A Semester of Life
Sang Froyd: Capers of the Balona Family Kuhl
and
A Little Honesty:
Trials and Triumphs of a Prince of Balona.

Balona Books are **POD**—printed and bound on demand (printed when ordered). All these books are available *through* any local bookseller who will do you the courtesy of ordering for you, by phone direct from the publishers (quickest!), or from Amazon.com, Borders, BN ("Balona Books"), or through the **Balona Website:** http://www.balona.com.